THE BALI ADVENTURE

A FEEL-GOOD ROMANTIC COMEDY SET IN BALI

KATE DASHWOOD

ABOUT THE BOOK

THE BALI ADVENTURE

Four best friends. Two ex-lovers. One amazing Bali.

In this modern retelling of Jane Austen's Persuasion, Lucy Green, an anxious bookworm from London, is travelling with her three best friends to Bali. They are going to spend a whole glorious month preparing one of her friend's wedding, exploring the island, and flirting with handsome locals. Sun, fun, and fun in the sun!

The only glitch? Lucy's sexy French ex, Antoine, is also coming to the island. They had an ugly breakup four years ago, and Lucy's heart still aches every time she remembers his cheeky smile and glint of humour from behind his Clark Kent glasses. Can Lucy and Antoine stay polite and distant for the sake of their friends' big day, or will they bring drama to paradise?

A perfect summer read for the fans of Debbie Johnson, Sheila O'Flanagan, and Marian Keys.

ABOUT THE AUTHOR

Kate Dashwood learnt how to write when she was five, and she hasn't stopped ever since. Her first literary crush was Sherlock Holmes, and the second—Mr Darcy. She worked for many years as an English teacher and translator until she ended up on a career ladder in a big corporation in London and Paris.

Kate's currently living with her French boyfriend in the South of France, where she took up new hobbies, like baking cakes, furniture renovation, and feeding her neighbour's donkey. *The Bali Adventure* is her first published novel, but she's already working on the next books in the series.

- Website: katedashwood.com
- Instagram: kate.dashwood
- Facebook: kate.m.dashwood

CONTENTS

To Anna, Edi, and Milena.
Thanks for all the fun, Chicas!

PUB NIGHT WITH A TWIST

"Where the hell is Mia?" Anna checks her watch for the fifth time. "It's not like her to be late, especially after such a dramatic message."

It's Friday night and Anna, Sylvia, and I are sitting in Approach Tavern, our favourite pub near Victoria Park in London. There's a pre-weekend buzz in the air, and the pub is filled with the familiar smell of stale beer and fried onions. Sylvia, dressed in a shocking red business suit, is checking work emails on her mobile and munching on chips, while Anna is observing people in the pub. I'm trying to read a book on my Kindle, the latest Comfort Food Café novel, but it's hard to focus with all the noise around me.

Anna, Mia, and I have been friends since high school, and sharing a house in East London during our college years cemented our bond. Sylvia joined our group three years ago, but she fit straight in, making me feel like I've known her my whole life. I'm not very close with my parents or brothers, so *"Las Chicas,"* or the girls, as Mia calls us in Spanish, have become my real family. Even though we're now all busy adulting with serious jobs and not-so-serious hobbies, we always try to meet at least once or twice a month to catch up on all our goss. But this meeting is completely unexpected.

Sylvia looks up from her phone and bites into a hand-cut chip with a dollop of mayo. "Lucy, can you call her again? This suspense is killing me."

"I already did. I'm sure she'll be here very soon." I turn off my Kindle and push away the plate of chips. I can't eat when I'm stressed, and I'm stressed almost all the time. Apparently, I've got something called GAD. Even though is sounds like an abbreviation of some fun reality show—*Gliding and Dancing* or *Glamorous and Divorced*—it actually stands for Generalised Anxiety Disorder. And it's a real pain in the ass.

"I just hope Mia's news is as important as she said it would be. I finished work early for her," Sylvia complains, as she keeps scrolling through her work phone.

"No, you didn't." Anna points accusingly at the phone. "What's so important that you have to work on a Friday night? It's not as if you're saving people's lives."

Sylvia immediately bristles, her Scottish burr getting stronger when she's angry. "The world of investment banking never sleeps. But of course, you wouldn't understand that."

Here we go again! Each of my friends is passionate about her vocation and thinks her job is the most important thing in the world. Sylvia is a bigwig in a bank, Anna is a therapist, and Mia runs her own yoga centre. Meanwhile, I'm a PA in a law firm, and the only person from our quartet who utterly hates her job.

I try to loosen my blond chignon bun, as I look with envy at Anna's casual olive sweater and Sylvia's perfectly tailored red jacket. I came to the pub straight from the office, so I'm still wearing my uncomfortable business outfit. The white shirt is chaffing my skin, the tights are glued to my legs like cling foil, and the high heels are giving me blisters. I can't wait to get back home, change into a black T-shirt and leggings, and curl on the sofa with the latest Marian Keynes book.

"Sylve, I really think you're using work to overcompensate for things that are lacking in your life. Like a stable relationship. Did you check out this Workaholics Anonymous group I recommended?" Anna is a great therapist, but she sometimes forgets that we're her friends, not clients.

"I think it's you who should join this group. You just can't stop analysing people around you!" Sylvia fires back.

I hate when people are fighting, even if it's just friendly bickering. Before their discussion has a chance to develop into a familiar quarrel about work-life balance, I ask, "You don't think Mia's ill or something?"

"Preggers more likely." Anna rakes her hands through her messy brown hair, as she takes a big swig of red wine. "I've heard she's back with Jack."

"Oh, I didn't even know they'd broken up again." Mia and Jack seem so happy together, so why do they keep breaking up and making up? Other people's relationships will always be a mystery to me.

"I hope she isn't pregnant. I'm too young to be an auntie." Sylvia finally puts her phone down and starts checking out a hot guy standing at the bar.

"Sylve, you're twenty-seven!"

"Exactly." She twirls a strand of ginger hair over her finger and sends the guy a welcoming smile. He takes it as an invitation and decides to make a move. But as soon as he takes a step towards our table, the creaky door opens, and Mia bursts into the pub with a huge grin on her face.

"*Chicas*, I've got news!" She walks towards us and makes a dramatic pause. With her petite body framed by long black locks, Mia looks more like a Flamenco dancer than a yoga teacher. "I'm getting married!"

Anna, Sylvia, and I sit in stunned silence. Mia and Jack have been going out forever, but we never thought they would tie the knot. Especially given Mia's disdain for the "misogynistic and oppressive institution," as her mother likes to call it.

"To who?" Sylvia seems as shell-shocked as the rest of us, but she tries to diffuse the tension by a feeble attempt at humour.

"Ha, ha, very funny, Sylve. Jack, of course. But this isn't the best part yet. Do you know where we're getting married?"

"Where? In Jack's family house?" I'm dying to finally see his parents' Georgian mansion in Hampshire.

"No, it's even better. We're going to Bali! And you're all invited!"

My head is still spinning from this unexpected news, but we all jump up to hug her, laughing and shrieking. If Mia is happy, we're happy. People in the pub look at us as if we were loonies, but we don't care.

"No more cider and chips tonight." Sylvia raises her glass. "Let's drink champagne and dance on the tables! We have to celebrate Mia's engagement and our trip to Bali!"

"So, how did it happen? How did he propose to you?" Anna asks, once we've calmed down and ordered a bottle of bubbly.

"*Dios mío*, it was lovely." Mia has a dreamy look on her face. "Jack invited me to this new fancy vegetarian restaurant in Shoreditch and said that he was tired of us playing cat and mouse, and now he wants us to catch each other for good."

"Ooh, how romantic." Sylvia grabs Mia's hand. "Now show us the ring!"

While my friends are admiring a simple silver band with a sparkling sapphire, I close my eyes and try to stop the stabbing pain in my chest. I'm really pleased for Mia, but her news brings so many unwelcome memories of my own engagement in Paris five years ago. I dig my nails into the palms of my hands to stop myself from crying.

"Luce, are you okay?" Anna touches my hand and massages it gently. I open my eyes and look at her with gratitude. She's my oldest and bestest friend in the world. We grew up in the same neighbourhood in a small town and we've become as close as sisters. I don't know what I'd do without her support throughout the years.

"Couldn't be better," I lie, as I start scratching my neck under the stiff collar. Bloody stress eczema. "Thanks for checking, sweetie."

Anna sends me a disbelieving look, but she drops the subject. At least for now.

"So, how many people are coming to Bali?" Sylvia has forgotten all about her work, and the hot guy at the bar, and is now fully focused on Mia.

"We want to book a boho restaurant next to the beach and invite just our closest family and friends. Thirty to forty people max. The ceremony will be small and casual, but I still need your help with the preparations."

"Of course you can count on us," Anna reassures her with a smile, while Sylvia is already on her phone, looking for the perfect wedding locations in Bali.

"If only we can take some time off from work," Sylvia adds. "I probably have a few weeks of carry-over holidays from last year. I was just too busy and important to leave the office for more than a few days at a time."

As they keep chatting and brainstorming ideas, there's one thought darting through my mind: *Oh my god, I just hope they won't invite Antoine.*

2

HUNGRY BIRDS

After months of hectic planning, shopping, and packing, we're finally sitting on the plane taking us on our Balinese adventure. We've all managed to convince our bosses to let us take our yearly holiday allowance in one go. Well, almost all of us. As a therapist and a good human being, Anna didn't want to abandon her patients and her elderly grandma, Misia, who has some health issues and has to undergo a few medical tests. I really hope it isn't anything serious, as I can't imagine my life without Misia's benign presence in it.

Now I'm sandwiched between Sylvia and Mia in a very cramped space, trying not to elbow them with my every move. We have about twenty hours of travel ahead of us, and we haven't even taken off from Heathrow yet. It's going to be a long flight.

"I can't believe it's finally happening." Sylvia swallows a big gulp of champagne and tries to make herself more comfortable in her tiny plane seat. "I've been waiting for this all my life."

"You sound like it's you getting married, not Mia," I reply, leafing through the Bali guidebook to distract myself from my fear of flying.

Sylvia doesn't pay any attention to my remark and just keeps babbling. "I can't wait to be there. Just think about it—a whole glorious month of beautiful beaches, beautiful food, and beautiful men. And I've never been the maid of honour before, especially on an exotic island."

"One of the maids of honour," Mia corrects her automatically. "Let's not forget about Lucy and Anna."

I can see that Sylvia wants to say something about the folly of having three maids of honour, but she eats one of the mixed nuts instead.

"It's a pity Anna couldn't go with us. It won't be the same without her." I turn towards Mia and almost knock off her guava juice.

"She promised to come at least a few days before the wedding. And Jack will join us in two weeks. But until then—" Mia retrieves from her handbag a blue file brimming with papers, "we have a lot of things to prepare. I've made a to-do list for each of us."

"Of course you have," I sigh. Mia is the queen of to-do lists.

"I am already prepared," says Sylvia defensively. "I've bought twelve new dresses, three swimsuits, and five pairs of stilettos."

"Five pairs of stilettos? Very useful on the beach. No wonder your suitcase was ten pounds over the limit," Mia glares at Sylvia and then steals one of her nuts.

There's a question that I need to ask, even though I've already asked it a million times since the engagement. "Mi, what about Antoine? Are you really, really sure he isn't coming ?"

Mia puts a hand on my arm reassuringly. "Don't worry, Luce. Just as I told you, the last time Jack spoke to him, Antoine was too busy on some environmental project in Singapore. You can relax, he won't be there."

I sigh with relief and sit more comfortably in my cramped seat. That's the problem with anxiety—it makes me worry about the same thing over and over again, even though the rational part of my brain knows that it won't happen. Antoine was the only black cloud on the horizon that could spoil my perfect Balinese holiday. Him and my fear of flying.

"Speaking of the guest list, have you invited your father after all?" Sylvia asks. "I know you aren't on the best terms, but it might be a nice way to offer him an olive branch."

"*Nunca en la vida!*" Mia sometimes switches to her native Spanish when she's angry. "I don't want him to spoil the best day of my life.

Also, my mum was already upset that I'm getting married at all—no need to also drag my father into it."

"Why was she upset? I thought she liked Jack," I ask.

"It's nothing personal against Jack." Mia fidgets with her blue folder. "But she thinks I should be happy on my own, as a strong, independent woman like her, not falling into a trap of patriarchy."

"Does your mum know that you can be a feminist, but still shave your legs and get married?" I really like María Carmen, but she's a die-hard hippie who spends most of her time taking care of orphaned chimpanzees in Zambia, and she sometimes loses touch with the modern world.

"Let's drop the topic of my parents and focus on the wedding preparations instead. Let me go through the list. First, your dresses."

As the plane takes off, my good humour evaporates. The higher we get, the more I panic. I know that planes are supposed to be safe, but what if this one isn't? What if there's a technical fault? Or the pilot gets ill? Or we fly into a turbulent storm?

I close my eyes and clutch the armrests as if they could save my life. I swallow hard a few times, fighting nausea and hoping that all the nuts I ate will stay put. As I realise that we might die soon, sweat trickles down my back, my body starts to tremble, and stress eczema breaks out on my forearms. I try to breathe normally, but I can't. I breathe faster and faster until my head is spinning from hyperventilation. I can't stand it anymore; I have to escape from here. But before I have a chance to stand up and shout, "Stop the plane, I'm out!" I feel someone's hand gently touching mine. I open my eyes and see Mia's face filled with concern. My friends have witnessed so many of my panic attacks when we lived together that they don't even have to ask what's happening.

"You okay, *cariña*?"

I blink a few times as I try to get my bearings back. I'm still on the plane, but I'm alive. At least for now.

"Maybe read one of your Bali guidebooks?" Sylvia picks up a book that I accidentally dropped on the floor and shoves it into my lap. "That will take your mind off the flying."

"I've already finished them all."

"Read them again?"

I look at Sylvia with incredulity. Can't she see that I'm fighting for survival here? I don't have the energy to even breathe, let alone focus on reading. I think I'm going to be sick. Which isn't the best thing to do while the plane is still zooming upwards and we aren't allowed to leave our seats.

"There, there." Mia is gently tapping my wrists with the tips of her fingers. Her touch is very soothing, and to my surprise, the nausea abides a little.

Sylvia decides to use another tactic. "Stop stressing, Luce. There's nothing to worry about. Planes are actually the safest modes of transport. Just don't think about this and relax."

I hate when people do this. Saying stop stressing to a person with anxiety is like saying stop drinking to an alcoholic. Thanks for the great advice, dude, why didn't I think of it myself?

"I know what can help." Mia stops tapping my wrists and sits straight in her seat. "It's a technique called Box Breathing, and it's used by Navy SEALS. I've tried it recently in my meditation class, and it worked really well."

I look at her with mistrust. I've joined a lot of her yoga and meditation courses in London, and they always helped me to relax, but I don't think a simple breathing exercise can stop a panic attack as powerful as this one. Especially now that I have a real reason to stress—our plane is going to fall, and we'll all drown in the English Channel.

"So, what is this thing?" I finally ask. I might as well die relaxed, not stressed.

"Close your eyes and get comfortable in your seat," Mia says, using her soothing yoga-instructor voice.

"Good luck with that! These seats are for skinny dwarves, not for fully-fleshed women like me," Sylvia complains.

"Sylve," Mia shushes her, then looks back to me. "Just close your eyes and focus on your breath."

I obediently shut my eyes, but then open them wide again. What if the flight attendants start some safety procedures and I don't see them? I need to stay alert.

Mia squeezes my hand and starts guiding us through the exercise. "Breathe in through your nose while slowly counting to four. One, two, three, four. Now hold your breath, counting to four."

I follow her instructions and almost suffocate. I can't keep the air in my lungs for so long, I might faint.

"Exhale for four. And then hold for four. Repeat this at least four times or until you feel calmer."

I close my eyes and try again. This time it becomes a bit easier. I just breath in—one, two, three, four. Hold—one, two, three, four. Exhale—one, two, three, four. Hold again—one, two, three, four.

Miraculously, when I open my eyes a minute later, I feel much, much calmer. Almost normal. "Wow, that really worked. Thanks, Mi!"

"I told you so," Mia beams with pleasure. "Sylve, are you feeling better as well?"

"Sorry, hun, I didn't do the exercise. I got distracted by this handsome guy across the aisle. He was checking me out the whole time. Do you think there's a bar on the plane where I can go and chat with him?"

"Sure, Sylve, there are bars at every corner." Mia rolls her eyes. "We're in the economy class, not on a bloody private jet."

In the meantime, the plane has levelled, and it's now almost noiselessly gliding through the white clouds. I've read somewhere that the take-off and landing are the most dangerous manoeuvres, so I should be safe at least until we're going to land at Denpasar Airport. Let's just hope that the Balinese gods will be protecting us by then.

"I can't wait to see all these amazing temples, museums, and palaces," I say, leafing through one of Balinese guidebooks one hour into the flight. Admiring the photos of all the exotic places I'm hoping to see helps me forget that we're in a huge sardine tin flying thousands of feet above the ground. Maybe Sylvia's advice wasn't so bad after all.

"And the food. Don't forget the food." Sylvia licks her lips. "Gosh, I'm starving. Must be the pre-wedding jitters."

"Sylve, you can't have the jitters if you aren't the bride," I point out.

"But I'm super hungry, nevertheless. Where's our in-flight snack?"

As if summoned by her remark, two beautiful flight attendants in turquoise uniforms materialise next to us with a huge trolley emitting delicious smells. They hand each of us a tray laden with small boxes covered in tin foil. I start with the biggest box, which includes my main dish: rice, steamed vegetables, and fried chicken. I'm no expert on Asian food, but this is really delicious. The rice is perfectly cooked, and the chicken sauce tastes of something lemony and coconut-y. It's a far cry from the soggy sandwiches I've been served on most of the flights within Europe. And then there's also a mango jelly for dessert. Not to mention all the mixed nuts and constant top-up of our tea. It's a much bigger, and tastier, dinner than I usually have at home.

"I was thinking of going on a diet," Sylvia says, her mouth filled with noodles and beef. "But if all Indonesian food is as good as this, I might ditch the idea."

"A diet? Why?" I ask.

Sylvia's always been a bit curvy, but she rarely worries about her weight. With her lush red hair and voluptuous body, she can't complain about a shortage of male attention. Quite the opposite, she's probably had more guys than Mia, Anna, and I combined.

"Because the last time I went on the scales, it told me, 'One person at a time.'" Sylvia chuckles at her own joke. "But who am I kidding? I'd rather die than go on another diet. I've had enough of them in my life. I'm healthy and happy now, so what if I don't look like a stick insect?"

"Good call, Sylve. Our bodies, our food choices." Mia finishes her vegetarian curry and yawns dramatically. "But if they keep giving us such big portions, I'm going to slip into food coma."

"Don't fall asleep yet," I poke Mia's arm with my guidebook. "I've got a fun fact for you about Balinese mythology."

"Is it about money, food, or sex? If not, I don't care," Sylvia declares.

"Do you know why our airlines are called Garuda?" I continue, ignoring Sylvia's sarcasm.

"Why? I think I've heard this word in an Indian ashram, but I don't remember the details," Mia replies.

"In Hindu mythology, Garuda is a mythical bird that's so always hungry," I reply. "And it also eats evil people."

Sylvia stops munching and looks at me with sudden interest. "Now it all makes sense. That's why they're feeding us all the time—to make sure we don't turn into hungry birds and eat all the other passengers onboard." She gestures across our aisle and whispers in a theatrical way, "Though, this guy is so cute that I could make an exception for him."

3

FIRST IMPRESSIONS

As soon as we arrive at Denpasar Airport and go to a bureau de change, we become millionaires.

"I've got ten million Indonesian Rupiah," I say, waving a wad of colourful banknotes depicting Indonesian national heroes. "Do you think this will be enough for the whole month in Bali?"

"Definitely not," Mia replies. "Probably not even enough for one day of Sylvia's shopping sprees."

"I've already bought all I need." Sylvia pats her ginormous red suitcase. "I'm not going to spend any more money on clothes."

"Fat chance of that." I laugh.

"Let's go, *chicas*, Bali awaits." Mia zips her boho handbag and leads us towards the exit. The arrival hall is modern—white and clean like any other airport in the world. If it wasn't for the exotic Balinese decorations made of stone, wood, and bamboo, I wouldn't even know we were outside of Europe. Dragging our suitcases behind us, we leave the air-conditioned arrival hall and emerge into a tropical night.

"It's like a free sauna here," I say, feeling that my tensed muscles automatically relax in the heat. "It's even hotter and more humid than I imagined."

"Hotter than the Central line during rush hours." Sylvia lives in a stylish studio in Notting Hill and commutes every day to Canary

Wharf in East London, so Central line – the hottest underground line in London – is her nemesis.

Mia doesn't say anything. She just takes a deep breath and exhales loudly, as if she was conducting one of her hot yoga classes.

"Oh, look at these Hindu sculptures." I walk over to a small stone statue of a Balinese god surrounded by sweet wafts of incense and tiny baskets filled with boiled rice, flowers, and coins. "I've read in the guidebook that everything in Bali is really mysterious and exotic."

"Yes, especially McDonalds and Starbucks." Sylvia points at the familiar logos lurking behind the sculpture and sniggers. "I think it's time to go to the hotel and finally get some sleep, Luce. We'll find you something mysterious and exotic tomorrow. Preferably in a form of a handsome man."

———————

Our hotel has sent a car to pick us up from the airport, and now we are zooming through the brightly-lit highway just outside the Denpasar Airport. I open the window and try to take in as much as I can. The night is hot, but a gentle breeze is swaying the palm trees lining the road. We go past a huge white statue of Balinese gods in a horse-drawn chariot fighting demons. It's a far cry from the modern minimalism of the small English town where I grew up. But at least we're driving on the left side of the road, so I don't feel completely lost here.

Once we've left the highway and entered a more residential area, the road becomes much narrower with small houses, cafés, and shops huddled on each side. I've read that the tourism in Bali concentrates mainly around three beach resorts—Kuta, Legian and Seminyak—but I didn't realise that this area started so close to the airport. Despite the late hour, the street is filled with cars and honking scooters, while both locals and tourists mingle on the narrow pavements. It seems that Bali, or at least its Southern peninsula, never sleeps.

When I notice an impressive orange building with black thatched roofs and a multitude of sculptures, I lean out through the window so far that I almost fall out of the car. "Look, Sylve, look, Mi, a real Balinese temple!"

"Watch out, Luce." Sylvia catches the waistband of my jeans and pulls me inside. "Don't lose your knickers over some old mouldy shrine."

Mia looks up from her phone and glances out of the window. "It's a pity I can't take a good photo at night, especially from a moving car. It would look nice on the Instagram profile for my yoga centre."

I slump back in my seat with a sigh. The island seems magical, and it would be nice to share it with someone who could appreciate it the same way I do. I wish Anna was already here.

Another stone statue welcomes us at our hotel in Kuta. With a serene smile, it watches over a young Balinese man sitting behind the reception desk. He's wearing a flowery shirt with a matching piece of fabric wrapped decoratively around his head. When he sees us enter, he puts down his phone and stands up with a broad grin on his face.

"Welcome, welcome!" The receptionist beams at us as if we were his long-lost cousins.

Mia puts on her polite-but-not-too-friendly smile and walks over to his desk. "Hello, we've got a reservation for three people: Mia Romero, Sylvia Mackenzie, and Lucy Green."

While Mia's dealing with formalities and Sylvia's trying to flirt with the receptionist, I decide to explore our new lodgings. The entrance lobby is almost completely open, with just a roof placed on four wooden pillars. I suppose in this hot climate walls become an expendable luxury. The lobby opens onto a noisy street on one side and the main hotel building behind a swimming pool on the other. The water in the pool is lapping gently against the marble rim while the cool breeze brings a faint sound of drums and the smell of boiled rice from across the road. Even though it's late and I'm still frazzled after the long journey, I feel a deep sense of peace that I haven't experienced in a long time.

"Here's your key, Luce," Mia dangles it in front of my nose. "We're on the top floor."

My room is very white and tidy with just a few Balinese accents, like a wooden sculpture on my night table or a burgundy runner placed across the bed. It would be nice to have more local decorations to cheer up the soulless bedroom, but at this point, I really couldn't care less about my surroundings. I'm just happy that I'm away from my normal life in London, my job, my anxiety. I fall asleep within seconds.

4

KUTA BEACH

The next morning, I step out onto the hot terrace where the breakfast is served and realise that the other side of our hotel is situated almost directly on the beach. Still dazed after the long trip, I rub my eyes, trying to get my bearings. I can't believe that instead of rushing to the office through rainy London, I can spend all day gazing at the golden sand and azure ocean on the horizon. Am I really in Bali, or is it just a beautiful dream? With the sun burning my pale skin and the sound of the waves in the distance, I'm starting to realise it's really happening. I sigh with pleasure, realising that this is the view that will welcome me every morning for the next month.

A smiling waiter crosses my way, balancing a big plate with delicious food that leaves a trail of mouth-watering smells behind. The buffet is laden with not only the typical Western breakfast selection, but also much more exotic Asian dishes that I can't yet name. They all seem to consist of rice or noodles, vegetables, and a lot of pungent spices. And there's even a separate table just for fruit set up in a rainbow of colours.

The terrace is packed with hotel guests, mainly couples and small groups of friends, almost no families with children. That's why Mia and Jack have chosen April for their wedding. They want to have nice weather after the end of the rainy season, while avoiding the holiday crowds that descend on the island later in the year. I spot Mia and Sylvia sitting at the table facing the waterfront. Ignoring the food, I start weaving my way towards my friends. Mia looks very casual in her favourite blue top and grey yoga pants, while Sylvia reminds me of a movie star in her signature red dress and auburn hair spilling from under a black straw hat. As I'm coming closer, I can hear snippets of their conversation.

"She should know. You told me that she hasn't been the same since the breakup." Sylvia is gesticulating with a sausage spiked on her fork.

"They broke up four years ago." Mia bites into a piece of a papaya. "I'm sure she's over him now."

"We should still tell her," Sylvia insists. "She's our best friend."

I can feel all the blood draining from my face, as I realise they're talking about me and Antoine. Suddenly, our whole relationship zooms through my mind. All the fun we had in Paris and London, all the dreams and hopes I had about our life together, and all the pain I felt after it was over. My emotions are as raw now as four years ago, and I'm on the verge of crying. Why do I have to be so emotionally unstable all the time? Why can't I just play it cool?

I probably should ask my friends why they're discussing my failed relationship and what they're trying to hide from me, but do I really want to know? Do I want to open this Pandora's Box of dead dreams? I decide to quietly return to my room and pretend I never heard this conversation. I take a step back, but at this exact moment, Mia looks up and notices me standing a few tables away.

"Morning, Luce," she puts on her friendliest, though not the most genuine, smile. "Did you sleep well? Are you still jet-lagged? Do you want some breakfast?"

"Yes, yes, and no," I reply on autopilot.

"No breakfast?" Sylvia lifts her oversized sunglasses and gives me a stern look. "Are you stressing again? We're in paradise, there's nothing to worry about."

"I'm still full from all the food on the plane yesterday," I lie.

My friends exchange meaningful looks, but Mia tactfully changes the subject. "Sylve, are you still up for a surfing lesson today? If yes, I think I've found a perfect instructor for you."

"Is he sexy?" Sylvia has her priorities straight.

"Very. If you can trust his Instagram photos."

"Good." Sylvia smiles. "I'm planning to have a lot of fun and sexy time on Bali. And you should do the same."

"Oh, I definitely will," Mia grins mischievously.

We both look at her with surprise.

"When Jack joins us in two weeks," she adds quickly. "It's our pre-wedding honeymoon."

"And what about you, Luce?" asks Sylvia. "You could use some fun."

"Let's see if your surfing instructor is really as hot as Mia said. Then, I'll decide."

I'm still a bit shaken after eavesdropping on my friends' conversation, but I don't have time to process all my emotions. Straight after breakfast, Sylvia realised that she'd packed a full bag of cosmetics but forgot the most important one: sunblock. Without factor 50, her white Scottish skin will burn like crispy bacon. So now Mia, Sylvia, and I are walking down a street full of noisy cars, motor scooters, and tourists, looking for a pharmacy. The air smells of incense, boiled rice, and fumes—an odd mixture, but not completely unpleasant. Some of the trees are decorated with white and black checkered cloth that symbolises the equilibrium of good and evil in the Balinese beliefs.

The narrow pavement is scattered with tiny baskets made of plated palm leaves and filled with rice, fruit, flower petals, and even candies and coins. These must be the offerings for the earth demons. According to my guidebook, evil spirits are so greedy that they'll eat everything that the local people will give them. Unless some stray dogs come first, which is exactly what's happening right now.

With our pale skin and surprised looks, we're immediately recognised as newcomers, and we get called out by vendors advertising their goods.

"Massage, massage?"

"Sarong, sarong?"

"Bintang, Bintang?"

"What is Bintang?" asks Sylvia "And why do they say everything twice?"

"No idea," I reply. "Maybe they just want to make sure we aren't deaf."

We're declining all the offers, but the sellers don't seem disappointed or angry. They just smile broadly, wish us a nice day, and move on to the next group of palefaces.

When we try to cross the busy road, there's another sight you won't see in most European countries. At least, not anymore. "Look at this poor creature," Mia points at a small brown horse pulling a carriage full of Western tourists. "This pony is famished and exhausted. He shouldn't be working in this heat, especially just for the pleasure of people who are too lazy to walk or take a taxi." She clenches her fists in anger. The first black cloud in our tropical paradise.

Finally, after fifteen minutes of the hot and noisy walk through Kuta, with a short stop at the local pharmacy, we arrive at the gate leading back to the beach. It consists of two massive pillars decorated with stone sculptures of some Hindu spirits and pyramid-shaped structures rising to the sky. We stop to contemplate the exotic architecture.

"Why does it look like one building split into two?" asks Mia.

This is when I can finally share my guidebook knowledge with my friends. My moment to shine. "To protect the city from evil spirits," I explain. "If a demon tries to go through the gate, the two parts will shut, trapping the evil spirit inside."

"I'll take it as a challenge," Sylvia swishes her long red hair and takes a step forward.

As if on cue, a big bird flies over our heads, flapping its wings and uttering a piercing scream.

"What was that?" Mia lifts her face towards the sky.

"No idea, but that was creepy as hell," I admit. "Like something from Hitchcock's *The Birds*."

"I always told you I was a Scottish witch." Sylvia smiles in triumph from the other side.

Mia and I follow her cautiously through the anti-demon gate, but thankfully, nothing uncanny happens this time.

The view that opens in front of us is breathtaking. The golden sand and blue water beckon invitingly. The part of the beach closest to the city is shaded by palm trees and dotted with little beach bars and makeshift stalls selling cold drinks from an icebox. Beachgoers, both pale tourists and bronzed locals, are strolling on the hot sand, lounging on sundecks, or playing in the sun. A few black women in colourful robes are selling fresh coconut juice, bracelets, and souvenirs. Everyone seems happy and completely relaxed. But the biggest eye-catcher is the wide expanse of the sea. Its colours range from deep navy blue close to the horizon to almost translucent ripples lapping the sand.

"It's too beautiful to be real," I sigh.

"Yes, it's definitely photoshopped," Sylvia quips.

We take off our shoes, and the hot sand gently massages our bare feet as we walk along the waterfront. The cool breeze from the sea brings the smells of seaweed and salt. I look at the azure waves crashing rhythmically on the yellow sand and feel utter peace. Maybe instead of taking anti-anxiety pills, we should just go for a walk on a beach? Though, good luck with that if you live in London.

"This is what I call a good life." Sylvia holds up the hem of her red dress and twirls around. "We should travel more often. Maybe Thailand next year?"

"Yep, why not," I reply half-heartedly. I love travelling, but I don't want to think about the dent this trip is making in my savings. I'm not an investment banker like Sylvia, or a successful entrepreneur like Mia, and I still have my student loan to pay off.

"Look at this guy!" Sylvia brutally interrupts my depressive musings in a theatrical whisper. She adjusts a strap of her bikini under the dress to make her boobs look even plumper.

I look up and see a handsome Balinese man standing a few meters away from us. He's wearing red Bermuda shorts and nothing else. He has short black hair, a charming smile, and dark eyes. I have a strange, hot feeling in my stomach, as if something has woken up inside me. Something that has been dormant for a very long time.

"Lust," whispers Sylvia. "I'm feeling lust at first sight. This guy is sex on legs."

"I think it's your surfing instructor," says Mia. "Let's go and introduce ourselves."

"So, Instagram didn't lie. He is gorgeous." I'm not an athletic person, but even I feel a sudden urge to take up surfing lessons. It seems that our stay in Bali will be even more eventful than we all expected.

5

RIDING THE WAVE

The sexy surfing instructor walks towards us with a broad smile revealing his perfectly white teeth.

"You must be Mia," he says with a cute Balinese accent. "The yoga teacher who contacted me on Instagram?"

"Yes, that's me. I'm actually the owner and director of a yoga academy," Mia explains with pride. "And these are my friends, Sylvia and Lucy."

"I'm Wayan." He shakes Sylvia's hand, and I can almost see a spark flying between them.

"My pleasure," murmurs Sylvia.

"And I'm Lucy," I croak.

Wayan gently takes my hand into his, and I melt as his warm skin touches mine. It's a very pleasant sensation. Sadly, he soon lets go of my hand and turns towards my friends. "Let's sit down in the bar and talk about your needs." He guides us towards a clump of palm trees away from the waterfront.

"A bar?" I look around, but I can't see anything except a few plastic chairs and empty beer crates.

"This is Sasak Bar," he points towards the chairs. "The manager will bring us some cold beer from the cool box."

"Who's the manager?" Mia sounds intrigued.

"It's just a joke between me and my cousin, Nyoman." Wayan laughs. "We run this surfing school and beach bar together. He's in charge of all the paperwork, so I call him the manager. And he calls me the coach ."

We follow Wayan to the little oasis under the trees. The plastic chairs aren't particularly comfortable, but the cool shade gives us a welcome respite after the hot street and even hotter beach.

As if summoned by a magic wand, a lean Balinese guy appears in front of us carrying a plastic ice box. He isn't as attractive as Wayan, but he still looks pretty good with his six-pack, tanned skin, and shoulder-length black hair.

"Ah, speak of the devil," says Wayan. "Nyoman will take care of you while I fetch some forms from our office."

"Welcome, welcome," he beams at us. "Do you want Bintang or something stronger?"

"What the hell is Bintang?" Mia eyes him suspiciously. "We've been hearing this word all morning."

"It's Indonesian beer. Very good. We've got lager or sweet radler."

"I'll take the radler," decides Mia.

"Same here." Sylvia smiles coquettishly at him. "If that's what you recommend."

"Isn't it too early for alcohol? It isn't even noon," I say, and am met with a surprised look from Nyoman.

"Relax! You're on holiday." He bursts out laughing and hands me a green bottle wrapped in a slightly damp beer holder, which is supposed to keep it cool. The beer is cold, sweet, and refreshing. Maybe he's right. Maybe I should stop overanalysing everything and start enjoying myself.

The manager and his ice box disappear behind the palm trees, as Wayan returns holding a bunch of papers with a big surfboard logo at the top.

"Before we start our lessons, I'd like to know a bit more about each of you." He sends us a charming smile and sits on a chair close by.

"Is it like a pub quiz?" Sylvia asks. "I love pub quizzes."

"Yes, just a bit more personal." Wayan replies. "Where are you from?"

"London," we reply in unison.

"So, you're all English?"

"Well, it's a bit more complicated than that, but we are all living in London right now." Mia takes a sip of her beer. "I'm half-Spanish, half-American, Sylvia's Scottish, and Lucy is English, but she comes from Milton Keynes."

The last sentence sounds a bit like an insult, which I suppose it is. My hometown is a soulless modern place near London, and it doesn't have the best reputation in the UK.

"And what about you, Wayan?" Sylvia asks.

"I come from Lovina, a surfing spot in the north of Bali. It's famous for black sand beaches and dolphin spotting."

"I love dolphins," Sylvia's twirling a strand of red hair around her perfectly manicured finger. "Such magnificent creatures."

Do you really? I want to ask, but bite my tongue. Sylvia has never shown any interest in wildlife, unless you can count handsome guys she's met at her wild parties.

"You should definitely come and see it. I'll be very happy to show you around."

Mia and I exchange meaningful looks. There's definitely something going on between Sylvia and Wayan.

"So, what are you doing in Bali?" Wayan moves to the next point in his questionnaire. I'm starting to suspect this questionnaire has nothing to do with surfing and has everything to do with flirting.

"We're preparing a wedding," I reply.

"And who's getting married? All of you? Is it some kind of a polyamory thing?"

"No, it's just Mia," Sylvia answers. "Lucy and I are the maids of honour."

"And where's the lucky groom?" Wayan puts down the forms on an empty beer crate, no longer even pretending it's business-related.

"Jack's still working in London, but he'll join us in two weeks." Mia raises her eyebrows. "Are you sure it's relevant to our surfing lessons?"

"Sorry, I was just being curious." Wayan grabs the questionnaire and clears his throat. "Have you ever surfed before? How many lessons would you like to take while you're in Bali? We've got some great packages available."

"To be completely honest, it was Sylvia's idea," I look at him apologetically. "We've never tried surfing before, and we're just tagging along."

"No problem at all. Would you like to start with a quick introductory lesson for each of you?"

"With pleasure." Sylvia's almost purring.

Wayan puts down the forms again and stands up. "Alright, let's go."

"Like right now?" I ask with alarm. Fantasising about lessons with a hot instructor is one thing, but getting on the surfboard in the middle of the huge ocean is quite another.

"Sure. Are you already wearing a swimsuit?"

Sylvia and Mia nod vigorously, apparently very keen to start their lessons. I look down at my black shorts and Pearl Jam T-shirt and shake my head. "Well, I'm not." Surfing lessons are way outside of my budget, so I didn't even bother with putting on a swimsuit.

"Go and change, Luce," Mia instructs me. "You can walk back through the city or take the shortcut through the beach. Just hurry up, the fun's starting now."

When I come back twenty minutes later, Sylvia is spread out on a beach towel, presenting to the world her Rubenesque shapes clad in a red bikini. As always, she's oozing so much sex appeal and confidence that she's attracting admiring glances from all male passers-by. She's funny and vivacious, and men just love her. With her in the spotlight, all other women just fade into the background, especially shy introverts like me. I sigh heavily thinking of the handsome coach. Maybe I should learn how to be more like Sylvia.

"Where's Mi?" I ask.

Sylvia opens one eye and immediately closes it again. "She's with sexy Wayan."

I shade the eyes with my hand and look towards the sea. I spot the coach's tall figure standing in waist-deep water, while Mia's gliding gracefully on the surfboard. She makes surfing look so easy and enjoyable. Soon, they both come back to the shore, dripping wet.

"You were amazing, Mi!" I say, when they join us on the beach. "I didn't know you could surf!"

"It was my first time, but I think it was easy because of my yoga practice. It was basically like coming from the Cobra position to Warrior II. Just on water."

"You're a natural," Wayan tells her with a smile and then turns his dark eyes towards me. "Who's next?"

I take a step towards him, but Sylvia's quicker. She springs from the towel, shouting: "I'm next, I'm next!"

Gosh, we've been in Bali for less than twenty-four hours, and she's already started saying everything twice. It's contagious.

"Why do you always have to be first?" I ask with sudden anger. Why is she always in the centre of male attention?

"Order of seniority," Sylvia puts her hand on Wayan's shoulder and bats her eyelashes.

"But you're three months younger than me."

"Exactly." She takes Wayan's hand and tags him towards the waterfront. "See you later, Luce."

They wade into the sea, walking so close to each other that their bodies are almost touching. With Wayan's support, Sylvia scrambles on the board. She tries to stand up but immediately lands back in water, helplessly waving her arms and legs. She gets back on the board, but then tumbles down again, headfirst, with her bum sticking up in the air. I sit down on the sand to watch, wishing I had some popcorn. This is going to be fun.

But Sylvia doesn't give up easily. Wayan is at her side the whole time, giving her guidance and helping her regain balance. And little by little, Sylvia's starting to make progress. She manages to stand on the board—first for a millisecond, then a second, then for two...

And when I think that she's finally got the hang of it, she falls down again with a huge splash, this time disappearing under the water for longer than before. When she resurfaces, I notice that something isn't right. As soon as she gets her breath back, she starts wailing. "Oh feck, oh feck, oh feck!"

Mia and I run into the sea to check what's happened. Wayan is already at her side, trying to comfort her.

"Are you hurt, Sylve?"

"Are you bleeding?"

"It's worse." Sylvia waves her arm dramatically. "I broke my nail!"

She shoves her hand in front of our faces, so that we can see a scarlet nail extension hanging limply from her middle finger.

We're huddled in stunned silence, unsure what to say. Finally, Wayan glances again at the broken nail and bursts out with laughter. Soon, we all find ourselves giggling. All except for Sylvia, who's still standing with her arm extended miserably.

"*Dios mío*, you're such a diva." Mia yanks the nail extension from Sylvia's finger and throws it into the sea.

"Ouch, it hurts." Sylvia's massaging the afflicted finger.

"Do you want to continue with the lesson?" Wayan asks gently.

"Yes, of course." Sylvia straightens her back, grabs the surfboard, and marches back into the deeper water. "Now even more than ever. I won't be defeated by some stupid waves."

She gets on the board and stands up without waiting for Wayan's cue. She wobbles but doesn't fall. We watch as she victoriously glides onto the beach with her wet red hair waving behind her. She looks like a fearless Celtic goddess.

"I did it, I did it!" She jumps off the board and starts to dance a wild Scottish reel on the golden sand.

Wayan also emerges from the ocean with droplets of water glistening on his bronze skin. "Well done, Sylvia! You were magnificent!" He gives her a big hug and then turns towards me. "Now it's time for Lucy."

———

I gingerly take the surfing board from Wayan. I feel a bit scared, but I'm sure surfing can't be too hard. After all, Mia mastered it without any previous experience, and even Sylvia learned how to do it. Eventually.

"You missed a short demo I did for your friends at the beginning. So let me explain how it works." Wayan places the board on the sand and shows me how to correctly stand up and keep my balance. It looks easy-peasy. "It's your turn," he says with a smile.

I'm lying face down on the wet board, trying to remember what Wayan has just demonstrated. First, I have to lift my head and chest. Then, I should put my left leg forward. Or was it the right one? Gosh, I'm such a clot. Wayan notices my confusion and comes to my rescue, patiently explaining once again what I'm supposed to do. After repeating the same sequence of movements about a gazillion times, I finally feel confident enough to venture into the water.

Further from the shore, the waves are surprisingly cold and strong. I look back at the hot beach in the distance beckoning me with the colourful parasols, palm trees, and refreshing beer. But if I chicken out now, Sylvia will be teasing me for the rest of our holiday.

When Wayan gives me the sign, I clamber up on the board and try to stand up. However, I've already forgotten the movements I learned on the beach just a minute ago, and I plop miserably into the water. Disgusting brine fills my mouth, nose, and eyes, almost wiping out my contact lenses. Yuck.

"Don't worry," Wayan tries to console me when I emerge back on the surface. "It happens to everyone for the first few times. But you'll soon get the hang of it. Just like your friends did."

I spit out salty water and obediently get back on the board. But when Wayan tells me to stand up, I just ignore him and keep surfing on my belly. That's nice. I can enjoy the waves without the risk of falling down. Perfect.

I do the same trick a few more times. Wayan is trying to motivate me by shouting, "Stand up, up, up, up!" but I don't even bother to move my clumsy limbs anymore. Floating on my belly is so much better.

Finally, Wayan gives up. "Are you sure you want to continue with the lesson?" he asks. "I don't think we're making a lot of progress."

"You're right, I'm useless at surfing," I reply, scrambling out to the shore. "But thanks anyway."

"Actually, what you were doing is called bellyboarding. I can put you in touch with a friend who's a bellyboarding instructor if you want."

"Sure, I'll think about it," I lie. I've had enough water sports for the next decade.

When we join Mia and Sylvia chilling out in the beach bar and drinking beer with the manager, they welcome me with sarcastic smiles.

"Well done, Luce, great performance," Sylvia mocks me.

"At least I spent most of my lesson on the surfboard, not under it," I retort.

"You all did a great job," says Wayan. "I hope you enjoyed your trial lesson. Would you like to sign up for the full course?"

I stare at my feet and slowly shake my head. There's no chance in hell I'm going back on this board of torture.

"I might sign up for a few more lessons," says Mia, "if I find time on top of my wedding preparations."

Wayan looks with hope at Sylvia, who sends him a seductive smile. Watching them flirt still brings a pang of disappointment, but I'm also secretly relieved. Maybe going out with a surfer isn't as cool as they show in films.

"I'm definitely in, coach," declares Sylvia. "When can we begin?"

6

SHREK VS. SHRINK

The next morning, I sit up disoriented in bed, with a thumping heart and metallic taste in my mouth, trying to shake off the nightmare that woke me up at this ungodly hour. I look around, but instead of my tiny room in East London, I find myself in the hotel room in Kuta. The super-clean, super-white space suddenly feels very oppressive. I get up and pad out onto the balcony, where I sit down on a lounger, as far away from the edge as I can. If I look down, my vertigo might trigger another panic attack.

The ocean is shimmering in the first light of dawn like melted gold. I can hear waves crashing onto the shore and, oddly, a rooster crowing. It's so peaceful and idyllic here. I'm in Bali, I'm safe.

The details of the weird dream—that were so vivid and frightening just a moment ago—are already slipping from my memory. I just remember that it involved my boss, Mr. Russell, who was chasing me in his perfectly pressed suit with an oversized butterfly net, while my ex-fiancé, Antoine, was watching us and laughing. When Mr. Russell finally caught me in his net, Antoine stopped laughing and started to fade away into the background like a Cheshire Cat. When he disappeared completely, I woke up.

I don't have to be Freud to understand the dream. The part about my boss is easy: I hate my job. Who doesn't? But I don't only hate it—I completely dread it. I majored in French literature, a very practical and profitable subject. So, when I ended up broke and unemployed—just like my mum had predicted—I took the first job that came my way and became a personal assistant in a solicitors office in London. This was supposed to be just a temporary solution for a few months until I found something better, but I've been working there for over four years now.

On the surface, I have no reason to complain. I know that a lot of people envy me the historic office in the Temple, regular hours, and decent pay. But I have a panic attack every morning before leaving the house. I'm scared of my stern boss, scared of making a mistake, scared of being fired. And every time I think of changing the job, I get paralysed, afraid that things might turn out to be even worse in a new workplace. Mia, Sylvia, and Anna love their jobs, but they are the exceptions, rather than the rule. And on top of that, I still haven't figured out who I want to be when I finally grow up. Which is sort of embarrassing, given that I'm already twenty-seven.

The part of the dream about Antoine is much more complicated. The dream opened up a door in my mind that had been locked for a very long time. Maybe I should pluck up the courage and ask Mia and Sylvia why they were talking about my ex over breakfast yesterday. The suspense is killing me.

I come back inside and walk into the bathroom. I take a hot shower and splash myself generously with the lavender shower gel. Jets of scorching water and the relaxing lavender scent sooth my frazzled nerves. I try to remember why the dream had left me so shaken, but the scary details have already evaporated in the steamy shower.

Instead, my mind decides to replay the montage of the happiest moments of my two-year relationship with Antoine. How I met him for the first time at a party in London. How smart and funny he was, with his cute French accent and irresistible charm. How we became almost inseparable for the next year, when I got on a student exchange in Sorbonne. We lived together in Paris, enjoying parties and picnics with our friends, and then getting engaged in the most romantic setting. How he moved to London for me when my exchange had finished. We had so much fun together. He could always find a way to make me laugh. The vivid memories flood my mind, completely ignoring the bitter end. The way Antoine broke up with me left me with a broken heart and broken trust.

———————

I turn off the hot water and wrap myself in a fluffy dressing gown. The shower calmed me down a bit, but I still feel restless after this roller-coaster ride down memory lane. Is it too late to call Anna? I check my phone. It's just after 7:00 am in Bali, which means 11:00 pm in London. I go back to bed and ping her a quick message: *Hi sweetie, are you asleep? Can I call you?*

I met Anna when we were both five and she moved to my neighbourhood in Milton Keynes. We've been inseparable ever since, hanging out in each other's houses after school, moving to London and sharing the house during our studies, calling each other every day during my year in Paris. She was my guardian angel during the horrible time after my split with Antoine. I stayed almost a month in her grandma's cottage, where I could regain my emotional balance and recover after the shock.

My phone starts vibrating, and Anna's name appears on the screen. I press the green button.

"Hi, Luce, what's up? How's Bali?" I can clearly see her face on the small screen, even though we're thousands of miles apart. Her brown hair is mussed, and she's nursing a glass of red wine in her hand.

"Anna, I'm so happy to see you! It's bloody amazing here. I can't wait until you come here and see it all for yourself." I notice dark shadows under her eyes and immediately think of her grandma's medical checks. "And how's Misia? How are you holding? Did you have a hard day?"

"Hard life." Anna grimaces and takes a swig of wine. "Misia's doing fine, even though the doctors told her she has to have even more tests. But I don't want to bore you with my moaning. How are you? Is Mia already in her full bridezilla mode?"

"Mia's cool, not bossing us around too much. Yet. But she's taking us shopping today—we have to buy our bridal dresses." I roll my eyes.

"They have to be blue to match the wedding theme. I'm sure I'll look like a Smurf."

"Always better than looking like a pink meringue during your cousin's wedding." Anna giggles and gulps down some more wine. "And how's Sylvia? Has she already found a new toy boy?"

"You bet she did. This time she went for her surfing instructor, Wayan. He's actually very cute."

"Wow, that's quick. Even for her."

"She doesn't lose any time," I say and make myself more comfortable in bed. Chatting with Anna has already helped me relax. She has this soothing quality about her.

"So, what's wrong, Luce?" Anna cuts to the chase. "Did you have another nightmare that woke you up and caused a panic attack?"

"How did you know?"

"I'm the Sherlock Holmes of psychotherapy." She laughs and takes a puff from an imaginary pipe. "Also, I've seen you in this state too many times to count. But I thought you've been feeling better recently?"

I try to smile, but fail, as another wave of anxiety hits my body and makes my blood freeze with fear. The truth is that I have nightmares almost every night, but I'm too embarrassed to mention them, even to my friends. My dreams feel like horrors, even though there's no usual menace. Instead of a werewolf or a serial killer, I panic because of a deadline at work, a missed train, lost wallet. Silly stuff, really, that gets completely blown out of proportion.

"Anna, I'm so anxious. And for no good reason. What's wrong with me?"

"Nothing's wrong, dear. It's just how your body reacts, trying to protect you from danger, even if it's completely imaginary. What was the trigger this time?"

I shift uncomfortably and avoid her gaze on the screen. "I had a dream about Antoine. And then I remembered our whole relationship. It was as if my brain decided to play a romantic comedy based on my life."

"Don't worry, it's normal. It's called an emotional vomit and happens a lot, especially on holiday."

"Emotional vomit?" I cringe my nose. "Is it a technical term?"

34

"I just made it up. But it's an accurate description, if I say so myself." Anna notices that I'm still not convinced, so she continues. "You know how people go on holiday, and suddenly, their sweat starts to smell funny? It's because their body is getting rid of all the toxins accumulated over the year. And it's the same with your mind—it's getting rid of all the memories and thoughts you were trying to suppress all this time. I know it's painful right now, but don't stop it. Let the emotional vomit flow, it'll help you heal."

"What a charming image," I grimace.

"You know what they say about toxins. Better out than in!" And she straight away contradicts her own words by drinking more wine.

"I think you're quoting Shrek now," I say. "The greatest psychologist since Freud."

"Now you're starting to get it." Anna stifles a yawn. "Okay, honey, it's getting late here. Hope you're feeling a bit better. If not, remember about your breathing and relaxation techniques. Or take the meds your doctor has prescribed."

"Thanks for the chat, it really helped," I say and yawn as well. "I can't wait till you join us here for the wedding. And I'll keep you posted about Sylvia's escapades."

"Send me the pictures of Bali, especially of this cute surfing instructor. At least I'll try to imagine that I'm there with you and not alone in gloomy London." She sends me a kiss and hangs up.

Just a few minutes of chatting with my best friend and all my anxiety is gone. But I'm so emotionally drained that I suddenly feel sleepy again. I put down my phone, cocoon myself in the white duvet, and fall asleep within seconds. This time, I don't have any nightmares—just dreams about Shrek, Freud, and lavender.

7

A LITTLE BLUE DRESS

"Luce, are you awake?" I hear Mia's voice and then a loud knock on the door. "Did you forget we're going shopping today?"

I open my eyes. 10.00 am. Shoot, I overslept! I was supposed to come to breakfast an hour ago.

"I'm almost ready, I'll be downstairs in five minutes!" I shout back.

"Okay, hurry up, the taxi is already here. We'll be waiting in the reception area."

I jump out of the bed and sprint to the bathroom. I splash my face with cold water and quickly brush my teeth. No time to put on makeup or even brush my hair. Not to mention the breakfast. Honestly, there's nothing new about this. Insomnia during the night and then over-sleeping in the morning. These are my twin passions.

I come back to the bedroom and snatch some random clothes from my suitcase. Unsurprisingly, it's a black T-shirt and skinny jeans. My wardrobe is rather monotonous. I quickly get dressed and burst out of the room.

The short taxi ride to the nearby town of Seminyak is a cultural experience in itself. I'm looking out the window while Sylvia and Mia are discussing potential designs of our bridesmaid dresses. Words like cornflower, indigo, and lapis lazuli are flying around the car. Gosh, who knew there were so many names for blue?

The traffic is moving at a snail's pace. We're constantly overtaking, or being overtaken by other taxis or noisy scooters that sometimes carry the whole family of five, including the dashing father in the front, the mother elegantly perched at the back and three cute children squeezed in the middle. Everyone is cheerfully ignoring the traffic lights and official rules. The only rule they seem to follow is that the priority belongs to the person who's honking the loudest.

We're driving from the party resort of Kuta, through more residential Legian, to posh Seminyak, though it's really hard to notice where one town starts and another begins. They just blend into one huge agglomeration that's also connected by a long strip of beach.

The driver drops us off in Jalan Raya, the main shopping street in Seminyak, which is lined with the same traditional Balinese decorations that we saw at the airport. They consist of very long bamboo poles with one end firmly planted in the ground and the other hanging in a semi-arch above our heads. I can see ornaments made of coconut leaves and colourful flowers hanging at the end of the pole like exotic Christmas decorations. I've checked in one of my guidebooks that they're called *penjor*, and they're not only ornamental, but they also express gratitude to the Hindu gods during religious ceremonies. I love how the Balinese bring a spiritual aspect to even the most mundane tasks like shopping.

The area is filled with stylish expats and tourists who prefer the artsy Seminyak to more popular and relaxed Kuta. I don't feel very comfortable in this crowded space filled with fashion shops, art galleries, and chic bars, but Mia and Sylvia are in their element.

"According to the wedding group I follow, there are some great boutiques with designer clothes and handmade jewellery hidden in this area. I made a list of places where we can find the bridesmaid dresses for you." Mia yanks her indispensable blue file from her bag. "I was thinking of something boho and romantic."

"I could do with some new jewellery." Sylvia's already scanning the busy street for signs of luxury. "A big golden necklace to go with my new dress." She twirls to showcase a red fifties dress with a sweetheart neckline and tie straps.

"The dress is gorgeous, Sylve," Mia says with genuine admiration. "Who is it? Dolce & Gabbana? Stella McCartney?"

"Actually, I made it myself." Sylvia is trying to hide her fake modest smile.

"Wow, I didn't know you could sew," I say with real admiration. Except for creating silly collages for my friends, I can't do anything artistic, and I'm always in awe of people who don't have two left hands.

"I don't have a lot of time for sewing now," Sylvia replies. "But I used to make my own clothes when I was in high school. I had no other option."

"How come? I thought your family was loaded?" I know that Sylvia's parents own a castle, so they should've been able to afford the basic necessities for their only daughter, right?

"It wasn't a question of money." Sylvia shrugs. "As a plus size teenager living in the middle of Scottish Highlands, I didn't have many shopping options. I could either buy horrible dresses that looked like potato sacks or make my own."

"Speaking of potato sacks," Mia is now scrutinising my clothes. "While we're hunting for the bridesmaid outfits, we should also find something nice and summery for Luce."

"I don't need anything new," I protest feebly, thinking of my suitcase full of black clothes and my empty bank account.

"Oh yes, you do." Sylvia folds her arms across her chest. "You can't spend the whole month in Bali parading in your old T-shirts and faded jeans."

"They aren't old, they're just from an outlet…"

Sylvia and Mia ignore my excuses, as they notice a tiny boutique filled with overpriced stuff. "This place looks promising. Let's start there."

The next three hours turn out to be an agony for me, but pure pleasure for my friends. I soon lose track of all the shops we visit and all the dresses I have to try on. All of them looked almost the same—boho and blue.

Finally, we emerge on the other side of the street, tired like hobbits going through Mordor, and loaded with more shopping bags than we can carry. The bags are brimming with Mia's and Sylvia's brand new clothes, shoes, and accessories, but we still haven't found what we were looking for.

"It's harder than finding your wedding gown back in London, Mi," I sigh and adjust the strap of my heavy shoulder bag.

"By the way, how did you transport it to Bali?" Sylvia shifts the batch of shopping bags from one hand to another.

Mia looks up from the map open on her phone. "I just put it in my suitcase. *Gracias a Dios* that I didn't go for a crinoline after all. Otherwise, I'd have to buy an extra ticket just to transport it." She glances again at the map and guides us towards a tiny shop nestled between an art gallery and a coffee shop. "I have a good feeling about this place. It has great reviews from other brides, and apparently, the owner is very friendly."

A little bell tinkles when we open the navy-blue door. The boutique is much bigger on the inside, and I almost expect to find myself in the Tardis. Instead, we step into a chic room with a creaky wooden floor, stone walls, and retro clothes displayed on old-fashioned brass hangers. Mellow jazz music and the scent of vanilla wrap us up like a warm blanket.

"Hello, ladies, my name is Melody. How can I help you today?" A tall woman with dark skin and a beautifully coiffed afro welcomes us in a smooth Australian accent. She's wearing a chic fuchsia dress and the biggest golden earrings I've ever seen.

"Hi, I'm Mia, and I'm looking for bridesmaid dresses for my friends."

"You've come to the right place." Melody invites us with a gesture towards a comfy plush sofa in front of the fitting rooms. "Do you have anything specific in mind?"

"I'm open to your suggestions as long as it's blue."

We drop all our bags on the floor and collapse on the sofa, gladly accepting flutes of champagne and roasted almonds. I close my eyes in relief. Maybe shopping isn't so bad after all. But this idyll doesn't last long. Soon, Melody returns with an armful of blue fabric, and Sylvia and I have to start our catwalk once again. Dress after dress is rejected by either Mia or Melody.

"Too short for Lucy, too long for Sylvia."

"Too boobsy."

"Not boobsy enough."

"This colour is weird. I don't even think you can call it blue."

I become so frazzled and overheated that I'm ready to burst into tears. I walk out from the fitting room for the umpteenth time, when I suddenly see a light coming into Mia's and Melody's eyes. At this point, I don't even bother to look at myself in the mirror, knowing that how I feel about the dress doesn't really matter. It's Mia's big day, and it's her call. But the glow on her face makes me check out the frock I'm wearing.

It's made of powder blue satin and reminds me of all the wonderful robes from Jane Austen adaptations I binge-watch with Anna. Sylvia looks, as always, stunning. With her curves filling the delicate blue fabric, she's ready to be swept away by some Scottish Laird. But even I don't look that bad. The dress has puffed sleeves, low décolleté, and a high waistband, making my tiny boobs look presentable. And it ends just above my knees, showing off my calves, which are probably the best parts of my body. To keep the Regency vibe, I'll have to arrange my shoulder-length hair into a high bun, but it can be easily done.

"You both scrub up well," Mia nods her head, as she and Melody give us the final look over. "We also have to order one dress for Anna, she's already given me her measurements." And then Mia comes over and gives us both a warm hug. "I'm so happy you'll be all at my side during the wedding. This will be the happiest day for me, Jack, and *las chicas!*"

———

Buoyed by our success with the bridesmaid dresses, my friends finally manage to convince me to buy some new summer clothes.

"You need a makeover, Luce," Mia declares.

"Absolutely," Sylvia agrees, glancing at her watch. "But let's hurry up. I have my surfing lesson later in the afternoon."

"Oh, the tricky second date." Mia looks at her with sudden interest.

"It's a surfing lesson, not a date," Sylvia replies with dignity. "But we might go out afterwards. Wayan invited me for a drink," she adds with a sheepish smile.

I have mixed feelings about this. I'm happy for my friend, but also a bit disappointed that sexy coach didn't choose me. Mia has Jack, Sylvia has Wayan, and I'm once again the odd one out. If only Anna was here. She's currently single and she always finds time to hang out with me. I know I can always call her, but it isn't the same over the phone. So I decide to find someone for myself, even if it's just to keep me company during our stay in Bali.

As soon as I think about this, Antoine's face flashes in my mind. It would be so nice to spend a holiday with him here. But that ship sailed a long time ago. If not Antoine, maybe Wayan's cousin Nyoman? He seems very friendly and not bad looking.

I'm so engrossed in making plans to find a summer love that I don't notice that Sylvia's talking to me. "Earth to Lucy, are you there?"

"Yes, I'm listening." I put down a black shirt I've picked up absent-mindedly from the hanger.

"Blue or green?" Sylvia asks, presenting two summer frocks.

"I can't stand blue anymore," I say and glance around to make sure Mia didn't hear my blasphemy. Fortunately, she's too busy talking to Melody about some shawls. "And I can't wear green because of my name."

"What's this haver?" Sylvia raises her eyebrows. "You're a blonde. You'll look amazing in green."

"Yes, but people are always teasing me about it. Lucy Green wearing green." I cringe internally remembering all the bullying I experienced at school.

Sylvia rolls her eyes. "Luce, grow up. We aren't in kindergarten anymore."

"Who isn't in kindergarten?" Mia materialises behind me with a beautiful silk shawl thrown around her shoulders. "By the way, you'd look smashing in that green dress, Luce."

When my friends join forces, especially at something as important for them as looks, resistance is futile. Resigned, I return to the fitting cabin.

"The dress isn't too bad, but it doesn't have a wow effect," Mia purses her lips when I walk out in a skimpy frock in the colour of spinach. "Try this skirt instead. I think it's got a potential."

The skirt is a mass of vibrant emerald satin. Long and flowy, it makes me feel as if I'm wading through silky water.

"Wow," Sylvia says when I opened the curtain.

"I think we've got a winner," Mia confirms.

I twirl around enjoying the sensation. "Thank you, *chicas*, I love it. Can I pick a matching top myself?"

"Okay," Mia graciously nods her head. "But only if it isn't black."

8

THE SURPRISING DOUGHNUTS

"Shopping was fun, but now I'm starving," Sylvia announces when we finally leave Melody and her chic boutique.

"Do you think we'll fit into a taxi with all these bags?" I look doubtfully at our spoils. "Maybe we should order a lorry? Or at least a van?"

"Don't complain, Luce. Your green skirt is a smasher." Mia effortlessly picks up a bunch of bags brimming with fabric. "You'll thank us one day."

"Let's go for a quick bite," Sylvia suggests. "I've seen on Facebook a nice café nearby. It's small, but full of doughnuts. We can walk, it shouldn't be too far."

We turn from the busy Seminyak high street into a quieter lane with almost no car traffic and just a few tourists in designer jeans and polo shirts ambling around. The posh shops give way to residential villas and stray dogs sleeping in the shade of the palm trees. The warm air smells of sweet, exotic flowers.

This world is as far away from my family home in Milton Keynes as possible, and I wonder what my parents would make of this place. For them, a holiday in Dorset was the height of exoticism, so I think they'd be completely lost here. I'm a bit out of my depth myself, buying beautiful clothes on a sunny island on the other side of the globe. But it feels good at the same time. I smile to myself, as I shift the heavy bags from one hand to another.

"It's here," Sylvia points towards a small café sandwiched between two residential buildings. "The best doughnuts in Bali."

With relief, we open the glass door and plop down on the high bar chairs, dumping our shopping bags on the floor, taking up almost half of the space. The smell of coffee and pastries fills the air.

"You were right, Sylve, your little doughnut place is indeed tiny and full of doughnuts," I say dryly. "How lovely."

"Keep your judgment until you've tried their goodies. They have very unusual toppings." Sylvia glances towards the counter, licking her lips.

The place seems surprisingly modern, with the glass walls letting in the sunshine from the street, simple white furniture reflecting the light, and the blasting AC creating a fake breeze. Other tables are occupied by Asian teenagers taking selfies with their coffee and posting them on social media. This seems like a good marketing strategy.

We go to the glass counter displaying perfect golden rings waiting to be devoured, while a fresh batch is frying in the back. A young man in a white apron and a retro diner hat is spreading white chocolate on the top of one of the pastries. He puts it down, sprinkles it with crushed pistachios, and then picks up another one. His rhythmical movements are mesmerising.

"Excuse me, can we have some doughnuts please?" Sylvia asks, interrupting his flow.

The man puts down the pistachio doughnut and turns towards us with a smile. "Sure thing. Do you want a sweet topping or savoury?"

"Sweet!" my friends cry in a unison.

"Savoury," I say at the same time.

"Today, our signature sweet toppings are apple pie, strawberry cheesecake, and white chocolate pistachio."

"I'll take one of each." Sylvia doesn't need a lot of time to make up her mind. "And a skinny latte."

"Is there anything that doesn't have too many calories?" Mia is scanning the rows and rows of pastries covered with whipped cream, chocolate, and caramel.

"Not really, miss. This is a doughnut shop." The young man smiles apologetically. "But I can prepare one with dark chocolate and hazelnuts if you want?"

"Thank you, that would be great."

"And what are the savoury options?" I ask impatiently, feeling my stomach rumbling. Maybe skipping the breakfast wasn't the best idea after all.

"Mozzarella, eggs and bacon, or salmon special."

"Salmon special, please. Whatever that is…"

As I bite into my doughnut with creamy cottage cheese, smoked salmon, capers and dill, I almost moan with pleasure. Relishing the unusual combination of the sweet doughnut and the savoury toppings, I take the second bite, but before I have a chance to swallow it, Mia wipes dark chocolate off her fingers and says, "Luce, there's something I have to tell you."

I put down the doughnut and wait. This sentence never bodes well. Why do people always use it to communicate something horrible and never to share good news? There's something I have to tell you—you look lovely today. Or you've won the lottery—

"It's about Antoine." Mia shifts uncomfortably on her stool. "He's coming to our wedding after all."

I almost choke on my capers.

Of course, I wasn't surprised that Antoine was invited, as he's an old friend of Jack's. Actually, that's how we met. Jack introduced us at a party just before my student exchange in Paris. Antoine agreed to show me the authentic city of love and ended up being my boyfriend, then fiancé, and finally an ex.

"Luce, are you okay?" Sylvia puts her hand on mine. "You're very pale."

"So, this is what you were talking about yesterday during the breakfast?" Their mysterious conversation suddenly starts to make sense. "Why didn't you tell me before?"

Mia's avoiding my eyes and starts nervously twisting her engagement ring. "Because I've just found out myself. His company signed a big environmental project in Singapore earlier than expected, and he's free to come after all."

I'm sitting in stunned silence with frantic thoughts darting through my mind. I will see Antoine again! The funny, gorgeous Antoine, who broke my heart into a million tiny pieces. Has he changed over the last four years? Will I even recognise him? Will he recognise me? On the scale from a broken nail to the Titanic, how much is this meeting going to hurt?

"He might even come to Bali a bit earlier, as he's just a short flight away, and he's keen to take some time off." Mia looks at me pleadingly. "But only if you're okay with this."

So, not only will I have to see him at the wedding, but I might be also forced to spend time with him before? The idyllic holiday with my best friends suddenly turns into my biggest nightmare—being stuck with my ex on a tiny island. For sure, he's moved on by now, and he'll be bringing some magnificent new girlfriend, like the ones I've seen on his Facebook profile when I cyber-stalked him during my moments of weakness. She'll be French and sleek and charming—all the things that I'm not.

At the thought of having to spend days, maybe even weeks, with Antoine and his new girlfriend, I feel physically sick. The doughnut, which was so delicious just a few minutes ago, now tastes like poison. Anna said that a holiday might bring an emotional vomit, but she never mentioned that there could be a physical one as well.

"Luce, how do you feel about this?" Mia's voice is gentle. "If you want, I can ask him to come only to the wedding. Or not come at all."

I shake my head and try to gather my thoughts. My first instinct is to book the next flight back to London and get away from this emotional mess. But this isn't about me. I can't make a scene and spoil my best friend's wedding. I have to act like an adult, not a scared child. So, I do what any responsible adult would do: I panic and run to the bathroom.

I wipe the eyes and splash my face with icy cold water.

"Breathe in, breathe out," I tell my pale reflection in the bathroom mirror. "Count to ten. Or do the square breathing that Mia showed you on the plane."

A few minutes later, I feel calm enough to come back to the café. I still don't look my best, but at least I don't have red dots spelling "Antoine!" flashing in front of my eyes.

When I return to the table, my friends look at me with concern.

"How are you feeling, hen?" Sylvia squeezes my arm with unusual sympathy.

"I think the capers didn't agree with my stomach," I lie. "I'm feeling much better now."

"Luce, I'm so sorry." Mia's wringing her hands. "I really thought you were over him."

"Of course I'm over him. It's ancient history." I force my muscles into a fake smile. "And don't be silly. It's a big day for you and Jack. You want to share it with all your friends, even if some of them have a complicated past."

"Are you sure? I can tell him that the guest list is closed, and this will be the end of it."

For a split second, I'm tempted to say yes. Without Antoine at the wedding, I'm safe. We can just keep our original plans and forget this ever happened. But then my loyalty wins—it isn't my wedding, it isn't my call. If inviting Antoine makes Jack happy, I can't spoil his and Mia's big day.

"Yes, I'm sure, Mi." I smile again, this time more honestly. "I think it's a great idea. It will be fun!"

"Thank you, Luce, you're the best. I'll tell Jack straight away." Mia gives me a quick hug and starts typing a message on her phone.

"I think we should celebrate with more doughnuts," Sylvia suggests. "They've just brought a new batch with lemon curd and basil topping."

I look down at my half-eaten pastry and push the plate away. I don't feel hungry anymore.

9

A GHOST FROM THE PAST

"Look at the lovebirds. Aren't they adorable?" Mia says, rubbing sun cream onto her shapely legs. We've been in Bali for four days, and her skin is already turning into a nice olive shade, while Sylvia and I are sporting the lobster look. That's the curse of blonds and redheads. If I get any more sunburnt, I'll have to sleep standing.

We're spending a lazy afternoon in Sasak Bar on Kuta Beach. Mia and I are stretched on comfy loungers that Wayan and his business partner Nyoman decided to add to the otherwise Spartan decor of their open-air beach bar. The drinks served by Nyoman are still placed on beer crates doubling as tables, but at least we don't have to sit on those horrible plastic chairs anymore.

I shade my eyes with my hand and spot Sylvia and Wayan playing in the ocean. Their surfboards have been long forgotten and are now bobbing on the waves, while our friend and her sexy surfing instructor are splashing each other with fountains of water, laughing and squealing.

"They look super cute together," I agree.

"*Dios mio*, I remember this sweet moment of falling in love. Everything is so new and exciting. Everything is possible." Mia smiles with nostalgia.

"Don't you miss this feeling?" I ask tentatively. "Now that you and Jack are tying the knot and getting all serious."

"Maybe a bit. But what I have with Jack is even better. We want to spend our lives together, building a healthy relationship and supporting each other. This means so much more than a surge of hormones when you fall for someone new." Mia has finished applying the sun cream and throws the bottle to me. "And what about you, Luce? Any new prospects on the horizon?"

"Not really." I shrug and rub the cream absentmindedly onto my crimson arms.

The truth is that I've never really recovered after splitting with Antoine. He's always been the most important man in my life. I thought we were soulmates, even though it sounds like a phrase from a cheesy book for schoolgirls. When I finally managed to pick up the pieces after the breakup, I tried dating again, but it was a complete disaster. I met a few Tindermen who were nothing like their internet personas.

First, there was Igor. He was funny and charming and clever. I was very happy until I discovered that he had a wife and a child. How did I discover it? Very easily. He told me.

"Darling," he said after we made love on a Sunday afternoon. "My cheating bitch wife decided to stop being so bitchy, and we're getting back together for the sake of our son. But we can keep having sex if you want?"

To his surprise, I refused his 'kind' offer and kicked him out from my flat and my life.

After that, I met Matthew. A very nice guy, but a bit boring. Especially in bed.

He was followed by Andrew, who was anything but boring. Especially in bed. We split up when he went backpacking for a year in Asia.

Then, I got matched with Quentin. There was nothing wrong with him, but you can't treat seriously a man with such a name. You just can't.

Finally, I dated Chris. He seemed perfect, and we spent a few wonderful weeks together. No weird name? Check. Great sex? Check. No wife and children? (As far as I knew) Check.

But then he ghosted me. He stopped answering my calls, didn't reply to any of my messages. I even suspected that he'd been kidnapped by aliens. That would have been a better option than dumping me without a word of explanation. But no, he was alive and kicking. A few months later, I bumped into him in a pub in Shoreditch, and he treated me like a distant acquaintance without once alluding to our brief but passionate affair.

For me, that was it. The last straw. I decided to take a break from men. At least if I stayed single, no one could cheat on me or disappear into thin air. Or dump me six months before our wedding, like Antoine did.

Speaking of Antoine, I still can't believe I will see him again. I take up my phone and ping a quick message to Anna, hoping she's already awake: *Guess who's coming to Bali!!!*

Who? Antoine? Anna texts me back immediately.

How did you know?!

The three exclamation marks gave you away, she replies. *Do you want me to come over and whoop his ass?*

That won't be necessary, but thanks for the offer, sweetie. I just hope he doesn't come with some new hot date...

If he does, more fool him.

I knew you'd say it! I type back and glance at the time, realising it's almost 9.00 am in London. *You probably have to go to work now. Take care and say hello to Misia x*

Will do! Call me if you need anything x

I smile, thinking how just a few short messages from Anna helped me cope with this stressful situation. I put down my phone and decide to ask Mia if Antoine is coming alone–when her phone starts ringing. She lifts her sunglasses and checks the screen. "Do you mind if I answer?"

"Of course not. I'll go for a walk to give you some privacy." I get up from my lounger with a quiet sigh. I have to find a new man and quickly. Hopefully, before my ex-fiancé arrives in Bali.

I'm strolling along the waterfront, feeling the tension in my muscles decrease with every step. There is something very soothing about the rhythmical sound of the waves and the patter of my bare feet on the wet sand. The heat, the sea, even the smell of the sun cream on my warm skin reminds me of so many happy holidays with my family in Dorset. The sandy beaches in Lyme Regis were always my happy place away from all the drama at home and school.

And after Antoine moved with me to England, I invited him to spend a long weekend in my favourite cottage close to the Cobb. It was late September four years ago, and the beach in Lyme Regis was almost deserted, even though the weather was still surprisingly balmy. We spent the whole day just walking on the sand, reading books, making plans for the future. In the evening, it started to rain, so we found shelter in a quaint pub with an open fireplace, where we had fish and chips washed down with some local cider. When we came back to our cottage, we made love in an old creaky bed while the rain was pelting down on the roof.

The bed was so old and creaky that it collapsed in the middle of our shenanigans. Can you imagine my embarrassment when we had to report it to our landlady the following morning.

I smile at this fond memory. Maybe it'll be good to see Antoine again after all? We had so many great adventures, and we broke up so long ago. After four years, we can be mature about this. I've had my Tindermen, and from what I've seen on Facebook, Antoine has had his own fill of girlfriends. If he's moved on (which he clearly did), I can do the same. Maybe we can even become friends again. Yes, this would be the right thing to do, just be nice to each other, talk about the good old times, forget the bitter ending—

I'm so engrossed in my imaginary scenarios that I don't notice a handsome man walking towards me. But I do see him now. I squint in the glaring sunlight. Where are my sunglasses when I need them?

There is something familiar about his slim frame, pointy chin, Clark Kent glasses, and oddly attractive face. Is it a dream? Am I hallucinating? No, it can't be him. But it is!

He's standing in front of me on Kuta Beach with his hands jammed in the pockets of navy blue shorts, the wind playing with his dark brown hair, slightly longer than I remembered.

"Bonjour, Lucy," he says, dispelling all my doubts. Only Antoine pronounces my name in this sexy French way. Loo-cie. As if it was a sweet bon-bon melting in his mouth.

Oh, the fucker! How dare he ambush me like that? I haven't had time to prepare myself for this meeting—neither emotionally nor physically. I glance down at my black T-shirt and denim shorts. Why didn't I decide to wear my green skirt that I bought in Melody's boutique? For once, I could look like a dignified human being, not like a victim of summer sales in a second-hand shop.

But let's not be shallow about this. It's not just about the looks. My emotional upheaval is much more important. I was just happily fantasising about our little reunion, and now I'm completely thrown off course. I want to hug and strangle him at the same time, which is a pretty accurate summary of our relationship. Or at least its final part.

What is the correct protocol when meeting your ex? Especially if the ex in question is looking at you intently with his twinkling green eyes. I'm frantically trying to think of something clever to say, but my wit-generator has failed me, and I am able to come up with only the most banal question.

"Antoine, what are you doing here?" I croak with a dry throat.

"I've just arrived to Bali, and I wanted to see how you're all doing. I called Mia, and she told me where to find you." To my dismay, his sexy French accent still gives me shivers. Though I'm not sure if I'm shaking from excitement or fury. "Can I walk with you a bit?" he asks, taking his hands out of the pockets.

"Actually, I was just about to go back to the beach bar," I say, trying to discourage him.

"Great, I'll walk you back," he replies, taking my snub for encouragement.

We're walking in an awkward silence. Or at least, awkward for me. Antoine seems completely at ease, looking at the horizon with a faint smile playing on his lips. Oh, the nerve of this man!

I'm trying to stop the vortex of emotions swirling in my head. I am so angry at him for turning up out of the blue and destroying my inner peace. But underneath all this, I'm also happy to see him. Some part of my brain (and body) happily ignores the years of separation and thinks we are still a couple. Walking peacefully side by side on a beach, like we did all those years ago in Dorset.

Antoine tears his eyes from the sea and breaks the silence. His tone is very neutral and polite. "So, how are you doing? How's life?"

Even when we were splitting, there was always warmth, even passion, in his voice, and now he turns into an Ice King. That stings.

"Life's good," I reply, equally polite, trying to come up with some news or accomplishment that might impress him. "I even got promoted. I'm a senior PA now."

As soon as the words tumble out of my mouth, I realise this is the worst thing I could say. Antoine has never been impressed by rank or economic status. That's probably one of the many benefits of coming from a rich and important family—you just take these things for granted.

"Congratulations, I'm glad to hear it." He looks at me again, this time a bit longer. "So, you're still working at the solicitors' office? I remember you always wanted to go into teaching."

Yes, I want to shout at him. This has always been my dream. To teach French in a language school in London or Paris. That's why I worked so hard and spent a fortune to get a degree in French literature. But after the breakup, I had an emotional breakdown and wasn't able to even dress myself, let alone pursue my dreams. I stayed in my job out of pure inertia, hating my life, but also unable to change it.

Hopefully, Antoine has no idea about all this. I take a deep breath and say, "Sometimes you have to grow up and change your plans, you know?"

"Yes, I know." His voice sounds unexpectedly sad.

He looks as if he wants to say something else, but at this point, we reach Sasak Bar, and Mia jumps out of her lounger to greet us. "Antoine, you made it!"

"*Bonjour*, Mia! Thank you again for the invitation!" He air-kisses her cheeks, as is the French custom. "And congratulations on your upcoming wedding. Jack's a lucky man."

"*Merci beaucoup!* Did you have a good flight? Where are you staying?" she asks.

"Yes, the flight from Singapore took just three hours. And it's still off season in Bali, so I've managed to get a good deal in the same hotel in Kuta where I stayed last time."

"Antoine, come meet Sylvia and Wayan." Mia points at our friends emerging from the sea with surfboards under their arms.

"Hello, hello, I've heard a lot about you." Sylvia drops her surfboard on the sand and gives him a full body hug, leaving wet stains on his polo shirt.

"I'm enchanted to meet you, Sylvia." He sends her one of his charming smiles.

"Hi, I'm Wayan." The two men shake hands, which seems weirdly formal on the beach. "Good to meet you."

"Mia told me you're one of the best surfing instructors in Bali. Maybe you could help me with my cutback? My surfing skills are a bit rusty."

"Anytime." Wayan beams at him and then glances at Sylvia. "Actually, I wanted to invite you all to a bonfire party on the beach tonight. Nothing too fancy, just some surfers getting together to drink beer and have fun."

I hate big gatherings of strangers. I never know what to talk about or how to behave. But before I even have a chance to think of an excuse, Sylvia makes an executive decision. "We are in! We'll bring some drinks and snacks. And if we have enough time to pop to Seminyak, we might even bring some delicious doughnuts."

"Sounds like a plan." Wayan looks so pleased that I know there's no way of getting away from the party now.

I can just hope that Antoine won't turn up there, haunting me like a ghost from the past.

10

BONFIRE NIGHT

"How did you feel seeing Antoine again? I didn't expect he'd fly from Singapore so quickly, he must have given you a shock." Mia asks while applying mascara on her already super-long and super-black eyelashes. We are preparing for the bonfire party in Sylvia's bathroom, as she has the biggest collection of make-up and accessories. Her hotel room is filled with so many eyeshades, lipsticks, and perfume bottles that she could easily set up her own store.

"Weird," I admit. "On the one hand, it felt as natural as if we'd never split up. But on the other, I realised we're now almost perfect strangers. It's all very unsettling." I add more foundation to hide my sunburnt skin. Even factor 50 sun cream didn't protect me from the burning tropical sun.

"After all you told me about him, I thought he'd be more handsome." Sylvia's trying to do the impossible feat of applying crimson lipstick and talking at the same time. To my surprise, she's succeeding. "Or maybe not even more handsome, just taller. Like Wayan!"

"What do you mean taller?" I bristle instinctively. "He's the same height as me. Not everyone can look like a Balinese god. And even if Antoine was a dwarf, so what? Who cares?"

Sylvia bares her lips to check that no lipstick stayed on her snow-white teeth. "At least you can be sure I'm not interested in him. You know what I call men under six foot?"

"What?"

"Friends." She smirks at me in the mirror. "But he's very cute in his own way."

I'm about to tell her not to call my ex-fiancé cute when Mia intervenes and changes the subject. "Sylve, how is it going with Wayan? I never thought he'd be your type. He's a far cry from your usual sleek lawyers and Canary Wharf bankers."

Sylvia pouts her perfectly red lips and admires the newly-applied make-up in the mirror. "Yes, but he's gorgeous and he makes me laugh. Something clicked between us, it's hard to explain."

Well, well, well, is it possible that our femme fatale likes someone for who he is, regardless of his job and social status? Don't get me wrong, Sylvia always chooses guys she fancies, and she would never date anyone she had no feelings for. But they always happen to be rich and handsome. Coincidence? I think not.

"What are you going to wear tonight, Luce?" Mia sprays herself with some ecologically produced perfume that smells pleasantly of lemon and verbena.

I glance at Mia's blue boho dress and Sylvia's strapless red mini. My friends look so marvellous with long hair cascading down their backs, their faces glowing from make-up and excitement. Then, I check my own mirror reflection. I think I look really well in my best jeans and favourite black T-shirt depicting the Hufflepuff coat of arms from Harry Potter. Why do they want me to change?

"Can't I go like this? Wayan said it was a casual beach party, and I want to feel comfortable."

"Luce, there will be surfers. Sexy surfers." Sylvia sighs with pleasure. "Not to mention your ex. You need to dazzle Antoine, so that he'll be sorry he ever let you go."

"Eh, do I? We don't even know if Antoine's coming, and if he is, if he's going to be alone. He might be bringing a hot date that will outshine us all." I cast a sidelong look at Mia, hoping she'd take the bait. And she does.

"Jack told me that Antoine isn't dating anyone at the moment. I think it's one of the reasons he didn't want to come to the wedding at first. He was probably as anxious of seeing you again as you were of seeing him." Mia sizes up my current outfit and comes to a wise decision. "Luce, if you want to wear something pretty, but still feel comfortable, why don't you try your new emerald skirt and white top you bought at Melody's boutique? It might boost your self-confidence."

"And I can fix your make-up and hair," Sylvia offers, pulling out the elastic from my short pony-tail. "You should let your hair down. Both literally and metaphorically."

I really hate dressing up, because I have to wear business formal outfits every day in the office. They're scratchy, uncomfortable, and they don't show who I am. But the green skirt is lovely—soft and flowy, completely different from the pencil skirts I have for work. So, why not try it? It's all for a good cause, right? Dazzling sexy surfers, and my ex.

"Just for the record, I don't want him back." I straighten my back and hold my head higher. "But a little make-up can't hurt. I'm in your hands, Sylve, do your magic."

It is already dark when the taxi driver drops us off at a hidden beach close to Jimbaran, a quaint fishing village south of Denpasar Airport. We are clutching bags full of drinks and snacks, not sure which way to go.

"I think I can hear the drums," I say, straining my ears. "Let's follow the sound."

We're walking silently on the cool sand with the moonlight skimming the ink black sea. I look up and see a myriad of stars twinkling above us. I wish I could say they look different than in the UK, but I don't spend a lot of time stargazing. I'm a homey person, and most of my evenings are filled with reading books, watching telly, or creating collages. I wouldn't be able to recognize the Big Dipper, even if it fell on my head.

The sound of the party intensifies. We can now hear not only the drums, but also peals of laughter and a lively chatter. The gathering is much bigger than I expected, about fifty young people standing around a big bonfire, chatting and dancing. Wayan and Nyoman are surrounded by a group of Balinese and Australian surfers holding beer bottles and looking very cool.

I immediately feel stressed out by the sheer number of strangers. But at least there is no sign of Antoine. One less thing to worry about. Though, if I am being completely honest, I feel a tinge of disappointment as well.

"I think we are a bit overdressed," I gesture towards our party outfits as I scan the crowd of bare-chested guys in shorts and girls wearing bikini tops with pareos. I regret not wearing my comfy jeans now. They'd help me blend into the crowd and avoid talking to people.

"Better more than less, that's my motto." Sylvia swishes her red hair and steps from the shadows, leading us towards the bonfire. "Let's get the party started!"

To my great surprise, I'm really enjoying myself. At first, I felt like a socially awkward penguin, but now I am on my third glass of Cuba Libre, and I'm chatting away as if I've known Wayan and Nyoman all my life. They're so easy-going and funny. The heat of the bonfire, the rhythm of the drums, rum cruising through my veins—they all help to lower my inhibitions and become more outgoing.

"So, how did you all meet?" Nyoman looks from Sylvia to Mia to me.

"Lucy, Anna, and I have been best friends since high school," Mia puts her arms around our shoulders, slushing a bit of beer on my arm. Luckily, I'm too tipsy to care. "And then we shared a house in East London when we were all at uni. But how we met Sylvia is a completely different story."

"Let me tell it." Sylvia's amber hair is glowing with the flames of the bonfire, and she looks like a Scottish witch. "It all started when I signed up for kickboxing classes."

Wayan's eyes widen with surprise. "Kickboxing classes? Why?"

"I was really stressed, doing a graduate program in a big bank, and I had to let off the steam. It was either that or punching all my colleagues in the face." Sylvia clenches her fists at the memory. "But I mixed up the rooms and joined one of Mia's yoga classes by mistake. I was furious. I thought they'd changed the schedule without letting me know. After the class, I went to make a massive row, but instead, I ended up having a chai latte with Mia and telling her all about my anger management issues. Mia invited me to one of their house parties, where I also met Lucy and Anna. And that's how I became a part of the gang." She grins.

"Did you ever come back to the kickboxing classes?" Wayan wants to know.

"Yes, but they turned out to be less helpful than chatting with Mia, so I quit them after a few sessions. Though, I can still deliver a mean front kick if I need to."

"What about you and Nyoman?" I ask. "How come two cousins decided to open a beach bar and surfing school together?"

"I spent a few years doing an office job, but I felt really miserable." Wayan shifts uncomfortably from one leg to another. "I quit the boring admin role and became a bartender in a posh hotel in Seminyak. I loved chatting to people, but I hated being confined in a closed space. I had to be outdoors, near the sea. At that time, Nyoman was working as a tourist guide, but he wasn't very happy, either. Finally, we realised that we had the same dream: to create our own space where people can just chill, have a drink, go for a surf. Something very simple like a beach bar. We put all our savings together, and we're hoping our business will swim, not sink."

I love stories like that. They give me hope that there's life outside of the corporate world.

"Do you sometimes think of leaving the island and moving some-where else?" Sylvia glances at him from under her mascaraed eyelashes.

"I love Bali, but I might move out if I have a good reason," Wayan replies without breaking eye contact with my Scottish friend.

"The air between the two of you is getting hotter than the bonfire." Nyoman winks at them and lets out a deep guffaw.

His amusement is contagious, or maybe it's the rum making every-thing seem hilarious, but I also start giggling. It's so good to feel happy and carefree. I have no worries in the world.

As soon as this thought crosses my mind, I freeze mid-laugh.

Antoine is looking at me from the other side of the bonfire, raising a bottle of beer in a salute. How long has he been watching me? How could I have missed him coming? Then, I notice that he's chatting with a black woman in a gorgeous fuchsia dress. She's standing with her back to us, but she seems familiar. Laughing at something he said, she playfully touches his shoulder. I feel a sudden stabbing pain in my chest.

"Your friend is here." Wayan also notices my ex and waves at him, oblivious of my mortification. "Let me bring him over. I'm sure you've got a lot of catching up to do."

"Antoine, I'm glad you finally came!" Mia greets him with air-kisses. "We started to lose hope."

"I wouldn't miss such a great party," he says with a twinkle in his eyes.

"And you even managed to find your own partner." Sylvia disentangles herself from Wayan's arms and points her chin towards the black woman, who's now dancing with her friends close to the congas. "Wait a second. Isn't it the lady from the boutique in Seminyak where we bought our bridesmaids dresses?"

"Oh, yes, it's Melody." Mia peers towards the group of the swinging women. "You don't lose any time, Antoine."

"We were just chatting." He shrugs and glances at me. "But she isn't the reason why I'm here."

I avoid his eyes as my cheeks are starting to burn. I hide my face by drinking yet another cocktail.

"And how was your business trip?" Mia asks. "Did your project in Singapore go well?"

"Yes, it all went much better than expected, we had some very successful meetings." Antoine shifts his gaze away from me, and I close my eyes in relief.

"What exactly do you do?" Sylvia leans against Wayan's six-pack, but her focus is just on Antoine. "I've heard you're a kind of lawyer, right?"

"Yes, I'm the director of a French law firm, but we're working closely with an international company that tests new technologies to protect the environment. I've been negotiating a deal in Singapore to install more smog free towers that can change smog into jewellery."

"No way! Jewellery made out of smog?" Nyoman eyes him suspiciously. "Are you pulling my leg, man?"

"Not at all. The carbon particles can be condensed to create tiny gemstones that you can then use to create a ring..."

While Antoine's explaining the pro-environment initiatives he's been involved in, I'm trying to understand why seeing him flirting with Melody has caused me physical pain. Can I be still jealous of someone who disappeared from my life four years ago? Why can't I just—

But before I have a chance to finish my thought, Nyoman is gently prodding me at the elbow. "Lucy, Lucy, what are you going to do tomorrow?"

"Hmm, I'm not sure yet. Maybe do some sightseeing. Why?"

Antoine has just finished a funny story about cleaning the coral reef with the help of local fish, and there's a pause in the general conversation. All eyes turn towards me and Nyoman.

"I can show you the island if you want." My Balinese friend sends me a wide smile that reaches his dark eyes. "I'm a certified tourist guide."

"That's a great idea." Wayan claps his cousin on the shoulder. "Nyoman has a minivan that fits six people, so you can all go on an adventure. It's still slow season, so I should be able to manage the bar on my own for one day."

"Where would you like to go? Temples? Monkey forest? Waterfalls? I can pick you up from your hotel and take you wherever you want," Nyoman offers.

Mia turns towards my ex. "Antoine, you've been here a few times before. What would you recommend?"

"Temples are a great introduction to the local culture," he replies. "There are over 20,000 of them. There's a reason why Bali is called the Island of Gods."

"Perfecto!" Mia clasps her hands. "Let's see the temples tomorrow. I suppose we won't have time to visit all 20,000, so I'll let you choose the best ones, Nyoman."

Sylvia puts her hand on Wayan's arm. "It's a pity you can't come with us as well. But, Antoine, you will join us, won't you?"

Antoine glances at me again, but I pretend to ignore him. "*Bien sûr, avec plaisir.* I'm sure it'll be fun."

11

THE TEMPLES

The following day, as soon as Mia, Sylvia, Antoine, and I pile out from Nyoman's minivan in front of the Taman Ayun Temple, we get drenched. It's the first rain we've seen since our arrival in Bali, and it's pelting down on us with a vengeance. Rain in Bali feels different to that in London—it's purer and warmer. But it still sucks to be wet.

We're a bit hungover after the bonfire party last night, and we're all quite grumpy. We hardly spoke to each other during the forty-minute car trip from Kuta to the royal temple in Mengwi. Nyoman opens the boot and gets three huge umbrellas. He hands one to Mia and Sylvia, one to Antoine, and then opens the last one above me.

"I hope you don't mind sharing with me, Lucy." He shifts closer to me, our bodies almost touching. It feels weird to be so close to another man, especially while my ex-fiancé is watching, but I just nod silently, too groggy to protest.

We walk across a bridge over a shallow moat surrounding the temple complex. It's so quiet here with almost no tourists. Probably, most of them decided to stay in their comfy hotels, rather than explore the island in the downpour. I can't say I blame them. I would like to crawl under a warm blanket with a nice book right now. I've just started *The Bridgerton* series and can't wait to get back to reading, even though I know from the start how each romance is going to end. Sometimes the most predictable stories are the most enjoyable to read.

Instead, I have to stand in the rain, huddled with my friends under the protruding roof of a small brick pavilion. Meanwhile, Nyoman goes into the pavilion to buy the entry tickets for us.

Sylvia peers at the sign on the wall and says, "Wait a minute, the tickets for tourists are much more expensive than for locals. That's a rip-off."

"Tourism is their main source of income," replies Antoine. "For you, it's just a few pounds, but the Balinese could never afford visiting their own heritage at such a price."

"I still think it's unfair." Sylvia folds her arms.

"Unfair?" Antoine raises his eyebrows. "You know what's unfair? That we all come here and invade this beautiful island, destroy its culture, and turn it into a tourist trap. That's what's unfair."

Sylvia narrows her eyes and takes a breath to defend her beliefs in free market and capitalism, as Nyoman comes out of the pavilion, holding some colourful fabrics.

"All good, we can go inside." He beams at us, completely oblivious to the tension. "But before we enter the temple, we all have to put on a sarong. Even you, Antoine."

"What's a sarong?" asks Mia.

"It's a special garment that both men and women have to wear inside the temples." Nyoman gives each of us a piece of silky fabric. Mine is bottle-green with golden swirls. "You wrap it around your waist like this." We all follow his instructions.

"It looks just like a long skirt. I expected something more exotic." Mia sounds disappointed.

"I like that men have to wear it as well." Sylvia swishes her red sarong around her. "Reminds me of Scottish kilts."

"It's actually very comfortable." Antoine looks down at his hairy legs sticking from under the silky fabric. "It's a pity that men stopped wearing kilts and togas."

Nyoman ignores our chatter as he leads us through another anti-demon gate that looks similar to the one in Kuta Beach. We enter a yard filled with wooden pavilions that have thatched roofs supported on wooden pillars, and no walls. In the distance, I can see pagoda-like towers with multiple black roofs stacked on top of each other.

"A Balinese temple is different from your Western churches," Nyoman explains. "It consists of three open courtyards with free-standing shrines and pavilions called bala. We're now standing in the first, least sacred courtyard. This is where we prepare offerings for gods and spirts. And here—" he guides us towards one of the wall-less huts, so that we can hide from rain, "is the cock-fighting pavilion."

"Cock fighting?" Mia widens her eyes. "*Dios mio*, are you still doing this in Bali?"

"Oh, yes. I have some of the finest fighting cocks in my parents' house. I've raised them from tiny chicks." Nyoman puffs up his chest. "It's our sacred tradition."

"But it's barbaric!" Mia's face goes very red.

"Not more than corrida ," Antoine interjects. "Bull fighting is very popular in Spain, isn't it?"

Mia turns towards my ex-fiancé with daggers in her eyes. "Just because I'm half Spanish doesn't mean I support this savage entertainment. You know I'm vegetarian. I can't stand animal cruelty in any form."

Mia stopped eating meat and fish in high school for ethical reasons, which was very progressive at that time, especially in Milton Keynes. Since then, she's joined multiple charities protecting animal rights, saving orphaned hedgehogs, and lobbying against fox hunting in England. I admire her that, but mentioning that she's vegetarian at every possible occasion sometimes becomes tiring.

"I'd like to see a corrida." Nyoman smiles amiably. "I think it's even more fun than cock fighting."

"How can you even say such a thing?" Mia puts her hands on her hips. "Do you want animals to suffer just because it's fun?"

I completely agree with Mia, but I don't have the energy to get involved in this inter-cultural argument. I knew that Sylvia could get easily excited in the presence of two handsome guys, but I didn't expect that Mia would get on her high horse about animal rights. If only Anna was here to smooth things over, she always knows how to diffuse even the most difficult situations.

According to my guidebook, visiting the temples was supposed to be a peaceful, soul-enriching experience. Clearly, the author hasn't met my hungover friends.

I sneak out from the cock-fighting arena, hoping to get a quiet moment to myself. Rain is dripping on my head, making my hair even more frizzy than usual, so I duck under a roof of a nearby pavilion, where I stand face to face with a monster.

It's staring at me with bulging eyes the size of ping-pong balls, baring its huge white fangs in a horrifying snarl. I almost get a heart attack before realising that it isn't a real animal. But it looks vaguely familiar—I must have already seen it in one of my guidebooks.

My friends finally stop fighting over animal rights and join me in the monster's hut.

"What is this?" I ask Nyoman, pointing at the horrifying creature.

"It's Barong," he replies, coming closer to me. "He's the king of good spirits, the symbol of health and good fortune."

"Good spirit?" Mia eyes the monster suspiciously. "Doesn't look very good to me."

"If you want, I can take you to see the Barong dance," Nyoman suggests. "It's a dance drama in which Barong fights with the evil witch Rangda."

"Oh, I love dance." Sylvia's eyes light up. "I spent five years in the National Scottish Country Dance group when I was at school."

"I remember the old photos you posted on your Facebook page," I say. "But you never told us why you stopped?"

"It's a long story. I'll tell you another time." She waves her hand dismissively. "But how can this Barong-thing dance? It's a big cow."

"It isn't a cow." Antoine smiles. "I think he's a lion. Isn't that right, Nyoman?"

"Barong isn't an animal. He's a spirit," Nyoman explains patiently. "And the costume is operated by two dancers—one at the front and one at the back."

"So, he's like a horse in a panto?" I say, finally starting to understand how it works.

"What's a panto?" Now it's Nyoman's turn to be confused.

"It's a Christmas show for children in the UK," I explain. "It's full of silly jokes, outrageous costumes, and people dressed up as animals."

"If this Barong dance is anything like the Christmas panto, I'm in," says Mia.

"I think you might be disappointed," replies Antoine and shifts his gaze from Mia to me. "We don't have it in France, but I saw a panto in London a few years ago. And it was a completely different kind of show."

I feel a blush creeping on my cheeks, as I turn my head away from my friends. We saw this panto soon after Antoine moved to London. When my student exchange in Sorbonne finished, I had to go back to England, and he decided to join me. We were living in a small studio in Shoreditch, and we loved hunting for discounted theatre tickets. I was trying to convince Antoine that the panto and West End musicals are better than his boring classical French plays, though he stayed unconvinced. But the evening itself was one of the best memories from that time. We were cuddled in the back of the theatre, laughing at silly jokes, munching on toffee, and drinking mulled wine.

"But is this dance Instagrammable?" asks Mia, as she's snapping a gazillion photos of the Barong thing on her mobile phone. "I need to keep my social media fresh and engaging. This is how most clients find my centre and decide if I'm the right person to help them with their personal development. Yoga and meditation are so much more than just physical activities. You need to trust your mentor before you can embark on the journey towards enlightening."

"Yes, you can take as many photos as you want. You can even pose with the cast when the show is over," Nyoman confirms.

"Good, then we should go." Mia nods her head enthusiastically.

Nyoman leaves the Barong pavilion and motions us to do the same. "Now let's go to the main temple courtyard, and you'll see *meru*, the soaring towers that symbolise the mountains. They're also very Instagrammable, even in the rain. And your clients might love them so much that they'll come not only to your yoga centre, but also to Bali."

12

THE BUTTERFLY EFFECT

"If I see one more temple, I think I'll explode." Sylvia slumps dramatically in the back seat of the minivan, while Nyoman drives us back to our hotel.

"Better not look out the window then," I reply from the front seat, turning towards my friends in the back. "I'm sure there are dozens of them along the road."

It's the end of our rainy temple trip, and we are now even grumpier than in the morning. Only Nyoman is still in a good mood, even though he's been doing all the hard work, driving us around and showing us the sights.

"But we visited only three temples today." Sandwiched between Sylvia and Mia in the back, Antoine is trying to defend the local heritage. "There are so many more to explore."

"Yes, and they all looked the same." Sylvia still doesn't sound impressed. "But at least it stopped raining at some point. That helped a little."

Mia takes out her phone and starts flipping through the photos from the day. "We saw one temple in the jungle and one in the village. And the very first one in the morning—the one with a weird horse from the Balinese panto."

"It was Barong," Antoine corrects her. "But it wasn't a horse, and it isn't a panto. It's a sacred dance that—"

"Yeah, whatever," Sylvia cuts him off. "The point is that we've seen a lot of temples today. And you know what they say about Balinese temples. If you've seen one, you've seen them all."

"Come on, Sylve," I protest. "It's like saying that all churches in Scotland look the same."

"Well, they kinda do," Sylvia shrugs. "I'm not a big fan of religious buildings."

"So, you didn't enjoy the trip?" Nyoman turns back to look at Sylvia without letting go of the steering wheel. Then, he shifts his sad gaze towards me. "Not even you, Lucy?"

I want to ask him to look at the road ahead, but he just keeps staring at me.

"I really enjoyed it. These were the best temples I've seen in my life," I reply. Not to mention the only ones.

"Good, good." Nyoman beams at me and focuses again on driving. "And now I have a small surprise for you."

Sylvia moans. "Not another temple, please."

"It's a butterfly sanctuary. I think you'll like it."

"A sanctuary?" I ask. "Like a place for homeless butterflies?"

"Yes, something like that. You'll see."

I feel like a Disney princess, twirling around in a garden full of butterflies. Bathed in the golden light of the afternoon sun, I'm caught in a whirlwind of fluttering wings. After the rain, the air smells of wet ground and exotic flowers. The only thing that spoils the view is a giant net above our heads, which stops butterflies from escaping the sanctuary.

"This is for you, Lucy." Nyoman gives me a tiny white flower with five thick petals and a golden centre. "It's frangipani, or *jepun*, as we call it in Balinese. We use these flowers in our temple offerings."

"It's beautiful. Thank you." I bury my nose in the flower. It smells like jasmine, but even sweeter and more fragrant.

Suddenly, I realise that my friends have wondered off, and I stayed just with Nyoman in this part of the garden. I don't feel very comfortable being alone with a man who's clearly interested in me. Don't get me wrong, I do like him. He's not only sweet, but also quite attractive. But is it a good idea to have a summer romance, especially with my ex-fiancé making an unexpected comeback into my life? Though, I did want to find someone to chase my loneliness away.

Oh, what the hell! Maybe I can do something crazy once in my life —I don't have to be sensible all the time. I come closer to Nyoman and inhale his salty scent mixed with smell of the flowers in the garden. He feels good, dependable.

"I want to show you something, Lucy. Something you've never seen in your life. Wait here," he says and disappears behind the shrubs, leaving me intrigued and a bit turned on.

Before I have time to enjoy a moment of solitude in this idyllic garden, another man materialises on the path ahead. This time it's Antoine. He walks towards me and looks at the white flower in my hand.

"So, you've discovered frangipani. I first saw these flowers when I went to Hawaii. They were everywhere." He gently takes it from my hand and tucks it behind my right ear. I always loved how much Antoine knows about the world. While I was reading about adventures in books, he was experiencing them in real life. "In Polynesia, if a woman wears a frangipani behind her right ear, it means she's looking for a relationship."

I immediately yank the flower out and drop it to the ground.

He ignores my childish gesture and changes the topic. "Do you remember how we went to Parc Floral and all the butterflies escaped from the insects' pavilion? It was so funny to watch the poor staff running around the garden with giant butterfly nets."

I smile at the memory. Maybe that's why my brain produced this weird dream about Antoine, my boss, and butterfly nets the other day. It was just replaying one of the most bizarre memories from my stay in France.

"And do you remember when fifty baboons escaped from the Paris zoo?" I ask. Life with him was never boring.

"Yes, the great baboon escape. Definitely, the best day of their lives."

We laugh, but I feel a stab of pain. Our life back then was so happy and carefree. Even though we were both conscientious students, we still had a lot of time for cycling trips to Bois de Vincennes, romantic walks along Canal Saint Martin, late-night parties with our friends in the Latin Quarter. What if that was the best time of my life?

I shake off the last thought. The best time of my life is now. I should move on from the past and make some new memories.

It's incredible how one small event can change the course of your life. If I hadn't met Antoine at that party five years ago, my life would look completely different now. Maybe I would be with someone else, living my best life without a broken heart. And what if Antoine and I had stayed together? Would we be happily married or bitterly divorced?

I lift my head and look into Antoine's eyes piercing me from behind his glasses. We are standing so close to each other that our bodies are almost touching. I don't believe in telepathy, but I can clearly feel that we're communicating without uttering a word. There are memories and emotions flowing between us. What if he decides to lean closer and kiss me? How should I react?

"Lucy, there's something I wanted to talk about—"

"Look at my new broach. It's moving!" Sylvia bursts out from behind the bend in the road with a huge butterfly sitting on her black top, with Nyoman coming close behind her.

Antoine shifts his gaze towards my friend and takes a step away from me. The magic of the moment is broken.

"Wow, that's impressive," he says. "Are you a butterfly whisperer?"

"Lucy, Lucy, I've got something for you." Nyoman proudly presents a huge beetle sitting on his open palm. It's black and shiny and has humongous horns. Disgusting.

"That's very interesting," I say with a fake smile. "Thanks, Nyoman."

"Do you want to hold it?"

"Definitely not." I flinch at the sheer thought.

"Oh, I see, I'll take it back then. But I thought you'd like it." Nyoman closes his palm around the beetle and goes back to wherever he's found this revolting creature.

I turn around again and see that Antoine and Sylvia are now in a deep conversation about butterflies and moths.

"It's the same species," Sylvia claims. "Moths are just Goth butterflies."

I'm not sure what happened between me and Antoine before Sylvia and Nyoman arrived, but I don't like this feeling. It's as if I'm falling under his spell again. I can't let it happen. Fool me once, shame on you. Fool me twice, shame on me. From now on, I'll avoid spending time with Antoine, especially alone. Hopefully, I don't have to see him too much until the wedding. And then we'll both go back to our own countries, safely divided by the English Channel and Brexit.

I notice Mia walking towards us, waving her phone in her hand. "*Chicas*, I've just been talking to Jack. He's coming next week, and he's got a great idea. He wants to hire a villa for all of us. It'll be cheaper and more comfortable than the hotel."

"Is there going to be a swimming pool and a breakfast?" Sylvia reaches for her phone to take a selfie, moving her arms gingerly not to scare away the butterfly still sitting on her chest.

"Yes, I suppose so."

"In that case, I'm in." Sylvia smiles.

"Sounds good," I agree. It would be nice to get away from people milling around the hotel and have some more privacy.

"What about you, Antoine?" Mia asks, and I look at her with horror. She can't be serious.

"That's very nice of you, but I don't want to disturb your holiday and wedding preparations. I'm sure you'll feel more comfortable with just Jack and your friends."

"Rubbish." Sylvia puts her hands on her hips, and the butterfly flutters away from her chest. "You're also our friend."

Antoine glances at me as if silently asking for my opinion. I want to shout, *No! I don't want to stay in the same house as my ex!* But I just look down at my sandals and stay quiet.

"Luce, are you okay with that?" Mia furrows her brow. "Sorry, I should have discussed it with you before. I didn't think it through. I was so excited."

She seems to be genuinely sorry, but at the same time, she exchanges a look with Sylvia. What are they plotting behind my back? Why do they want me to spend more time with Antoine?

"Yes, sure," I lie. "No problem at all."

"Great! In this case, it's all settled!"

As we're leaving the butterfly sanctuary, I notice the white frangipani still lying on the ground, and I crush it under my foot. A small gesture, but very satisfying.

13

LOVING HELL

"Lucy, we've got a problem." Sylvia bursts into my hotel room without knocking. At the beginning of our stay, we exchanged our spare hotel cards, as we're in and out of each other's rooms all the time anyway, but now I'm starting to regret it.

I'm still half-asleep, chilling in my pyjamas before breakfast and reliving the magic moment that I experienced with Antoine in the butterfly sanctuary yesterday. The last thing I need right now is my friend's drama.

"What is it, Sylve? Another broken nail?"

"This is serious this time." She slumps on my bed and makes a dramatic pause. "Mia wants to cancel the wedding."

"Oh no, not that again." I sigh and bury deeper under my duvet.

"At first, I thought it was just pre-wedding jitters. But now I'm starting to worry."

"What is she worried about? Just yesterday she was so excited about Jack arriving and moving to the villa." I sit up and shiver. I still can't believe that in less than a week I'll be living under the same roof as Antoine.

"I think there's something she's not telling us. Should we ask Anna for help? Maybe she knows some psychological tricks to convince Mia to be more reasonable." Sylvia must be really worried if she's thinking of getting help from a therapist. Even if the therapist in question is also our best friend.

I check the time on my phone. "It's after midnight in London, too late to call Anna. And besides, why does Mia have to marry Jack? Maybe it's a good idea to call off the wedding if that's what she really wants?"

"How can you even say that?" Sylvia stands up and starts pacing around my room. "Mia and Jack are perfect together, they're made for each other. The wedding is the confirmation of their love and dreams."

"Apparently, they are not that perfect if Mia wants to cancel it."

"What do you know about true love? You've been almost celibate for the last four years. You forgot how to be with a man."

I clench my hands into fists. "At least I had a serious relationship with Antoine. It didn't work out, but we spent two happy years together. And when was the last time you stayed with the same guy for more than a few weeks?"

Sylvia stops pacing and narrows her eyes. "Yes, I'm having fun with men, so what? But I do believe in real love. I know it's hard, but not impossible. My parents have been happily married for over thirty years."

"Good for you, Sylve. But not everyone is so lucky." I turn my head towards the window and blink back the tears. "You don't know what it means to live with people who hate each other."

"I'm so sorry, Luce. I forgot about your parents." Sylvia sits down again on my bed.

"Sometimes breaking up is a good idea. Especially if staying together means a loving hell for you, your partner, and your children."

"I know you were relieved when your parents finally got divorced. But Mia and Jack are different. I think they're genuinely happy together."

She's right. I throw off the duvet and get out from the bed. "Okay, let's go to see Mia. We need a *chicas* intervention."

75

We find Mia at the hotel swimming pool. It's still early morning, but the air is already getting hot and heavy. Mia's lounging on a deckchair, reading a book on her Kindle, and sipping a drink. She probably saw us coming over, but she doesn't acknowledge our presence. Sylvia and I sit down on a deckchair next to hers, while she's still ignoring us.

"Hi, Mi, how are you?" I ask. "What are you reading?"

She puts down her Kindle and finally looks at us. "A new Stephen King. Reading about serial killers always calms me down."

We sit in silence for a minute or two. I can hear a faint sound of brass music coming from the temple across the road. I wonder what kind of ceremony is taking place at this ungodly hour.

Finally, Mia breaks the silence. "Sylvia told you that I want to cancel the wedding?"

"I think you're making a mistake." Sylvia points an accusing finger at her. "Even though you like to break up and make up, I think you and Jack should finally settle down. You give us hope that true love is still possible."

"Before this conversation goes any further, I'm calling Anna." I pull out my phone and tap my best friend's name on the screen. I hope she's still up. But after a few beeps, my call goes to her voicemail. I try again, with the same result. "She's not picking up." I put the phone back into my pocket. We'll have to deal with this situation without reinforcements. "What's happened, Mi? Why this sudden change of heart?" I ask, racking my brain and trying to come up with something that Anna might say in this situation. "Express your emotions. Better out than in."

Mia gets up from the lounger and starts stalking around the swimming pool like an angry lioness. "It's not about Jack. I still love him and want to be with him. But I'm scared that the wedding will be the beginning of the end of our relationship."

I look at her with concern. "What do you mean?"

"Married people become lazy and complacent. You start taking your spouse for granted, treat them like a piece of furniture, stop making an effort. It's no longer romantic dinners and roses, it's quarrels about bins and dirty socks. No wonder that almost a half of marriages in the UK end in divorce."

"But it also means that more than half of them stay together," Sylvia observes, the finance whizz that she is.

"Exactly. They stay stuck in loveless marriages that make them angry and miserable." Mia stomps her foot and then continues her angry pacing.

"Did you quarrel with Jack? Did you find out something about him?" I ask.

"I'm telling you, it's not about Jack."

"Have you met a handsome Balinese guy, and you're planning to elope? If yes, I won't blame you." Sylvia suggests, taking a sip of Mia's drink.

Mia clenches her teeth. "No, it has nothing to do with men. I just don't think that marriage is for me. Look at my parents. My mom has never married, and she's much happier than my dad, who's just moved to wife number three. I can't even keep up with the names of all my stepmothers."

"Have you talked to your dad recently?" I ask, starting to put the pieces of the puzzle together.

Mia nods. "He called me today at dawn, forgetting about the time zone differences between Bali and New York. He's just divorced Mandy, and he's already married Candy, or whatever her name is. *La puta.*" She quickly wipes a tear rolling down her cheek. "He even threatened to come to Bali with her and walk me down the aisle."

"Aren't you glad that your dad will be here?" Sylvia finishes the drink in one big gulp.

Mia swipes off the rest of the tears. "He's never been there for me. He always promised to come to my birthday parties, my school recitals, my graduation. But he never made it. His work and his lovers were more important than me. And now he wants to come to the most important day of my life and pretend that he's the father of the year. So, no. I'm definitely not glad about this."

"But maybe it's for real now? Maybe he's changed?" Sylvia still doesn't lose faith in happy families.

Mia shrugs again. "It's most likely he wants to showcase his new wife. And pretend in front of the whole family that he's a good and caring father. Which is complete *mierda*."

"And what about your mom?" I ask. "Does she know your father wants to come? Do you think she'll have anything against this?"

"My mum cares more about orphaned chimpanzees in Zambia than about men in her life. She's very supportive, but I think she's secretly upset that I'm getting married at all, especially to someone as posh as Jack."

Sylvia shifts uncomfortably on the deckchair. "Maybe you can ask your mom to give you away at the altar, Mamma-Mia style? That might make her happy."

"I don't need to be 'given away.' I'm not a piece of *puñetero* property." Mia takes the Kindle from the lounger and smashes it with a bang on the wooden coffee table. I shudder—that's not how you treat books, even electronic ones. "And there will be no altar, it's just a civic ceremony in a restaurant."

"What exactly is the problem, Mi?" I ask gently. "Is it really about the wedding? Or are you just upset about your father?"

"I don't know anymore. I'm so confused." Mia rakes her hands through her long black locks. "I feel I need to do some yoga or meditation to get my inner balance back. But I'm too angry to even read a bloody book, let alone meditate."

I look at her with concern. Mia has always had a fiery temper, but I've never seen her so upset. I really want to help her find a solution to her dilemma—whatever the outcome.

"Yesterday during our trip, Nyoman offered to take me to his village and show me a temple where you can have a private meditation," I say. "Apparently, it's a holy place that can bring you inner peace, even in the times of great distress. Do you want me to call him and ask if he can take us there tonight?"

Mia brightens up. "*Sí*, that's a good idea. Thanks, Luce."

"Do you want me to go with you?" Sylvia asks feebly, as if hoping that the answer would be no. "I'd like to give you my moral support, but I've never been a meditation fan. No offence, Mi, but even your yoga lessons put me to sleep."

"Yes, come with us, Sylve. Group meditation might be even more effective. And don't worry, I'll guide you through this."

"I was planning to have drinks in Sasak Bar and then some sexy time with Wayan. Now I'll have to swap it for a visit to yet another temple. But I'm not complaining." Sylvia sighs theatrically. "The things we do for our friends…"

14

POO COFFEE

As soon as I leave Mia bickering with Sylvia at the swimming pool, I call Nyoman. Fortunately, he can make himself available today and is more than happy to take us to the meditation temple near his house. Of course, I don't tell him that the real purpose of the trip is to decide the fate of Mia's wedding. Will she go back to Jack as she always did? Or is she so upset about her father that she'll cancel the ceremony just to spite him?

Later, Sylvia, Mia, and I are getting out of Nyoman's minivan in a small village whose name I couldn't even find on the map. I just know that it's a one-hour ride away from our hotel in Kuta, hidden among the jungle and rice paddies near Ubud. Mia spent most of the morning locked in her room and is clearly still shaken after her outburst at the pool, but Sylvia is in the exploratory mood.

"Wow, look at all this rice." She walks towards young emerald leaves growing out from shallow water on the other side of the road. "There's so much mud. I wonder if they have any mud spa treatments here?"

"You can probably have them for free if you slip in the field," I reply. "I just hope we don't have to go through all this dirt."

"Don't worry, Lucy, there's a path to the temple," Nyoman says with a smile. "It shouldn't be wet. Well, at least not too much."

I look at the muddy path and then at my white sneakers and heave a big sigh. This day is getting better and better.

"The meditation will start at sunset," he continues, "so we have time for a coffee in my parents' house. Balinese coffee is the best in the world."

"Is it *luwak* coffee?" Mia asks suspiciously. "The one that's made of animal poo?"

"No, sorry, *kopi luwak* is too expensive." Nyoman smiles at us apologetically.

"Animal poo?" Sylvia scrunches her nose. "Sounds delicious."

"Apparently, it's one of the best and most expensive coffees in the world," I explain, remembering the food section in one of my guidebooks. "The coffee beans are pre-digested by little cat-like creatures called civets, which gives them a milder flavour."

"Yes, and the poor civets are kept in horrible conditions." Mia puts her hands on her hips. Now she's starting to look like her usual self, fighting for environmental rights and asking a million questions. It's a good sign. "Can you imagine eating coffee beans all day long? That's animal abuse."

"Sounds like a normal day for a Canary Wharf banker," Sylvia replies wryly.

"But civets like coffee," Nyoman protests at the same time, probably once again unable to understand why Westerners are making so much fuss about their local traditions. "But we don't have *kopi luwak*. Too expensive, too expensive."

We're on the veranda of Nyoman's house, eating sweet biscuits and drinking bitter coffee that has never touched animal poo. Or at least, so I hope. It's started raining again—a sudden warm downpour of the tropics—but it's nice and cosy here. We're sitting cross-legged on cushions placed directly on the floor, listening to the rain beating on the thatched roof above us.

Just like the temples we saw yesterday, the Balinese house consists of a big courtyard protected by a stone wall and filled with numerous pavilions, most of which have a thatched roof and a wooden floor, but no walls. All the pavilions are surrounded by a lush garden filled with trees, flowers, and chickens roaming freely in high grass. I can also see Nyoman's famous fighting cocks sitting miserably in small wicker cages close to the gate. Poor creatures.

"Welcome, welcome!" Nyoman's parents join us on the veranda, beaming as widely as their son.

"I'm Gunawan." His father has a small black moustache, and he's wearing a traditional white robe with an *udeng* headdress. "This is my wife, Ida Ayu, and our youngest grandchild, little Ketut."

A stunning woman, clad in a purple blouse and a long matching skirt, is cradling a cute toddler in her arms. She must be in her late forties or early fifties, but her skin is flawless, and her long black hair looks so lush that I want to ask about her beauty regime. Maybe she could help me tame my blonde mop of frizzy hair.

Nyoman's parents sit down next to us, and there's an uncomfortable pause in the conversation. It reminds me of the times when I had play-dates with my schoolmates, and their parents decided to join us for small talk. Awkward.

I look at Ketut, who also has magnificent black curls, probably inherited from her grandmother. The toddler's munching noisily on a biscuit and looking at us with her big dark eyes. When she leaves Ida Ayu's lap and crawls into my direction, probably in a search of another treat, I decide to break the silence. "What a beautiful girl! How old is she?" I blurt out the first thing that comes to my mind.

"He's actually a boy," Nyoman explains with a smile. "My sister's youngest child. He didn't have his hair cutting ceremony yet. That's why his hair is so long."

I can feel my cheeks burning with embarrassment. Why do Balinese give the same name to both girls and boys? It's so confusing.

Ignoring my blunder, Nyoman's father asks the standard question that we hear almost everywhere we go. "Is it your first time in Bali?"

"Yes," we nod in unison.

"And we absolutely love it here!" Sylvia adds with a hint of her Scottish burr.

"Nyoman told me that one of you is getting married," says Gunawan, as he straightens his headdress.

"That would be me," Mia replies, but without much enthusiasm.

"Ida Ayu and I have been married for thirty years," Gunawan states with pride. "We have three children and five grandchildren. Marriage gives you a purpose in life, it's your most important duty. That's what I keep telling Nyoman—that he needs to find a wife, become an adult, be an active member of the community."

"What do you mean?" Mia asks. "Can't he be a member of the community if he's single?"

"Only married men have a right to speak at a Banjar meeting, the community council," Nyoman explains. "But I don't even have time to go to Banjar meetings. I'm too busy in Kuta running the bar with Wayan."

"Ah, the young people nowadays—" Gunawan waves his hand dismissively. "Ida Ayu and I had a beautiful wedding ceremony and have a beautiful life together. And we always fulfil our duty in front of gods, our ancestors, and the community."

"And what about happiness?" Mia asks, glancing at the cocks in the cages. "What if being married doesn't make you happy anymore?"

"Fulfilling your duty brings you happiness," Ida Ayu answers solemnly.

I wonder if she's right. This idea sounds so foreign in our individualistic society, in which the pursuit of happiness has become a new god. Is getting married really our duty to the society? And if so, does it really make us content? But what about people who can't find their soulmate? Or are a part of the LGBQ+ community and live in a country in which the same-sex marriage is illegal? Or were jilted at the altar like me?

Okay, I wasn't really jilted at the altar, we broke up almost six months before our wedding was going to take place, but you get the picture. Did Antoine have a moral duty to keep his word and marry me, even though he didn't want to do it anymore? I shudder at the thought.

And is it really so important to tie the knot and spend the rest of your life with the same person? What if you're a social butterfly, like Sylvia, changing men like she changes her stilettos? Though, judging from our conversation this morning, even she seems to be secretly fascinated by long-term relationships.

"So, how was your wedding ceremony? What were you wearing? What did you eat?" Sylvia asks Nyoman's parents, and they gladly satisfy her curiosity.

I'm surprised that so many Balinese people speak fluent English, even an older generation in a remote village in the middle of the jungle. But maybe it's because Nyoman comes from a well-educated and quite wealthy family. He told me that before retirement, his father was a distinguished tourist guide, employed by the government to organize tours for foreign officials and celebrities. And his mother is still working as a teacher in a local school, where she organizes a lot of international programmes.

I glance at Mia, who's tapping her fingers on a coffee cup and gazing into the rainy distance. I wonder if she's serious about calling off her wedding just three weeks before the date. This would be such a horrible mess, especially for poor Jack and all the wedding guests who are flying to Bali to see the big day. And then I notice the familiar symptoms—pale face, shallow breathing, trembling hands. I think Mia's heaving an anxiety attack.

"Mi, are you okay?" I move a bit closer to her, so that the others can't overhear us. "Are you scared?"

She looks at me and nods without a word.

"What are you scared of?"

She swallows hard and blinks back the tears. "Following in my dad's footsteps and messing up all the important relationships in my life. After talking to him, I feel like a complete mess."

I punch her arm playfully. "Hey, that's my job. Don't steal it from me!"

She looks at me and smiles feebly. And at that moment, I know there's still hope for her and Jack.

15

MEDITATION FROG

Once we've finished the coffee at Nyoman's house, we thank his parents for their hospitality and set off for the meditation temple. We're lucky the afternoon rain has stopped, and the setting sun is drying off the steaming jungle. We walk through a sleepy village, followed by curious looks of locals who aren't used to Westerners outside of touristy destinations.

Nyoman turns onto a little country lane leading straight into the rice paddy we saw from the minivan. My white sneakers are turning wetter and darker with every muddy step. Why didn't I put on my old, faithful trekking boots? This is punishment for my vanity. I wanted to look nice for Nyoman, but he didn't even notice.

There's no one else here, just us, the gurgle of the stream, and the smell of wet plants. The black silhouettes of palm trees against the pink background of the setting sun remind me of a landscape from a Disney cartoon. We walk in silence until we reach a temple hidden behind a group of trees.

The temple looks similar to the other shrines we saw with Nyoman and Antoine, though this one is much smaller and less ostentatious. I notice orange walls protecting the inner courts and free-standing pavilions covered with black thatched roofs inside. It smells of old stone and wet moss that is gently growing on the white sculptures of Hindu gods and spirits.

"This is the high priest of the temple," Nyoman introduces us to a handsome Balinese man in a long white rob and a matching headdress.

For some reason, I always assumed that a high priest of a Hindu temple would be an old wise man with a bald head and three teeth. But he's quite young, probably in his early forties, has plenty of hair, and his pearly teeth are in a better condition than mine. Actually, he's quite handsome.

"Welcome to the temple of Ganesha." His white teeth are gleaming in the falling dusk. "Please put on the sarongs, and in the meantime, I will prepare the offerings for you." He bows and walks swiftly towards a wooden door, while we're tying on the colourful pieces of fabric.

As soon as he disappears inside the temple, Sylvia turns towards Nyoman and asks innocently, "Can Hindu priests have wives?"

"Yes," he replies, and Sylvia's eyes light up. "For example, the high priest of this temple has a wife and three children."

Sylvia's interest immediately evaporates.

The man in question beckons us through the gate, and we obediently waddle towards him in our tight sarongs. Everyone except Nyoman.

"Aren't you coming?" I ask.

"No, I can't," he says, sitting down on a stone step in front of the gate. "My neighbour died last week, and the whole village came together to prepare his cremation. We sacrificed some chickens and ducks, while the women made the offerings. I also helped build the cremation tower and then we threw the ashes into the river which leads to the sea. It was a beautiful and joyous ceremony, but now I'm impure and can't enter the temple."

We leave Nyoman behind with our heads filled with images of a 'beautiful and joyous' cremation. Not morbid at all.

We kneel down on the bamboo mats in front of an altar filled with offerings in little baskets. The air smells of boiled rice and burning incense. Golden shafts of light put the sculptures into almost theatrical spotlights. A giant stone turtle with yellowish ivory teeth is staring at us with his vacant eyes. I think it's Bedawang, a giant turtle on whose back the island of Bali is resting in the cosmic ocean.

"The turtle gives me creeps," Sylvia whispers.

"I know, me too," I whisper back. "Why do you think his teeth are so dirty?"

"I know nothing about reptile hygiene, but he should definitely invest in a toothbrush and whitening toothpaste."

The high priest coughs politely. "The main altar is actually this way."

We all scramble back to our feet and turn around to face a sculpture of an elephant with a benign face and a broken fang. It's Ganesha, the Hindu remover of obstacles and god of new beginnings. What a relief— I won't have to spend a whole hour looking at a psychedelic turtle in an urgent need of a dental appointment.

After a short incantation and offering, the high priest bows towards the stone altar and leaves through a side door, giving us space to meditate. Mia's sitting on the mat in a perfect lotus position. I try to imitate her, but my legs resemble more a cabbage than a lotus flower. And Sylvia crosses and uncrosses her legs a few times until she puffs out in frustration and just sits on her haunches.

"So, what do we do now?" she asks, shifting uncomfortably.

"Let me guide you through the meditation." Mia straightens her spine even further and instructs us in her best yoga teacher voice. "Close your eyes, and focus on your breath. In through the nose, out through the mouth."

I've gone to so many classes in Mia's yoga centre that I quickly slip into the familiar routine. Actually, meditation is one of the few things that really helps me cope with my anxiety. With every deep breath, I feel tension rolling away.

"Let the thoughts come and go," Mia continues in her soothing tone. "Don't focus on them, just observe them like clouds gliding through the sky."

My problems don't exist at this moment. It's just me and my breathing. My work? Gone. Anxiety? Gone. Weird attraction towards my ex-fiancé? Gone. A hope that one day—

"Ouch!" I shriek involuntarily, opening my eyes and swatting at a mosquito. Unfortunately, shrieking isn't the best way to repel insects, and I'm soon besieged by the little buzzing buggers.

I open my eyes and see that Sylvia is in the same predicament. She's scratching her arm and muttering, "Bloody vampires."

"Let's refocus." Mia seems to be in a zone, where no insects dare to enter. Or maybe she spent years in a Shaolin monastery practicing self-restraint. Who knows? "Close your eyes again and mentally scan your body to check if you have any tension. Start at the top of your head and continue until your feet."

I like this part of meditation the most. It helps me reconnect with my body, which I rarely do outside of the yoga practice. I'm starting to feel fully focused and relaxed, with a stream of warm energy rushing through my whole body—

CROAK!

Okay, one little frog isn't going to ruin my meditation. I just ignore the frog and the mosquitos and focus on the energy stream in my body….

CROAK! CROAK!

I try one last time to forget about the distractions, and start chanting the Om mantra in my head. But the amphibian is becoming more and more vocal.

CROAK! CROAK! CROAK! CROAK!

Finally, I give up and open my eyes. A big fat frog is sitting next to me, facing the altar with half-closed beady eyes. It seems to be meditating as well, repeating her CROAK! mantra.

I can't help myself and start giggling. It doesn't take long before my friends join the merriment, and our meditation is completely ruined. Even Mia abandons her cool poise.

The high priest must have heard our peals of laughter, because he comes back and quickly finishes the session with a short ceremony involving chanting and raising his hands full of frangipani flowers. But the final word belongs to the frog, which utters one last CROAK! and jumps into the bushes.

As soon as we bid goodbye to the high priest and leave the temple, Nyoman welcomes us with a huge grin on his cute face. "So, how was it? Did you like it?"

"It was magical," Mia says with dreamy eyes. "I've never felt so peaceful before."

"I can't meditate," Nyoman shakes his head. "I just can't focus. My thoughts jump like a crazy frog."

Poor Nyoman doesn't understand why we suddenly start laughing like loonies.

When we stop giggling, I look around the temple courtyard, getting dark in the failing sunlight. "Is there a toilet? I desperately need to pee."

"Why would you need a toilet here?" Nyoman raises his eyebrows. "We're in the middle of the jungle and rice fields. You can pee wherever you want—just apologise to local spirits first. If you pee on a spirit, it might get angry and bring bad luck on you."

I'm not sure if he's pulling my leg, but I don't want to take any chances. Bali is supposed to be an island of gods, after all.

"You go ahead, I'll catch up with you guys later," I say, as soon we reach a respectable distance from the temple and the local spirits.

"Actually, I need to wee as well," Sylvia admits.

"Me too," Mia joins us.

Nyoman goes alone towards the van, while we're peeing in companionable silence.

"Do you think we'll find the way alone in the dark?" My old friend anxiety is back.

"Don't worry, Luce, we have torches in our phones." Sylvia's voice is reassuring

"What did you decide, Mi?" I ask, trying to navigate my way through the dark rice field. "Are you calling off the wedding?"

"No, I don't think so." Mia releases a loud exhale towards the stars twinkling in the ink-blue sky. "Maybe I overreacted a bit."

"A bit, my ass." Sylvia snorts. "You bolted like a jumpy frog and for no good reason."

"I had a good reason," Mia protests. "During the meditation, I wasn't actually thinking about Jack, but about my father and how much he hurt me by his absence." She shakes her head. "I just really don't want my dad crashing my wedding. Especially because I know he doesn't really care about me. He just wants to flaunt his new trophy wife. I'm sure it was her idea, so that she could sneak into our family. I don't have to do anything drastic. I'll just tell them to stay away. End of story."

On the way to the hotel, I get a text from Anna: *Everything okay, honey? How are things with Antoine? I saw your missed call, but haven't had time to reply until now. A hectic day at work. x*

I reply quickly. *All good, sweetie, sending all my love to your grandma. Antoine's polite, but distant. Feels weird being around him. In other news, Mia made a small drama, but she's calmed down now. Apparently, there's nothing better than listening to frogs and peeing in the rice paddy to help you think straight again. You should recommend it to your patients...*

16

THE VILLA

A week later, Mia, Sylvia, and I are standing in the crowded arrival hall at the Denpasar airport, waiting for Jack. It's hot and humid, just like the night we arrived in Bali two weeks ago. However, it's morning now, and the modern airport, with its wavy white roof and grey marble floors, looks much less exotic and mysterious than I thought. Also, while we were driving here, I realised that the airport is actually much closer to Kuta than to Denpasar, so its name is very misleading.

I can't believe we've been here for just two weeks—it feels much longer. I miss Anna more and more with every passing day. Talking on the phone and texting doesn't feel the same and she's missing out on so many things. Sylvia starting a passionate romance with sexy Wayan, Antoine popping up from nowhere and trying to reconnect with me in the butterfly sanctuary, visiting all the temples with Nyoman, Mia wanting to call off the wedding because of her dad. And speaking of Mia, she's now jumping with excitement, scanning the crowd flowing out from the arrival gates. The meditation has really helped.

"Jack, Jack!" she exclaims at the sight of a tall, burly man with a well-trimmed brown beard. He notices us above the heads of his fellow travellers and starts making his way, followed by a big mountain backpack.

Mia runs through the airport and leaps on Jack. Literally. Her petite body is clinging to his huge frame with her arms wrapped around his neck and her legs around his waist. They're kissing as passionately as if they've just started their relationship. Which in a way they have, given that Mia almost cancelled the wedding. They look really happy together.

It could be me and Antoine. I shake my head to get rid of this unwelcome thought. Antoine is a distant past. Though he doesn't seem so distant now, especially as we're going to share the house for the next two weeks. He's going to check out from his hotel and join us directly in the villa later today. I haven't seen much of him over the past week, as we were busy with wedding preparations, but it's going to change now.

As soon as Jack disentangles himself from Mia's embrace, he takes her hand and they walk towards us.

"And how's my delicious dumpling? My chilli con carne?" As a chef, Jack loves food. He also loves Mia, but not as much as food.

"Just not con carne." She wags a finger at him. "You know I'm vegetarian."

"Hello, Sylvia. Hello, Lucy." He squeezes us both in a bear hug.

I always wonder why petite girls like Mia are drawn towards huge men like Jack, leaving us taller women fewer choices. But I quickly dismiss this thought. As long as you don't play basketball or have to pick a jar from the top shelf, height doesn't matter.

"Thank you so much for taking care of my little paella. She looks even more radiant and delicious than in London." Jack takes off his heavy backpack and puts it on the stone floor. "Do you mind if I leave it here for a second? I need to exchange money and pick up our rental car."

While Jack goes to a bureau de change to become a Balinese millionaire, Sylvia and I surround Mia, demanding answers. "How's it going, Mi? Is everything okay with the two of you? No more second thoughts?"

"None at all." She shakes her head. "As soon as I saw Jack, I realised I can't imagine my life without him. I missed him so much," Mia says with a sheepish smile. "And you were right, Sylve, Jack and I are good together. And yes, we break up sometimes, but it's just tiffs, never anything serious. It keeps our life spiced up, and we always have amazing make-up sex." She beams at the memory.

"And what about your dad?"

Mia's face hardens. "I told him that he and his new wife are not welcome. I don't think he'll bother me ever again."

When Jack comes back, dangling car keys in his big hand, Mia plants a big kiss on his lips and turns towards us with a huge grin. "Let's go! Jack and I have a lot of catching up to do."

<hr />

Hidden behind a high wall, our rented villa is surrounded by a garden filled with sweet smelling bougainvillea and red hibiscus. It's a pretty two-storey building with a wooden roof and floor-to-ceiling windows. Jack chose the quiet town of Legian sandwiched between the party-going Kuta and posh Seminyak, so we're close to all the fun, but not too close. And the beach connecting all three towns is just across the road, so we can still easily walk to Sasak Bar. A perfect location.

"Home, sweet home." Jack drops his suitcase on the gravel path and unlocks the intricately carved wooden door.

Mia, Jack, and Sylvia go inside the house, while Antoine and I stay awkwardly behind. He arrived by taxi a few minutes after us, holding a black leather suitcase that screams money and elegance. It contrasts with the pile of our luggage in different colours, shapes, and states of disrepair. The disrepair applies specifically to my old suitcase that's been serving me faithfully since the university and looks as if it's been through a lot of battles. But despite the frayed edges and worn canvas, it's still working perfectly well, so why splash a fortune on a new one?

"After you," I say, hoping that the door actually leads to Narnia, so he'll spend the rest of the holiday drinking tea with Mr. Tumnus, disappearing forever from my life.

"*Vas-y*," he motions with his hand, as he did so many times in Paris, holding the door for me like a real French gentleman.

Wonderful, now we're stuck in a politeness limbo. Finally, I walk inside the villa, getting dangerously close to Antoine. Our forearms accidentally brush, and an electric shock jumpstarts my body. I quickly turn away my head, so that he can't notice a blush creeping on my face and neck. How am I supposed to keep my cool for the next two weeks if my face turns into a beetroot every time I see him?

I shake my head to clear it and enter a spacious living room tastefully furnished with two leather sofas, a low coffee table, and a jute rug. It feels cosy and welcoming. I walk across the wooden floor to the other side of the room and step through French doors to join my friends, who are already making themselves comfortable on the patio.

"*Mira*, we have a swimming pool!" Mia squeaks with excitement. She turns towards her fiancé and throws her arms around his waist. "Jack, you thought about everything. You're the best, *mi amor!*"

I walk towards the swimming pool and bend to check the water. It's crystal clear and pleasantly warm. I look around and notice rattan loungers strategically placed around the garden. The green lawn is lined by exotic trees and bushes and there's a dining area with a huge modern barbecue close to the villa. I think we'll be very happy here. For a moment, I don't even mind that I'll need to share this space with my ex, who's chatting with Sylvia as if they were old friends.

Once Mia lets go of Jack, his attention is immediately drawn towards the barbecue. "We can buy some sausages and steaks in the market and grill them for dinner." He opens the cover with a loud metallic noise and glances at Mia. "What do you think, my juicy sirloin?"

"You know what? Grilled sausage is the only thing I've missed since I've become vegetarian." Mia admits with a big sigh. "But I'm sure we'll find some vegetables and halloumi cheese for me."

Sylvia sits on one of the loungers and stretches her voluptuous body. "Who's going to cook for us here? Do we have a private chef?"

"Definitely not me. I also need a holiday." Jack snaps the barbecue close with a huge bang. Jack works for one of the best French restaurants in Covent Garden. He studied law at Oxford, but then, to the horror of his aristocratic family, he decided to become a chef. His relatives, who for centuries have been land-owners and dandies, couldn't understand his passion for cooking and creating new flavours. They thought he was a lunatic.

Lunatic or not, Jack dropped out from Oxford and started working in various London restaurants, learning the trade on the job. When his family realised Jack was determined to become a chef one day, they decided that he would at least be a decent one. More Heston Blumenthal than the Swedish Chef from the Muppets. They sent him to Paris to study in Cordon Bleu, probably the best, or at least the most expensive, cooking schools in the world. This is when he and Antoine became friends, bound by the law—Antoine's love for it, and Jack's complete hatred of it.

It's a pity that this time we won't have a chance to eat one of his *filet mignons* or *confit de canard*, but honestly, I don't blame him. It would be like a busman's holiday.

"So, what are we going to eat for the next two weeks?" Sylvia sounds disappointed.

"There are many nice restaurants around Legian, and we aren't far away from Kuta and Seminyak." Antoine sits on a lounger next to Sylvia's. His skin is already bronzed from the week in the sun.

"Or we can cook something healthy ourselves." Mia takes off her flip-flops and sits down on the edge of the pool, swinging her legs in the azure water. "It could be fun."

"And what about the drinks?" Sylvia doesn't give up easily.

"I can be in charge of the drinks," Antoine volunteers. "I'm sure the local store will have everything we need to prepare some decent cocktails."

"*Merci*, Tony." Sylvia sends him her best smile.

"*De rien*, Sylvie."

Sylvie? Tony? Honestly? Since when have they been using pet names for each other? Also, Antoine's nickname isn't Tony, it's Anton. Or at least, this is what I called him when we were still together.

I huff quietly and clench my teeth. Is it possible that I'm jealous of my ex-fiancé and my best friend? It doesn't make any sense. Sylvia is in a sort-of-relationship with the sexy surfing instructor and Anton—sorry, Antoine—is just someone I used to know.

"Let's go and choose our bedrooms," Mia suggests leaving the pool and walking back to the house. "Who wants the big room upstairs?"

We all follow Mia up the wooden stairs to the master bedroom, which takes almost all of the first floor. The room is dominated by a four-poster bed with a muslin canopy and burgundy runner with frangipani flowers scattered over it. There's also a beautiful mahogany wardrobe and a huge bathtub facing a wall of windows overlooking the sea.

"Wow!" I can't stop myself from gaping at the bathtub in the middle of the room. I imagine myself taking a hot bubbly bath with a sea view and then lazily lounging in the huge bed. Unwelcome, racy thoughts gallop through my head, some of them involving me, Antoine, and a bathtub filled with melted chocolate. I glance at Antoine and blush when I realise he's also looking at me. I'm glad he can't read my thoughts at this moment.

Sylvia turns towards Mia and Jack, who are already testing the king-size bed. "It looks like you two will have a hell of a pre-wedding honeymoon. Bridgerton style."

"Are you sure that you don't want to stay in this bedroom?" Mia shifts her gaze from Sylvia, to me, then to Antoine, without moving from the bed.

"It would be wasted on Luce and Tony, given that they barely talk to each other," Sylvia replies. "And I can think of a few nice scenarios with Wayan, but you definitely deserve this room. Getting married has to have some perks."

Mia and Jack stay in their royal bedroom, while Sylvia, Antoine, and I walk downstairs to check out the rest of the house. Sylvia walks through the hall and opens the first door on the right. It's a kitchen. It has ecru walls, a wooden table for eight, and probably more cooking equipment than Jack has in his London restaurant.

"Looks decent. Maybe we won't starve here after all." Sylvia leaves the kitchen and opens the next door. It's a bedroom with a view of the front yard and almost the same furniture as the master suite upstairs, minus the bathtub.

"It's close to the kitchen, I'll take it." Sylvia jumps on the bed, without giving me or Antoine a chance to protest.

Antoine and I exchange an amused look and leave Sylvia's bedroom, closing the door behind us. We walk across the hall to the other side of the house, where we find two bedrooms next to each other divided only by a thin partition wall.

"Do you have any preference?" he asks, exploring one of the rooms.

"They look almost the same. You can choose."

We stand for a moment in awkward silence until Antoine reaches a decision. "As I'm already in this room, I can keep it, if it's okay with you?"

"Sure," I agree. "I'll bring my suitcase to the other one."

"Let me help you," he offers gallantly.

"Thanks, but I brought it myself from London, I should be fine carrying it from the driveway."

"But I really want to help, Lucy." He takes a step towards me.

"I've been doing great without you for the last four years. I will be fine now." I storm away from the house and slam the door behind me. I've spent less than an hour in Antoine's company, and I already want to run away.

THE SOUND OF SILENCE

It's siesta time. It means that most tourists in Legian, including us, are inside their hotels or houses, digesting lunch and avoiding the hottest time of the day.

After the morning hustle settling into our new lodgings, the villa is so quiet that I can hear my stomach growling from food overdose after our take-away Balinese lunch. I used to think that food in this tropical climate would be light and fresh, but the calories and oil swimming in my stomach prove otherwise.

Rubbing my belly, I sit up on the bed and look around my new room. It's very welcoming and cosy, especially compared to the white austerity of our old hotel in Kuta. I love how the three main colours used in the décor complement each other: the stout mahogany of the wooden furniture, the calming white of the walls and the canopy, and the bold burgundy of the cushions and the bed runner. Not to mention the greenery of the garden outside my window. Yes, very cosy indeed.

I get up from the bed and walk towards a beautifully carved desk facing the window, wondering what my friends are doing right now. Mia and Jack are probably testing their bed upstairs, while Sylvia is getting some beauty sleep in hers. And Antoine is suspiciously quiet on the other side of the wall. Maybe he's sleeping as well?

Meanwhile, I decide to create a hand-made wedding card for my friends. I've cut out some photos and pictures from glossy magazines I bought back in London, and I want to assemble them into a nice collage.

When we were kids, Anna and I spent hours in her grandma's kitchen, drawing and painting, feeling like young Picassos. But I soon realised that I had zero artistic talent, so I decided to make collages instead. There's something calming and almost therapeutic about spending long winter evenings browsing through old magazines, snipping up images and words, and pasting them on Bristol boards. They also make great low-cost gifts for my friends and family. Like the birthday card I made for Anna's grandma depicting a chimpanzee eating a birthday cake in a bathtub with a caption: "Never too old to party!" Misia couldn't stop chuckling when she got it for her seventieth birthday.

Now I'm trying to create something beautiful for Mia and Jack's wedding, but I have no idea where to start. I want it to be so perfect that the pressure is blocking all my creativity. I push away hearts and flowers I've cut out from one of the magazines. They were supposed to remind them of love and marriage, but I think they're too cheesy and cliché for my boho friends.

Also, I'm getting constantly distracted by the sounds that started flowing from Antoine's room. So, he's awake after all. He isn't particularly noisy, it's just that the wall is very thin. While I'm rearranging for the zillionth time a bouquet of blue dahlias on the page, my ex-fiancé is walking around his room, opening and closing a squeaky wardrobe and shuffling his suitcase on the wooden floor.

When he finally finishes unpacking and slumps on the bed, I give out a big sigh, but I stop myself half-way. If I can hear him, it means he can hear me as well. At least the ensuite bathrooms are on the opposite sides of our rooms and seem to have solid doors. Otherwise, this situation could become really embarrassing.

I focus back on my collage, but before I get a chance to make any progress, there's a new source of auditory distraction. Antoine's started playing music on his phone. Very softly, but I can still hear it. And which song did he decide to play out of all the songs ever created?

"Cheek to Cheek" by Ella Fitzgerald and Louis Armstrong. Our song.

Damn this man. What is he thinking? I want to go and bang on his door and tell him to switch it off immediately. But what exactly should I tell him? That this song brings too many bittersweet memories?

No, I can't do it. I would just expose my wounds that I thought I had healed long ago. But he's either teasing me on purpose, or he has clearly forgotten what this song meant to me. To us.

I've always loved Ella Fitzgerald. Her velvety voice often filled the house which Anna, Mia, and I shared during our uni days. And this particular song was playing when Antoine and I met for the first time.

It was the summer before my student exchange in Paris, and our posh friends, Victoria and David, invited us to a birthday party in their massive house in Hampstead Heath. I noticed the *Ella and Louis* album while browsing through David's collection of vinyl. Yes, vinyl. That's how posh they are—they don't listen to music on their laptops or mobile phones like other mortals. David plays music only on the highest quality record player with the most powerful stereo he could find on the British market.

"Dave, can you put this on?" I handed him the vinyl. "It's my favourite album."

As soon as Ella and Louis started singing "Heaven, I'm in heaven—," Mia burst into the room, followed by Jack and some attractive dark-haired guy with glasses.

"Luce, you've got to meet someone. This is Jack's friend from France. Maybe he can show you around Paris when you move over there?"

And this is how it all started. Antoine and I spent the whole evening talking about literature, films, and music, oblivious to the party around us. He was two years older than me and travelled a lot. I was in awe of his knowledge of the exotic places like Haiti or French Polynesia. In turn, he listened with a keen interest when I explained that books helped me discover people and places from the safety of my own sofa.

We didn't share the same taste in literature—I preferred Jane Austen, while he was more of a John Grisham guy—but we agreed that life without books would be unbearably dull.

When we got engaged a year later, we chose "Cheek to Cheek" for our first dance.

I slam down my scissors and glue on the table and decide to go outside. Maybe a quick swim in the pool will chase away the unwelcome memories. I swing the door open and bump into Antoine, who's just left his room with a French magazine tucked under his arm.

"Oh, sorry." I take a step back into my room.

"*Excuse-moi. Vas-y.*" He gestures to let me go first.

"No, after you."

We're standing in the narrow corridor connecting our rooms, once again paralysed by politeness and embarrassment. It starts to feel like a Groundhog Day.

"I just wanted to read on the terrace." He explains, holding up the magazine. He's still reading *Le Monde*. Some things never change.

He sends me a warm smile, and for a split second, my brain forgets that Antoine and I are no longer together. I feel a sudden urge to put my head on his shoulder and just let him embrace me. But then, like a lightning strike, the memory of his rejection shoots through my body. The pain is fresh and raw. I can't breathe, I just can't breathe.

I need to hide before he notices my panic attack. I retreat into my room, mumbling, "Sorry, I have to go," and shut the door in his face.

I don't dare to move, as he's standing in silence on the opposite side of the door. I fear, or maybe hope, that he'll knock and check how I'm feeling. But after a while, he walks away. I lean against the smooth wood, breathing heavily until I can no longer hear the echo of his footsteps.

18

FLOATING UNICORNS

Our first evening in the villa is unexpectedly chilled. I was afraid that Antoine might make some comments about my strange behaviour earlier in the day, but he keeps a safe distance.

Mia, Jack, Sylvia, Antoine, and I are sitting on the patio behind the villa in the humid night. The air smells of sweet flowers growing in our garden and the chlorine water in the swimming pool. And if we all stay silent for a second—which doesn't happen a lot—we can hear the roar of the nearby ocean and some noisy cicadas.

Jack broke his no-cooking-on-holiday rule and fired up the barbecue to prepare delicious fish for us. True to his word, Antoine is mixing exotic cocktails, while Mia, Sylvia, and I are relaxing around the pool.

"Handsome men serving us food and drinks. I could get used to that." Sylvia murmurs, taking a gulp of mango juice mixed with rum.

"Jack's family thinks that I'm marrying him for his money and status." Mia swirls rose vodka and sprite in her glass. "But I'm actually doing it for his cooking skills."

"I don't blame you," I reply and lick my lips at the memory of the tender barramundi fish with lemon juice and garlic that Jack grilled for us tonight.

As we didn't manage to find any halloumi cheese, even vegetarian

Mia agreed to make an exception and eat some freshly caught fish. "At least it led a happy life in the ocean and hopefully didn't suffer too much after it got caught," she explained, trying to appease her own conscience.

Jack winks at Mia from behind the barbecue. "And I'm marrying you for your fiery Spanish temperament and great yoga moves, my spicy gazpacho. I still can't believe how you can be so passionate and poised at the same time."

"It's all a matter of balance," Mia explains. "Yin and yang."

"Just like in the Balinese philosophy." Antoine's shaking the drinks mixer with some new concoction. "You have to keep the balance between good and evil, life and death, light and darkness. That's why the Balinese put the offerings on the altar for the gods. And on the ground, for the demons." He pours some violet liquid into a flute glass and hands it over to me.

"But the offerings on the ground are eaten by stray dogs, not spirits." I take a sip and recognise the sweet flavour with a fruity twist. It's my favourite drink called *kir*, white wine mixed with blackcurrant liqueur. It brings so many memories from Paris.

"I think dogs are angels in disguise," argues Mia. "We're going to adopt a puppy from a shelter when we come back to London."

"Oh, how sweet." Sylvia drains the last drop of her drink and looks expectantly at Antoine, who quickly refreshes her glass. "Can I be the godmother?"

"Of our dog?" Jack has just finished cleaning the barbecue and comes over to lie down on a lounger next to Mia's. "Why not?"

"More drinks, anyone?" Antoine hands Jack a tumbler of his favourite Old-Fashioned cocktail, smelling of zesty lemon and musky brandy.

"Maybe one more." Sylvia extends her glass that's almost empty again. "Who knew that mango juice and rum go so well together?"

Antoine fills her glass, saying, "Actually, this afternoon, I had a look into the garden shed and found something that you might like, Sylvie. But I need Jack's help to bring it out."

"Now I'm intrigued." She sends him her most dazzling smile. "You're a very mysterious man, Tony."

I want to stand up and pour my drink over Sylvia's head. She's already dating sexy Wayan. Isn't that enough? Does she have to flirt with every damn man in Bali? But instead of attacking my friend, I sip my kir muttering French invectives under my breath.

———

While Antoine and Jack are rummaging in the garden shed hidden behind the bushes, I decide to take this opportunity to check on Mia. The best way to get distracted from my own drama is to focus on someone else's.

"Did you tell Jack about your doubts, Mi?" I ask quietly enough to make sure the guys can't hear us.

She toys with her glass before answering. "Yes, I finally did. I talked to Anna yesterday and she advised me to come clean. I felt much better afterwards."

"And how did he react?" Sylvia whispers, leaning closer to us. Oh, so now she's pretending to be our friend, instead of an ex-snatcher? *Salope.*

"He said I was a silly pancake, and as long as I still loved him, he wouldn't let me cancel the wedding."

"Well, at least one of you has some gumption." Sylvia slumps back on her deckchair. "I told you so from the very beginning."

"And what does he think about barring your father from the wedding?" I ask. "Is he okay with that?"

"He doesn't care one way or another. It's completely my call. What-ever makes me happy." Mia twirls a strand of her black locks around her fingers. I know for her it's a sign of stress. "So, it's definitely a no."

"Are you sure it's the right decision? Maybe you could invite him after all?" Sylvia suggests.

"No, absolutely not! *Nunca en la vida!*" She slams her glass on the coffee table next to her deckchair. "I don't want my father to spoil the best day of my life."

Before Sylvia or I have a chance to reply to Mia's outburst, Jack and Antoine come back, holding two huge inflatable unicorns.

"Now you can enjoy the swimming pool without getting wet."

Antoine puts one of the unicorns on the surface of the blue water, and it floats away from the pool's edge.

"Perfecto." Sylvia jumps out from her lounger and tries to mount the unicorn's back. She fails miserably, landing bum-first in the water. She resurfaces laughing like a loony. "Come here, guys. Join me in the unicorn quest."

We are all so tipsy that we just follow her instructions, trying to push her on top of the slippery creature. It's lucky that most of us are already wearing swimsuits, or at least very skimpy clothing. After a lot of splashing and laughing, Sylvia's sitting astride the floatable creature with her arms extended to the sides, as if she was flying.

"I'm the queen of the world!" she shouts out with triumph.

I throw my head back and laugh. Life is so much better with a unicorn.

While Sylvia is blissfully floating on a unicorn, sipping yet another drink, the garden party is slowly dying. Mia and Jack are cuddling on two loungers pushed together. Antoine has abandoned his bartender's duty and is standing on the edge of the swimming pool gazing into the darkness, while I'm trying not to look at his sportive body. He has strong arms and the toned calves of an experienced swimmer. I gulp.

"What are we going to do tomorrow?" I ask, hoping that we can split into groups and I won't be forced to spend another full day with Antoine. Inadvertently, I check out his slim back, broad shoulders, and shapely bum. Hmm, maybe spending time with him isn't such a hardship after all.

"I'm so jet-lagged, I could sleep all day." Jack yawns loudly to prove his point.

"I know, *mi amor*." Mia gently rubs his arm. "But we still have a lot of things to prepare. We need to go to Kuta to check on our wedding venue. The Boardwalk restaurant looks amazing in the photos and has glowing revues on the internet, but I just want to make sure it's as good as everyone says." Mia's now massaging Jack's neck. "And then, we're going to Seminyak to have the final cake tasting."

The mention of the cake wakes Sylvia up from her unicorn nirvana. "Ooh, I can help you with the tasting. I'm good at it. Eating is my superpower, especially desserts."

"Sure, you can be our official menu consultant," Jack agrees with a smile on his bearded face. "We're going to order a three-tiered wedding cake, exotic fruit salad, and sorbet to refresh our guests in this heat."

"And what about tiramisu?" Sylvia demands. "It isn't a real wedding unless there's tiramisu."

The azure water in the pool is lapping gently against the edge, with bigger ripples riding the surface every time Sylvia gestures broadly with her glass and throws the floating unicorn off balance. While our friends continue chatting about cakes, flowers, and wedding venues, I observe Antoine. As if sensing my gaze, he turns around and sends me a wistful smile. I wonder if he's thinking what I'm thinking.

19

PARIS, PARIS

This hot night air, the sound of water, Antoine's silhouette in the dark — it all makes me think of the evening when we got engaged and began to plan our own wedding. I feel as if it had happened in a different lifetime, not just five years ago.

After the fateful birthday party at Victoria and David's house, Antoine and I kept in touch. And when I moved to Paris a month later, we were already an item.

We spent the first few weeks of my student exchange exploring the city and having mind-boggling sex. Thanks to him and his friends, I was no longer shy and boring Luce from Milton Keynes. I turned into sophisticated and elegant Lucy living her best life in Paris.

I almost completely changed my wardrobe, though I still preferred black clothes. But thanks to a side job as a babysitter for a loaded Parisian family, I could afford chic onyx dresses from second-hand boutiques in Montmartre. With Englishness painted all over my Anglo-Saxon face, I was an exotic bird for Antoine's French friends. My social life bloomed.

"So, in England, you pronounce it as happiness?" his friends would wonder, while I was trying to give them free elocution classes. "Not a-penis?"

But most importantly, my anxiety also took some time off. It was always close to me, lurking in the shadows, but rarely making a full entrance on the stage. And if I did get a full-blown anxiety attack, Anton always managed to find a way to calm me down. Or even better, to make me laugh.

I've had panic attacks since I was a kid, but my parents would brush them off, saying that I was just "oversensitive" or "exaggerating." Anton understood that my turbulent emotions were real, though he always encouraged me to take some distance from them.

"How was your drama today, Lucy?" he would ask, rubbing my shoulders, after I'd stopped crying after some small slight or hurt. "What point did it reach on the drama-metre?"

"Not as good as last week, I think. I'll give it just five points out of ten," I would reply with a faint smile, tension already diffused.

I couldn't believe how Anton and I were compatible on so many levels: intellect, humour, sex. He, a party animal, helped me overcome my shyness and enjoy the company of other people, going out to restaurants and bars, drinking *kir*. Me, an anxious introvert, showed him that staying at home from time to time, reading books or watching a film, could also be nice.

I was always his *chouette*, a little owl, because I liked staying up late at night to read or create my collages. And he was my *dauphin*, a dolphin, because he loved swimming and laughing. His sense of humour was so contagious that I spent the best part of my year in Paris chuckling with him.

I soon moved into his art nouveau apartment in Vincennes, a beautiful area close to a big park, a zoo, and a *château*. We spent lazy weekends secretly feeding baboons with smuggled bananas, browsing through flea markets, or cycling around the park on rented *Velib* bikes. *La vie en rose*.

And when a few months later, we got engaged, life couldn't have been more perfect. Anton and I were strolling through Paris on our way back home from a lovely date. We'd gone to the cinema and then grabbed a late dinner in a small bistro in the Latin Quarter.

It was a balmy Friday night just before the summer holiday, and Parisians were already in a party mode. We walked past groups of friends chatting, drinking, and even dancing along the River Seine. But despite the festive atmosphere, gloom started seeping into my heart. I knew that my time in Paris was coming to an end, and in less than a month, I'd have to go back to London to finish my degree.

Also, I wasn't sure how a year apart would affect us. Would we have enough time, money, and determination to take the Eurostar train every few weeks to keep our relationship alive? Or would we slowly drift apart, losing the connection we'd been sharing for the past year?

Holding hands, we were walking and chatting about the film we'd just seen, a rerun of *Marie Antoinette* directed by Sofia Coppola.

"It wasn't madness," Anton argued, gesticulating with his free hand. "It was avarice. Greed for power."

We stopped on Pont Neuf, the oldest existing bridge in Paris, and leaned against the stone wall, gazing at the Conciergerie, a part of the old Medieval castle that served as a prison during the French Revolution. This is where the fashionable French queen spent her final weeks as a prisoner before she lost her head. Literally.

"But isn't fixation on just one idea a sign of mental issues?" I replied, breathing in the warm air that smelled of the river. "Don't you think that with a proper emotional support and guidance, Marie Antoinette could've led a happy and healthy life? Even in Versailles, the capital of vice?"

"Capital of vice?" Anton raised his eyebrows in mock horror. "So, this is what you English Redcoats think of the most magnificent palace in the world? Versailles was the epitome of culture and refinement, not vice."

"Maybe. But it had no toilets, and it stank."

"*Touché.*" His eyes twinkled with humour. "But let's not quarrel about history anymore, Lucy. The evening is too beautiful to think about dead people and their *merde*."

"What a lovely image!" I swatted him jokingly on the shoulder.

"Well, you started it." He put an arm around my waist, as we looked in silence at the beautifully lit Conciergerie, standing proudly over the dark waters of the River Seine, centuries after the head of poor Marie Antoinette rolled down from the guillotine.

"In fact, I wanted to talk about us." Anton's voice was no longer playful, and my stomach lurched. Was this the moment? The moment of truth. Are we going to part ways now? Or find a way to stay together long-distance?

Anton took my hand in his and kissed it gently. It was a good sign. Unless it was customary in France to kiss a person's hand before dumping them? Who knew. The French were known for their savoir-vivre.

"*Ma petite chouette.*" He looked into my eyes and smiled. "I'm so happy with you. You're the loveliest, kindest, funniest person I've ever met, and I can't imagine my life without you. Would you like to get married?"

For a moment, I couldn't believe my ears. Marriage? So soon?

Anton's eyes were unusually serious, his eyebrows raised in a silent question. A slight breeze was playing in his dark wavy hair and moving the unbuttoned collar around his neck.

"What do you say, Lucy? Do you think we can be happy together?"

Oh god, yes! Joy filled my whole body. It was as if glitter had just exploded inside of me.

"Yes, *bien sûr! Oui*, of course!" My brain, unused to so many positive emotions at once, was too confused to create a coherent sentence. But it didn't matter. Nothing mattered anymore. We were getting married!

I was intoxicated by him, by our love, by Paris. And even though he didn't go down on one knee or offer me a diamond ring, it was the most perfect proposal I could've imagined.

Anton took me in his arms and whispered "*Je t'aime*, Lucy. *Tu es l'amour de ma vie.*" And then he kissed me in front of all the tourists, Parisians, and historical ghosts standing with us on Pont Neuf.

As soon as we celebrated our engagement by having the best sex in Anglo-French history, we started our wedding preparations. We found the perfect venue—a Baroque chateau in picturesque Brittany.

We also chose our witnesses. In France, you needed not two, but four witnesses, so Anna and Mia were supposed to be mine, while Jack and Anton's younger brother were his. Our friends were delighted for us and also excited about the prospect of the first wedding in our circle.

We sent out invitations that I'd designed myself, a funny collage of an English bulldog kissing a French poodle with "Love is in the Air" scribbled above them.

I even found my wedding dress, a beautiful ivory gown in Regency style. Thank god I didn't buy it. I was waiting until I could save a bit more money, but before I'd saved enough, our engagement was over. No more castles or French lovers for me.

I blink a few times and look around our garden in Bali. Mia and Jack are cuddling in the deck chairs, while Sylvia, still riding the inflatable unicorn, is telling Antoine some anecdotes from her banking life. Antoine is laughing with his head thrown back and his white teeth gleaming in the dark.

Physically, he's almost as close to me as he was on Pont Neuf. But emotionally, he might as well be on Mars.

20

SEA SURPRISE

We're still a bit hungover after last night's drinks in our villa, but Sylvia's decided that we can recover in Sasak Bar, while Mia and Jack have a lie-in.

Armed with water bottles, straw hats, and very dark sunglasses, Sylvia, Antoine, and I walk the short distance from our villa to the beach. My ginger friend is leading the way, with me and my ex walking behind her, a safe distance from each other.

The main street in Legian is filled with car fumes and the smell of hot asphalt. It's so busy we have to wait a few minutes before we can cross to the other side. The noisy scooters and blue taxis are overtaking each other in the narrow road between the buildings and the wall that shelters the beach from the traffic.

With a sigh of relief, we finally cross the street and reach the shade of palm trees lining the beach. But when we step through one of the anti-demon gates, Sylvia stops dead in her tracks, and Antoine and I bump into her like a slow-motion human domino.

"What the feck has happened?" Sylvia takes a few steps towards the sea and shakes her head in disbelief.

I peak from behind her and freeze in shock. The beautiful golden sand, that just yesterday was pristinely clean, is now covered with disgusting litter. A strip of bottles, plastic bags, and even flip-flops snakes along the waterfront. It's impossible to walk towards the sea without stepping on rubbish.

"Who did this?" I turn towards Antoine, hoping for some logical explanation of this unnatural disaster.

"The ocean," he replies. "Or rather the people who dumped the garbage into the water or left it on the beach."

"Barbarians." Sylvia's swearing with a strong Scottish burr. "Fecking eejits. Clarty bastards!"

We start walking again, trying to navigate our way through the plastic debris, while Sylvia's lifting her legs like a curvy flamingo.

"But how is it even possible?" I ask, almost losing my own flip-flop that got stuck in the wet and dirty sand.

"During the high tide, the ocean spits out all the litter left on the beach," Antoine explains. "All the garbage thrown directly into the rivers and sea ends up on the land."

"Someone should clean it up," Sylvia declares, as she continues her flamingo dance.

"The Balinese are very tidy, and they clean as much as they can. But the sea just keeps bringing more and more."

"Then, why don't we do it?" I suggest.

"This isn't our island." Sylvia gestures towards other tourists and locals sunbathing in deckchairs or playing football on the dirty sand. "See? No one else cares."

"But this is our world!" I reply sharply. "Isn't it weird that all these people are doing nothing, just lounging on a landfill?"

"I'm going to do some lounging myself." Sylvia gestures towards Sasak Bar that's just appeared in the distance. "I work really hard all year long. I deserve to have a break during my holiday."

I drop my head and sigh. Maybe Sylvia is right. Maybe it's best not to get involved. I'm sure there must be someone hired to keep the island clean.

"I'll help you, Lucy."

I lift my head at the sound of Antoine's voice.

"I think it's a good idea," he continues. "Of course, we need more systematic solutions, but if everyone took care of at least the area around them, the world would be a much cleaner place."

That's the Antoine I remember. Always supportive, always getting involved in some good cause. I nod and send him a small smile.

"Do whatever you want. Whatever tickles your pickle." Sylvia shrugs her shoulders. "But if anyone's looking for me, I'll be in the bar, drinking Bintang and making out with Wayan."

"Lucy, Lucy!" As soon as we've reached Sasak Bar, Nyoman envelops me in a big hug. He smells of sand and salt. "I haven't seen you since the meditation in the temple. How are you? My mom sends her compliments. She said I should invite you for another coffee whenever you're free."

"Good to see you, Nyoman. And thanks for the invitation." I pat him on the back. There is a frisson of attraction between us, and it feels good to be hugging his bare, muscled body. But then I notice that Antoine is sending me one of his sardonic smiles, and I gently push Nyoman's chiselled chest away.

I look around the bar and realise that Sylvia and Wayan have no issues expressing their sexual energy. They're kissing as passionately as if they haven't seen each other for two years, not two days.

"Get a room!" Shouts one of the patrons, a middle-aged Australian guy with a beer belly and a serious sunburnt. "And bring me more Bintang, mate!"

Wayan untwines himself from Sylvia's embrace. "Nyoman, bring the gentleman some cold beer, please. It's time for Sylvia's surfing lesson. I need to teach her the forehand bottom turn."

"Oh yes, my bottom turn requires your undivided attention," Sylvia murmurs. They grab their surfboards and quickly disappear in the blue waves.

Nyoman swallows hard. "Are they talking about surfing or sex?"

"Both, I suppose," I answer with a laugh.

"Nyoman, I have a small favour to ask," Antoine interrupts our chit chat. "Lucy and I would like to clean all this horrible plastic from the beach."

"I've cleaned everything myself." Nyoman gestures with pride

114

towards the plastic-free area around the bar. But I can still see heaps of garbage lining the sand in the distance. "It's all rubbish from Java and other islands." He shakes his head. "Balinese people are very clean. Very, very clean."

"Do you know where we can get some bin bags and gloves? Is there a shop around here?" Antoine asks.

"Don't worry, I've got everything." Nyoman beams, happy he can be of use. He reaches under the counter and pulls out the cleaning gear. "There you go!"

"Thank you, Nyoman, you're the best," I say, and he grins. But before he has a chance to reply, we hear the Ozzie accent again.

"Mate, where's my bloody Bintang? Do you want me to parch here to death?"

21

FAMILY MATTERS

Antoine and I have left our friends in Sasak Bar, and we're now walking on the beach, picking up the rubbish on the way, though I find it a bit ironic that we're using plastic bags to get rid of plastic. Antoine lifts a purple flip-flop that looks almost like new. Was it lost by some beach Cinderella?

"How are your parents?" he asks conversationally. "Still living in Milton Keynes?"

"Yes. And still divorced. Thank god for that." Now that we're alone, I feel self-conscious again. I wish I had Sylvia's natural charm, or Anna's ability to easily connect with people around her. I hate being shy and tongue-tied in so many social situations. Maybe that's why I escape into books—they don't judge me and don't ask me questions in a sexy French accent.

The sun's blazing, and I feel hot and dizzy, despite the straw hat protecting my head. Inside the rubber gloves, my hands start to sweat. But there's something very soothing about our unhurried rhythm. Bend, pick up a piece of litter, put it in the bag. Repeat.

Antoine looks at me with sympathy. "Yes, I remember how upset you were by your parents' fighting. Maybe that's all for the best?"

I shrug and pick up a tangled mess of plastic tubes that smells of dead fish. I don't even know what it is, but it's completely revolting. I throw it into the bin bag with disgust.

"And your brothers?" Antoine tries to continue this one-sided small talk.

I shrug again. The truth is, I'm not really a big fan of my brothers, especially Leo. They used to bully me when I was a kid, though back in the day it was called brotherly affection.

"Luke's fine," I reply after a pause. "He and his boyfriend opened a hair salon in North London. For some reason, they've become very popular with the local Jewish community. So, now they specialise in twisting peyot, even though you couldn't find a more Goy family than ours."

"Maybe they should rename the salon the *Gay Goy?*" Antoine laughs, showing the neat row of his perfectly white teeth. "And what about Leo?"

"I'm not really close with him. Apparently, he's still trying to find his place in life, even though he's almost forty now."

"Aren't we all, though?" Antoine asks philosophically.

"And what about your parents?" I ask in return. "Did your father fully recover after the heart attack?"

"Yes, he quit smoking, drinking, and eating red meat. Well, almost quit. Can you imagine my dad without a cigarette in his mouth?"

"No, not really." I shake my head.

"And my mom sends her love. She's always been very fond of you."

Has she now? That's one way of putting it.

I will never forget how Anton invited me to a Sunday lunch with his family a week after our engagement on Pont Neuf. It was the first time I would meet his parents and visit their elegant apartment in a Haussmann building close to the Arc de Triomphe.

Anton squeezed my hand reassuringly, while we were waiting in the spacious hall that smelled of lemons and some wax-based cleaning product. His mum opened the door, invited us inside the apartment, and air-kissed my cheeks.

"Lucy, so nice to meet you at last! Antoine told us all about you!" She welcomed me in English.

"*Bonjour, Madame Dechampe. Enchantée.*"

"Oh, call me Monique!" She waved her manicured hand in dismissal. "You're almost a part of the family now."

I instantly liked her. Apparently, we form our impressions about others in the first seven seconds of meeting them. Mine were very favourable so far. Under her very chic looks, Monique seemed to be a genuinely warm and friendly person.

Meanwhile, Anton's father emerged from the kitchen and came to greet us. He was wearing an impeccable three-piece suit protected by a navy-blue apron. He smelt of expensive eau de cologne, cigarettes, and, faintly, fried onions that he was probably preparing for lunch.

"*Bonjour*, Lucy. I'm Jean-Pierre." He planted a wet kiss on each of my cheeks and then air kissed Anton. "Good to see you, son."

"I've brought something for you." Proudly, I gave Monique a box of Lindt chocolates. The biggest and most expensive I could find.

"Oh, you've brought us chocolates from a supermarket," she said in a sweet voice. "How lovely."

I blinked a few times. She'd clearly offended me, but she did it in such a polite way, that I had no idea how to react.

"Don't be rude, Monique," Jean-Pierre admonished his wife. "The girl is English, of course she has no taste. But it's the thought that counts, *n'est-ce pas?*"

I felt as if I'd stepped into a parallel universe. Sure, my family also had issues, and my parents and brothers could be really rude, but only to each other, not their guests.

I was so paralysed by the rules of politeness and my own embarrassment that I stood there like a muppet, unable to defend myself.

Fortunately, Antoine came to my rescue. "*Maman, Papa! Ça suffit!* Stop offending Lucy, she's my fiancée and your guest."

"Offending?" Monique opened wide her baby blue eyes with long eyelashes. "*Mais*, no one's offending Lucy. We're just joking. Innocent bantering. Don't be so touchy."

"The roasted chicken is almost ready," Jean-Pierre announced, as he peeked into the kitchen. "You can go to the dining room and get some champagne for the *apéro*. We've bought Veuve Clicquot to celebrate your engagement."

"What does your father do?" Monique asked when we were all seated, cutting through the chicken's breast with a surgical precision. "Is he involved in the law like our family?"

"Oh no, not at all." I tried to swallow a boiled baby potato and almost chocked. "He's a production supervisor in a food factory."

"And your mother?"

"She's an assistant manager at Lidl."

"Lidl?" Monique spit this word out as if it was a rotten potato. I instantly started regretting that my mom didn't work at Harrods. Or at least Marks & Spencer.

Jean-Pierre pushed away his empty plate and lit a cigarette. In a closed room. While we were still eating. I glanced at Anton, but he didn't seem to mind having lunch in the billows of toxic smoke. I, on the other hand, felt as if I'd landed in a film noir shot in the 1950s.

"Antoine tells me that you have to go back to England." Jean-Pierre puffed out the smoke with visible pleasure. "So, what are your plans for the next year?"

"I need to finish my uni first and then we'll see what to do next. I'd like to move back to Paris, but there are more job opportunities for me in the UK."

"And what about you, son? Are you going to let the girl go all alone?"

"Actually, I've just found a job in a law firm in London," my fiancé announced proudly. "It will be good to get more international experience and live in the same city as Lucy."

"A law firm in London?" His father squeezed the cigarette in a crystal ashtray. "*Pah*! You should work in our family firm, or at least some other respectable law company in Paris. What's the use in learning the Common Law? Roman law, Code Napoléon, that's what you should be studying, not some Anglo-Saxon nonsense."

"Don't be so harsh on the Anglo-Saxons, *mon cher*." Now it was Monique's turn to soothe her spouse. "I'm sure they're doing their best, though they don't have the same culture as us."

And so it continued throughout the whole lunch. Cruelty, sugar-coated in fake politeness.

When Anton and I left his parents' apartment, I burst into tears. Anton took me in his arms and stroked my back.

"*Désolé, ma chouette.* I'm so sorry for my parents. I'm not sure why they were so mean today. Usually, they're lovely people…"

This lunch with Monique and Jean-Pierre was the first crack in our perfect love bubble. And our relationship just went downhill from there until we broke up with a bang almost a year later.

I wonder how Monique and Jean-Pierre would react if they discovered that their son and I are now picking up garbage on a Balinese beach?

22

SLEEPING DOGS

"I think it's enough for today." Antoine heaves the heavy bin bags brimming with plastic and dumps them on the ground in Sasak Bar. He wipes sweat from his brow, smiling victoriously. How does he manage to look so sexy even while playing the garbage collector in the 30-degree heat? "We've done a good job." He gestures towards the small strand of the beach that we've managed to clean.

"But what should we do now with all the plastic?" I ask.

"Don't worry, I'll send it to the recycling centre together with our usual waste," Nyoman assures me with the never-fading grin on his bronzed face.

"*Suksma!*" Antoine says in Balinese. "Thank you."

"Yes, thank you, Nyoman. How can we repay you for your help?" All this physical effort helped me work up an appetite, and my stomach is rumbling. "Maybe I can invite you for lunch?"

"With pleasure, Lucy, but not today. Too many clients." He gestures towards a group of sunburnt holidaymakers chilling in the white plastic chairs and drinking beer.

"And where are Sylvia and Wayan?" I turn around to scan the sea, but I can't spot our friends among the surfers gliding on the waves.

"Sylvia forgot her sun cream, so they both went back to your villa.

But it's taking them very long. Very long." Nyoman shakes his head while Antoine and I exchange an amused look. A typical Sylvia move.

"I'll go for lunch with you, Lucy," Antoine offers. "I know a very good *nasi goreng* place. And we still haven't finished our conversation."

I send Nyoman an apologetic smile and walk away with Antoine. The hot sun, hunger, and fatigue make me dizzy. After a few minutes of walking, I sway on the uneven sand, and Antoine takes my elbow to help me regain balance. "Are you feeling unwell? You look very red."

I instantly feel embarrassed, which probably makes my face even redder.

"I'm fine," I lie.

"The restaurant isn't far away, but let's cool down in the shade for a while."

We sit down under the palm trees with a few stray dogs playing nearby. They all have pointy noses and pointy ears. They remind me of dingoes, just smaller and with more diverse coat colours.

Antoine tilts his head towards me, then takes off his sunglasses and pierces me with his blue eyes. "There's something I wanted to talk about."

My heartbeat starts to race, and I can feel the familiar metallic taste in my mouth. What does he want to tell me? That he got married and has five children? That he decided to become a Catholic priest? That he fell in love with Sylvia? Do I really want to know the answer?

I turn away and observe the dogs chasing each other on the sand and barking loudly at all the passers-by. Are they warning us about the presence of malignant spirits? Apparently, Balinese dogs possess second sight that allows them to see *niskala*, the unseen magical world.

"I've read somewhere that one of the Dutch colonisers was breeding Dalmatians in Bali," I say, stalling for time. "One day, the Dalmatians ran away and started mating with the local dogs. Apparently, that's why a lot of Balinese dogs are black and white. I wonder if it's true or just an urban legend?"

"Do you remember how we were thinking of adopting a dog? You were so excited about having a new pet, even though you still missed your tortoise Theodora." He smiles at the memory, but his face quickly becomes serious again. "Actually, that's what I'd like to talk to you about."

"About pets?"

"No, about us. I'm so sorry how our relationship ended. I'm sorry I screwed up." He looks at me almost pleadingly.

Uncomfortable, I shift a few inches away from him. "This is ancient history. There's no need to come back to this."

My mother used to say "Let sleeping dogs lie." Don't bring up the old problems. I don't have to stay here and talk with Antoine. I'm as free as these Balinese dogs. Even more so, because I can take a flight back to London and never see him again. But that's exactly what I've been doing for the last four years. Burying my head in the sand, ignoring my problems and pain. And where did that get me? Literally, to Bali, which is nice. But emotionally? Nowhere.

I swallow hard and decide to finally ask him some questions that have been brewing in my mind, even though I might not like the answers. Let's start with an easy one.

"Why have you come to Bali, Antoine?" I try to speak in a casual tone, but my voice sounds more like a squeak.

He turns away and stares at the blue expanse of the sea. "For Mia and Jack's wedding, of course."

Yes, that's the official answer, but I feel there's something more behind it. Or maybe I'm reading too much into it?

"But you didn't want to come initially," I press him. "What's changed?"

He looks down at the hot sand. "If I'm completely honest with you, I was nervous about seeing you again. I was afraid you'd come with some handsome guy."

"And I thought you'd come with a sleek French girl. The type that surrounded you in Paris."

He sighs. "Yes, there were many girls like this. But they didn't help me forget you." He lifts his head and looks me straight in the eye. "I came to apologise. And to explain what exactly happened four years ago when I broke off our engagement. Can we talk about this?"

I reluctantly nod my head.

"Do you remember how we used to give ratings to our quarrels?" he asks with a small smile. "Five out of ten on the drama-scale. That always made you laugh."

"I do remember." The memories of our breakup, together with all the pain, are starting to rise to the surface. A shot of hot pain crosses my chest. "But it was before you decided to cancel our wedding and bugger off to France."

I can see he's also upset, but his voice is calm when he finally replies. "I buggered off to France, as you put it, because my father had a heart attack, and I had to take care of my family."

"I know all that, but why did you have to dump me as well? I wanted to support you during that time, but you didn't let me." I swallow the tears and the bitter taste of rejection that has been my faithful companion since the breakup.

He sighs and looks away. "I didn't want to involve you in my family issues, you had enough of your own problems. I had to focus on my father and taking charge of our law firm while he was ill. That was my priority at the time. And I couldn't give you my undivided attention. It wasn't fair to stay with you if I couldn't give you what you needed."

"But you didn't even give me a chance to say anything!" I explode. "You treated me like a child, making the decision for me. That's not how a healthy relationship should work."

"I know." He hangs his head. "I thought I was protecting you, but now I know I was just being a coward. Do you think you can ever forgive me?"

His words bring me back to the last evening I spent with Antoine in London. To the time he broke my heart.

After Anton and I moved from Paris to London, our honeymoon period was over.

He had to work long hours in one of the top law firms in the City, while I was focusing on finishing my degree in French literature and working part-time jobs to pay the bills. We moved from Antoine's spacious apartment in Vincennes to a cramped studio in Shoreditch, where we could barely fit in a bed and a wardrobe. We went out more rarely, had less sex, even laughed less. It was as if the adult responsibilities slowly sucked out all our energy and passion. But I was in denial, telling myself that it was just a difficult phase, another small crack in our otherwise perfect relationship.

I thought we were still going strong, until the fateful night in June four years ago. I was in our studio cooking a very elaborate meal of boiled pasta with tinned tomato sauce, when Anton came back home late from work. He was pale, almost grey, and there was no trace of his usual cheerfulness.

I left the pasta on the cooker and ran towards him. *"Mon amour,* what's happened? Is everything okay?"

I tried to hug him, but he gently pushed me away and went to the wardrobe to find his suitcase.

"Is there anything I can do to help you, *mon dauphin?*" I asked him with panic rising in my voice.

He shook his head and, with his face turned away from me, started packing.

"I'm sorry, Lucy. I'm so, so sorry," he whispered without looking at me.

"Why are you sorry?"

"My father has had a heart attack. We don't know if he'll survive. I have to go home. Now." He was still standing with his back towards me.

"Oh, that's horrible. How can I help you?" I tried to embrace him, but he moved away. "We'll go through this together. For better or for worse, in sickness and in health."

"I can't deal with this right now. I have to focus on my family." He was packing clothes and books with almost robotic moves.

"Let me pack real quick and go with you to Paris. I'm sure Jean-Pierre and Monique will be relieved to know that you're not alone during this difficult time."

"No, please don't." He shook his head. "You don't understand. It's much more serious than you think. We can't be together right now."

"What do you mean? Why can't we be together?"

Without answering my questions, Antoine closed his suitcase and finally turned around to look at me. His face was ashen, his lips almost white. He looked like a ghost.

"I have to go, I'll call you soon." He kissed me briefly on the cheek, then picked up his suitcase and walked out from my life, leaving me with a shattered heart and overcooked pasta.

I blink back the tears and look at Antoine sitting next to me on the hot sand of Kuta Beach. He jams his fists into the pockets of his shorts, and I think he also has tears in his eyes. Or maybe these are just drops of water blown from the sea?

2 3

NASI GORENG

These memories are excruciatingly painful, but Antoine's apology brings a sense of catharsis. It's like opening a festering wound, so that it can finally start to heal. I've been thinking about our breakup so many times, looking for clues, trying to figure out if there was anything I could have done differently.

Now I realise that—even though I was in total denial back then—our relationship was already on the rocks, and Antoine took the first opportunity to abandon the ship. There wasn't anything I could have done to make him stay.

"Apology accepted," I say after a very long pause. "But I still don't understand why you jilted me in this cruel way? You pushed me away and turned into a complete stranger, as if two years together meant nothing to you."

"This is the part I'm most ashamed of," Antoine admits, digging his hands into the hot sand. "I have nothing to say in my own defence, except that I was in a shock after receiving the news about my father's illness. And my mother said—"

"Yes?"

"Never mind." He shakes his head. "It was completely my fault and I shouldn't put blame on others. *J'ai été un connard.* I was a jerk."

"Yes, you were." I cast a sideway glance at him, sensing sarcasm. But he seems genuinely sorry. "Though, the situation wasn't easy for you either. You were alone in a foreign country and your father's life was in danger. It must have been very distressing."

"I wasn't alone—I had you." He smiles and I feel a shift in the mood. The skeletons have left the closet, we can move on. "Are you feeling better now? Do you still want to go for lunch?"

To my surprise, our talk didn't kill my appetite. Actually, I'm more ravenous than before. "Okay, let's go. Eating out with you is always an adventure."

"Are you sure this is the right place?" I say, looking around the hole-in-the-wall in a small alley that Antoine has proudly announced as the best nasi goreng restaurant in Kuta.

"Trust me. The food here is really delicious," he assures me with a smile.

"How do you know Bali so well?" I ask, wondering how many times he's been here already. And with whom.

"I've been working on a lot of environmental projects in South-East Asia, and every time I had a chance, I spent some time in Bali. I like this island, it helps me relax."

"I didn't know your company is now operating outside of France. What does your father think about it?" I ask.

"He's always been happy working just for Parisian snobs. But he isn't in charge of the company anymore, and I've decided to expand outside of our bubble. That's why I work on many projects for free, especially if they have environmental or social impact. Saving the planet and helping people is more important than making even more money."

Wow, Antoine has really cast off the stuffy bourgeois ideals he was taught as a child. Just imagine how furious Monique and Jean-Pierre must have been when they discovered that their son had become a social justice advocate. I smile with satisfaction.

"Good for you! And you always liked to travel, so this is an extra bonus," I say, while my stomach rumbles. I peer at a small decrepit sign above the entrance. "Should we go into this—warung?"

"Warung is a small restaurant that serves home-cooked Indonesian dishes," he explains. "You can find a lot of them in Bali, and they usually offer great prices for delicious food."

Calling this place a restaurant is a bit of a stretch. It's a small pavilion with a tin roof and no front wall, furnished with just four plastic tables and a few uncomfortable chairs I've already seen in Sasak Bar. The kitchen area is separated by a low wooden wall, so that we can clearly see a motherly woman stirring food in big metal pots. The place looks shabby, but I have to admit that the smells wafting out from the pots are very promising.

Curled up under one of the chairs, there's a little dog that looks much fatter and happier than the strays we saw on the beach. Probably living in a restaurant has its perks, especially for dogs.

We step through the non-existent front wall, and Antoine greets the cook in Balinese as we sit at the table in the corner. I pick up the laminated menu and stare at it for a few seconds. It has only two main dishes: *nasi goreng* and *mie goreng*. Well, that makes my choice easier. If only I knew what the heck they were.

Antoine must have noticed my hesitation, as he provides a helpful translation. "Nasi goreng is fried rice with vegetables and fish or meat, often served with a fried egg on top. It's one of the national dishes of Indonesia. Mie goreng is very similar, but you get noodles instead of rice."

"In that case, I'll take the noodle thing." I know that the risk of getting food poisoning from boiled rice is very low, but I don't want to take any chances, especially in a shabby place like this. "And a freshly pressed pineapple juice."

With a big smile on her face, the owner comes out from the kitchen to take our order. "Welcome to my warung. My name is Made," she says, examining Antoine's face. "I think I've seen you here before. You ordered a big portion of nasi goreng with double eggs."

"Yes, that's right. I was here last week, and the food was delicious, especially with the sambal sauce. It was spicy, but not too hot," he says. "I have a colleague based in Singapore who's recommended your restaurant. Maybe you know him as well, he's native to Bali."

While Antoine is chatting with Made, I shake my head. I've been in Bali for over two weeks, but I still can't believe how genuinely warm and friendly the locals are. How come they never get tired of tourists invading their island? Is it because of the always sunny weather or their hospitable culture?

I also notice how easily Antoine fits in here. Despite his upper-class upbringing, he always chooses places that are budget-friendly and authentic. Thanks to him, I discovered that the best food in Paris is served not in the five-star hotels, but in small family-run bistros outside of the city centre.

"How do you manage to become friends with everyone around you?" I ask Antoine once Made has gone back to prepare our meal.

He shrugs with a smile. "I don't know. I'm just curious about the people around me. You can learn so much listening to their stories. For example, Made has just told me where we can find the best Balinese dessert in Kuta. We can go there after lunch if you want."

"Sure." Another thing I learned while being with Antoine—always follow his food recommendations. They might be unusual, but always worth it.

"Lucy, there's more I'd like to explain about what happened four years ago."

I raise my hand with an open palm to cut him short. "Remember the first rule you taught me about food etiquette? Never discuss difficult topics on an empty stomach."

"You're right." He starts tapping his fingers on the table as if he was playing an invisible piano. We sit in silence, as Antoine continues his internal piano concert, until Made places our food and drinks on the table.

"*Selamat makan!* Enjoy your meal!" She beams at us before returning to the kitchen.

My mie goreng looks very appetizing. It's served on a banana leaf, with a fried egg on top of noodles, mixed with spices and veggies. The smell of garlic, onion, and soy sauce makes me realise how hungry I really am, as I dive into my dish. It tastes very exotic, but also comforting at the same time, like something a Balinese grandma would prepare for her sick grandchildren.

Antoine twirls a strand of his own noodles on the fork. "Do you like it? You look famished."

"It's delish," I mumble with my mouth full. I quickly polish off my food and have to refrain from licking the plate. Instead, I wash down my meal with the pineapple juice, which is sweet and tangy, clearly made from fresh pineapple, not the canned sugary water we get back at home. My lips and tongue start to tingle.

I don't remember the last time I enjoyed my food so much.

When Antoine left for Paris to take care of his father, I still thought it was all just a horrible dream, and we'd both wake up from it. That as soon as his father got better, he'd come back to London, and we'd resume our life together as if nothing had happened.

During this time, we had just one phone conversation that I replayed a million times in my head.

"I can't give you what you want, Lucy. I'm not in a position to get married, at least not now. And it's not fair to keep you waiting for something that might never happen."

"So, why did you even propose to me?" I asked, as I swiped away the tears that were streaming down my cheeks. "Why have we been planning a wedding?"

"Because I love you."

"But not enough to marry me?"

"The circumstances have changed. And we're too young to make a serious commitment like this anyway."

"Too young to get married, but not too young to get engaged? What kind of bullshit is that?" What was he even talking about? I was twenty-three, and he was twenty-five. Maybe we weren't wise old people, but we weren't some delusional teenagers, either.

"I'm sorry, *ma chouette. Je suis vraiment désolé.*"

Even after this phone call, I still didn't lose hope. I was trying to convince myself that it wasn't the end, just a misunderstanding we could clear up. Communication breaks happened all the time, especially with international couples. Right?

2 4

BITTER DESSERT

"Lucy, can we talk now?" Antoine looks at me pleadingly while I bite into a piece of fresh mango. My mouth is filled with the sweet pulp and an oddly resin-like flavour, so I just nod my head.

We've just bought some traditional desserts in a place recommended by Made, and now we're strolling through busy Legian streets towards our villa. The idea was to share the treats with our friends, but I couldn't resist the temptation, and I started eating my coconut porridge with fresh mango just outside the shop. As I'm trying to lick off the sticky juice trickling down my hands, I realise that choosing fried bananas or sticky rice cakes would have been a wiser choice.

"I understand that bringing up the past is painful for you," Antoine continues, as I'm desperately trying to find some clean tissues in my bag. "But I'd like to explain. I'd like to come clean."

No tissues. Great. I'll just have to behave like a real lady and wipe my hands on my denim shorts. I stuff my mouth with more mango, hoping that the sweet dessert will stop the bitterness I feel on my tongue.

"Okay, I'm listening," I finally say, cleaning my mouth with my forearm. Classy, I know.

He heaves a big sigh. "Let me start by saying that I was an idiot. A young and immature idiot. I wanted to act as a grown-up and build a life with you, but adulting was harder than I'd expected. I didn't like my work, I hated living in London, I missed my friends back in France." He sends me a pleading look from behind his glasses. "And when the crisis came, I was so confused and stressed that I didn't know how to choose between you and my family."

I tilt my head, not sure if I've heard him right. "I don't know what you mean. I never asked you to choose."

"No, *you* didn't."

"I still don't get it." I shake my head. Is it possible that Monique and Jean-Pierre asked him to break up with me? They never liked me, but I thought they didn't want to meddle in their son's love life.

"It was a difficult time for my family. We didn't know if my father would survive the heart attack. My parents told me to come back home and devote my full attention to our law firm. They wanted me to take over as the senior partner. They said that being in a relationship at that time would distract me from my new duties."

Oh, the nerve of those horrible people! How did they dare interfere? "Is it because I come from the working class?" I spit. "Because I don't have a family full of lawyers?"

Antoine looks away, which confirms my suspicions. His parents were always intellectual snobs.

"It's not just about that," he finally admits.

"So, what was it about?"

He looks at the dusty pavement, evidently uncomfortable with whatever he's going to say next. "It's because you're British."

I stop dead in my tracks, ignoring other tourists walking around us. I didn't see that one coming.

"Don't your parents know that the Napoleonic wars are over?" I'm boiling inside, but I'm trying to keep the cool facade. "That the British and French can be friends again?"

"Please, try to understand them. They wanted me to focus on expanding our business in France, not on starting a new life with you in London." He runs his hand through his black hair. "Also, they believed I was too young to get married. That I should get more experience before committing myself to one person, especially a foreigner."

Ah, at least one mystery has been solved. Over the last four years,

I've been analysing our relationship from all the angles, trying to understand why he suddenly thought that we were too young to get married. Playing the age card was his parents' idea.

"Now I know that it wasn't a real ultimatum," he continues. "That together we could have found a solution. But I didn't want to add another layer of complications to this already hard situation. So, I listened to their persuasions and broke off our engagement. But if it's any consolation to you, I've regretted it ever since."

So, he didn't break up with me because he didn't love me anymore. He did it because his parents asked him to do it. I'm not sure which reason is worse. I start moving again, but it's more like a zombie walk.

"As soon as my father got better, I wanted to come back, but it was too late. I tried to call you, I sent you countless messages, but you never replied. And I don't blame you, I know that I deserved it. I even went to your family house in Milton Keynes trying to find you. But Leo told me to bugger off and never come back."

Hold on a second. It's true that I blocked Antoine on all communication channels, but I've never heard of him coming to my home. Did Leo really try to protect me from Antoine? Maybe my oldest brother wasn't so useless after all.

"He also said that you'd already found someone else and moved in with him," Antoine continues with a slight hurt in his voice.

"What?" I lift my head. "Why did he say that?"

"I don't know. But I thought that you'd moved on very quickly. Maybe you didn't care for me so much after all."

I clench my fists and try not to spit out a bunch of curses that are stinging my tongue. "Listen, Antoine. Leo is a very poor excuse for a brother." I say through gritted teeth. "The truth is that I was unwell and stayed for some time with Misia, Anna's grandmother. I was in Milton Keynes all the time."

"Are you saying that you weren't dating anyone back then?" Antoine raises his eyebrows in disbelief. "Why did Leo lie to me?"

"Because his middle name is Asshole?" I suggest.

"I didn't know, *je ne savais pas.*" Antoine shakes his head, as if trying to process this new fact.

So, Antoine did come back after all. We could have had this conver-

135

sation much, much earlier, and spare each other four years of pain. But, after all, maybe it was all for the best? Back then, I was in no fit state to see anyone, especially not him.

Saying that I was unwell is the understatement of the year.

After our breakup call, the days passed by, and I didn't get any more news from Antoine. Two weeks later, I was at work, filing some boring legal papers, trying to occupy myself with mindless tasks. I was on a constant alert, waiting for another call from him.

Finally, a message came. I grabbed my phone, as soon as I'd heard the familiar ping, hoping it was Antoine saying that it was all a big mistake, and we were back together. But instead, his words made my blood freeze.

"Just cancelled our booking at the chateau. Please inform your family and friends that the wedding is called off. I hope you'll forgive me one day. A."

I sat in stunned silence for a few minutes, feeling as if my whole life had just collapsed. On autopilot, I sent an email to my manager telling him I was sick and had to take a few days off. I left the office, went straight to Euston Station, and took the first train I could get to Milton Keynes. I didn't even bother to go to my parents' house, I knew they were too preoccupied with their own divorce at the time. Also, they're useless in crisis situations. Instead, I went to Misia, who was always my safe haven whenever I was in trouble or needed a refuge from the turbulent life at home.

Just like countless times during my childhood, Anna's grandmother opened the door to her quaint cottage and let me stay as long as I wanted. She didn't judge, she didn't make any comments, she just listened to my tales of woe and prepared countless pots of strong tea with lemon and honey.

"There's nothing that can't get better with a good cuppa," she would say, adding extra honey to my teacup.

Once I stopped blubbering about Antoine and our broken engagement, she offered just one piece of advice: "A clean wound heals faster."

So, I blocked Antoine's phone number, unfollowed him on all the social media, asked my friends not to tell me any news about him. A clean break. And then I collapsed. Denial that helped me survive the two worst weeks of my life had now evaporated, and I was unable to perform the simplest tasks. I didn't cry, I didn't talk, I didn't sleep. I was just lying in bed staring at the ceiling like a plant.

Misia was the best nurse I could imagine. She took me under her wing and cared for me as if I was her own granddaughter. She called my boss to explain the situation and ask for an unpaid personal leave. Surprisingly, Mr Russell agreed and he even kept paying my wages. Maybe he wasn't such a heartless prick after all.

For almost three weeks, Misia would help me go to the bathroom and take a shower, washing my hair with a chamomile shampoo. I still find the smell of chamomile very soothing. She would spend hours next to my bed, stroking my hair and telling me about her life as a Polish immigrant trying to make a new life in the UK. And she forced me to eat some Polish comfort food, smuggling anti-depressants prescribed by the GP in a fruit pudding called *kisiel*.

My parents and brothers visited me from time to time, but they were too busy with their work and own lives to take care of me full-time. Also, they didn't understand how serious my depression really was. "It's all in your head," they kept saying. Yes, of course, it was in my head, it was a fucking mental issue. Where else would it be? In my ass?

Anna, a conscientious psychology student, was trying to explain that my breakdown was so severe not only because I felt betrayed by Antoine, but also because my guard had gone down and I finally stopped hiding all the bottled-up emotions about my family, my work, my life in general. She told me that I'd depended too much on Antoine for happiness and the feeling of safety. That I should be able to stand on my two own feet before getting so emotionally involved with another human being.

It all made sense on the intellectual level, but emotionally, I still felt as if Antoine had bulldozed my heart. It was easier to blame him for my misery than to admit that I had some real issues to resolve.

"Lucy, Lucy, are you still there?" Antoine puts his hand on my arm, and I almost jump out of my skin. "I'm so sorry, I really didn't want to hurt you."

Well done, Antoine, mission accomplished. You didn't hurt me at all!

25

BARONG DANCE

There's a buzz in the air. People are chatting animatedly while all our villa crew plus Nyoman are waiting for the Barong dance to start. We're in an open amphitheatre in the middle of the jungle close to Ubud, and the air is heavy with humidity and heat.

"It looks a bit disappointing," Mia points towards the empty open-air stage with a dropout of a brick wall but no decorations.

"These plastic seats are super uncomfortable," Sylvia complains.

"And I have no space for my legs." Jack is trying to squeeze his long limbs under a seat in front of him.

"It'll get better, don't worry." Nyoman smiles encouragingly. "You won't think about the discomfort when the dance starts."

"Yes, the Balinese dance drama is really impressive," Antoine agrees. "I've seen it already in Ubud a few years ago and still can't believe how skilled the dancers were."

By some cruel trick of fate, or maybe just my own lack of caution, I'm sandwiched between Antoine and Nyoman. I can smell Nyoman's salty scent on the left, and Antoine's musky French cologne on the right. I accidentally brush against Antoine's leg, and an electric current rushes through my body, raising the hairs on my arm. Typical. I haven't had any action for over a year, and suddenly, I'm surrounded by two attractive guys at once. It never rains, but it pours.

Our long conversation yesterday cleared the air and helped me see our breakup from a new perspective. I'm still angry at Antoine for breaking our engagement off, but I've started to realise that not everything was as black and white as I thought. And I'm quite relieved that he did come back to apologise in person after all. Clearly, he came too late and was scared off by my stupid brother, but at least he had cared enough to make the effort of travelling back to England and even visiting my family. It makes me feel less like a discarded old shoe and more like a heroine of some romantic story.

"I hope you like the Barong dance," Antoine whispers into my right ear. "It's not the same as Opéra Garnier, but it's beautiful in its own way."

It's true that we spent a lot of our weekends buying cheap student tickets to see *The Nutcracker* or *The Magic Flute*. But it doesn't give him a right to get so close to me now, pretending we're best buddies.

It also makes me realise that my life has been a cultural desert for the past few years. I'm usually so exhausted after work that the most exciting place I want to visit is my bed. And unless the girls convince me to go and see a West End musical or spend a night in a pub, I don't even leave my flat during the weekends. Going out is expensive, while reading books in bed is free. Well, almost free, if you don't count the library fees and the price of e-books I buy on my Kindle. Also, the tube or bus in London seems like too much bother—getting anywhere takes you at least an hour. The French call this existence "Metro, boulot, dodo"—commute, work, sleep. That's my life.

A tinny tune interrupts my musings. I'm not a music expert, but it seems to be some brass instrument. At first it sounds like tinkling bells, but then it gets louder and louder. Now it's not just the bells, but also my ears that are ringing.

"*Dios mío*," Mia covers her ears with her hands. "Is someone hitting a spoon against a garbage lid?"

"It's a *gamelan*," Nyoman whispers into my left ear, as he takes my hand into his. His palm is warm and strong. It makes me feel safe. My heart starts beating faster, and it's not just because of the thumping rhythm produced by the Balinese orchestra.

Antoine shoots us a piercing glance. Is it possible that he's still jealous? Men can be so possessive, even long after a relationship is over.

"What's a gamelan?" I must have read about it in one of my guidebooks, but I can't remember in what context. "And why is it so loud?"

"It's a drum and percussion orchestra that plays during religious celebrations in the temples," Nyoman explains. Ah yes, that's why it sounds so familiar. I heard it many times flowing from the temple in front of our hotel in Kuta. "And if you play gamelan very loudly, it'll drive the evil spirits away."

Are we really supposed to spend the next hour listening to this racket? If they keep banging like this, they'll drive away not only the evil spirits, but also all the spectators.

The play begins. The musicians, hidden under a thatched roof on the right side of the stage, are playing an eerie tune, increasing and slowing down the tempo. The music is much quieter and less aggressive than in the intro, but it still has the same nervous energy. The rhythm of the drums and gongs becomes so hypnotic that I just hope I don't fall asleep in this heat and embarrass myself in front of all my friends.

Actors in outlandish costumes enter and leave the stage while Nyoman is whispering into my ear, trying to explain the complicated plot full of kings, queens, princes, monkeys, good spirits, and wicked witches. Apparently, this is a re-enactment of an ancient ritual that's very important in the Balinese culture. I'm trying to pay attention, but I quickly lose track of who's who and just enjoy the play for its mesmerising dances and outlandish costumes.

Two beautiful girls with long black hair and flowery crowns glide onto the stage and start moving in a synchronised twin-dance. They're wearing pink strapless tops and golden sarongs tightly hugging their slim bodies. With utmost precision, they're rhythmically moving their arms, bare feet, and even their eyeballs. It reminds me of a Bollywood dance performed by pretty robots.

Since his last remark about Opéra Garnier, Antoine has stayed silent and aloof, though he keeps glancing at me and Nyoman still holding hands. I'm trying to ignore him. He has no right to be upset because I've moved on with my life.

Barong, the leader of good spirits, stumbles onto the stage to cheering and clapping from the audience. He looks almost exactly like the "panto horse" we saw in the Taman Ayun Temple. The two dancers hidden inside his body are moving rhythmically, their bare feet with little bells strapped to their ankles. I know that with his long body covered in white thick hair and savage face with sharp fangs, Baring is supposed to look like a lion. However, he reminds me more of a big Pekinese dog, frolicking around, snapping his wooden mouth, and chasing his own tail. I can't help but laugh at this silly creature with protruding eyes and huge red ears.

"Don't be deceived by his appearance," Antoine whispers into my right ear. "He looks cute, but he can also bite. You can't mess with Barong."

As if on cue, Barong becomes angry and starts chasing the evil witch, who, according to Nyoman's running commentary in my left ear, is called Rangda. The goofy doggo is gone, replaced by a mighty lion.

When the performance finishes to an enthusiastic ovation, I feel as if someone woke me up from a beautiful dream. The soporific music, rhythmical dancing, and exotic tales transported me to a magical world.

"So, how did you like it, Lucy?"

"Did you enjoy it, Lucy?"

Like the synchronised dancers, Nyoman and Antoine fire the same question at me and then glare at each other across my seat. I'm starting to enjoy this male rivalry. Makes me feel important.

"It was amazing," I reply with a dreamy smile on my face. "Much better than British panto or French opera."

Maybe I should start to be more like Barong, protecting my boundaries and fighting for what is right in life? If I only knew how to do it—

26

LIFE ON THE SWING

"Luce, where are you sneaking out to so early?"

Two days after the Barong dance, I stumble upon Mia doing yoga on the terrace of our villa. She's fixed in a perfect cobra position, and then with one fluent move, goes into the downward dog.

I straight away recognise the salutation of the sun, the yoga sequence that we did together hundreds of times during her yoga classes or—even before she had her own yoga centre—in the living room of our shared house in London.

"I'm not sneaking out," I reply with as much dignity as a sneaking out person can muster. "I'm going on a trip with Nyoman. He wants to show me something interesting close to his village. He's being very secretive about it."

"But you remember that we're going to check the wedding venue today, right? And then Jack and I are going for cake tasting."

"Oh gosh, I'm so sorry, I thought it was tomorrow!" I've completely lost track of time here. A day feels like a week and a week feels like a day. Maybe Bali is a time warp? "In this case, I'll cancel my trip with Nyoman and go to the restaurant with you. That's more important."

"Nah, don't worry. Jack and Sylvia are coming, we'll be fine." Mia stands up and plunges into the swan dive, dropping her upper body towards the ground, so her words are a bit muffled. "And I'm happy to see you going on your own adventure. Three days ago, you had a date with Antoine, and now you're going out with Nyoman. You're a real player, Luce."

"It wasn't a date," I say defensively, glancing at my watch. It's almost 8:00 am, and Nyoman will be here any moment. "We just cleaned the beach together and then went for lunch."

"That sounds like a date to me." Mia's forehead is now pressed to the mat in the child's pose, and I can barely hear her. "So, what was it then?"

Yes, what exactly was that hot afternoon I spent with Antoine? It was the closing of a chapter, a conversation we should have had four years ago, but one I was too scared to face. I realise now that splitting with Antoine became a convenient excuse, so that I didn't have to do anything about my miserable life. Whenever I was unhappy with my job, my relationships (or the lack of them), the world in general—I could always blame it on my broken heart and not on my own reluctance to start living again. Anna was trying to tell me this all the time, but until now I wasn't ready to listen.

I glance at Mia bent like a pretzel on her yoga mat and probably not really interested in my self-analysis, so I simply reply, "It was just a meeting with a man I know."

And then I leave the villa to meet my Balinese guide.

Nyoman parks his minivan and swiftly jumps out to help me get out from the passenger's seat. We're in a makeshift parking lot in the middle of the jungle, somewhere between Legian and Ubud. The air outside is hot, humid, and suffocating. I miss the sea breeze that makes even hot days so pleasurable on Kuta Beach.

He takes my hand, as we follow a muddy path between the palm trees leading to a little bamboo hut on the top of a hill. My sandals are slipping in the mud, and I still have no idea what we're going to do here. The palms are swaying menacingly above our heads, and despite the heat, I shiver. I just hope he isn't going to sacrifice me to some cruel Hindu god and then eat my beating heart. No, wait, I'm thinking of the

Aztecs. But what if the Balinese have a similar ritual and my guide-books failed to mention it?

We finally reach the top of the hill and enter the bamboo hut, which —similar to most of the Balinese buildings—doesn't have a front wall. A young man comes from behind a wooden counter and greets us with a big grin. "Nyoman, good to see you, man!" He shifts his gaze to me and raises his eyebrows. "And I can see you've brought a friend."

"This is Lucy," Nyoman introduces me with pride in his voice. "I wanted to show her a different side of Bali. I hope you can help us, Gede."

"You're in the right place, man. Come with me."

Gede leads us outside the bamboo hut and then down the steps carved on the other side of the hill. Ahead of me, Nyoman and his friend are jumping down the slippery stairs with amazing agility, chatting amiably in Balinese, while I'm clinging desperately to the bamboo rail. The path is lined with some exotic shrubbery, so I still can't see our destination, but I start to hear horrible shrieks. It sounds as if someone was trying to survive on a roller coaster or had their heart ripped out alive. Who knows what's really happening there?

Finally, we reach the bottom of the stairs, and I realise that we're on the brink of a steep cliff opening towards emerald rice paddies below. The cliff is lined with very high swings hanging from the tall palm trees. Flying high above the edge, people on the swings are shrieking with fear or delight. Or both. It looks like a safety nightmare.

"That's amazing, man." Nyoman is scanning the rows of swings with awe. "You've done a great job here since my last visit." He reaches again for my hand. "Come on, Lucy, this is the best place to swing in Bali."

I instinctively take a step back and clutch tighter the bamboo rail.

"What's wrong?" Nyoman's face falls. "Don't you like my surprise?"

I shake my head. "It's lovely, Nyoman, but I can't do it. I'm scared of heights."

Nyoman's friend comes closer and puts a reassuring hand on my shoulder. "I was also scared at the beginning. But it's great fun, very exciting. And we make sure everything is very safe."

From what I've seen in Bali so far, safety isn't very high on the priority list. But even if these were the safest swings in the world, I still wouldn't be able to do it. At the sheer thought of it, my panic attack is having a panic attack.

I swallow hard, trying to stop the trembling in my body. "I'm really sorry, but I can't."

"No, I'm sorry I didn't ask you before. It's my fault." Nyoman drops his head. "But maybe we can just sit down on a bench and watch others? As we're already here?"

"Sure." That's the least I can do for him.

Gede directs us towards a wooden bench away from the cliff edge and then goes away to take care of other customers. I have to admit that the place looks lovely. There are five or six swings made of wood and long manila ropes. Most of them are designed for just one person, but there's also one wider plank for a couple, and even a suspended bed for a group of friends. Emerald grass covers the ground, and the whole area is peppered with white and pink flowers.

A group of Korean models arrives and I look on with jealousy as they start a photoshoot in an oversized bird's nest huddled between two palm trees. The nest models and people on the swings seem to be having a really good time. Why can't I be more like them?

Next to me, Nyoman shifts on the bench and sighs. Poor guy, it's clear that he wanted to impress me with his friend's place, but he doesn't know me well enough to realise I suffer from vertigo. Antoine once tried to take me to the Eiffel Tower, but he had to give up when I started shaking from fear, even before we managed to buy the tickets.

At the thought of Antoine and our conversation in the nasi goreng restaurant, I feel blood pumping faster in my temples. I realise that I wasted so many years being a coward and avoiding the confrontation with him. Clearing the air between us didn't mend my broken heart, but it gave me a sense of closure. Now that I know the full truth, I can finally stop playing the victim and take charge of my own life.

Without thinking too much, I stand up and pull Nyoman's hand. "Okay, let's do it. But I'll feel safer if we do it together."

"Are you sure?"

I can see hope lightening his face. "Yes." To be honest, I don't feel sure at all. But I have to try. I don't want to bury my head in the sand and live a half-life anymore.

Nyoman's friend helps us get comfortable on the double wooden plank and puts on some safety harnesses that don't seem to be adding much protection.

"Ready?" Gede asks.

"As ready as I can be," I reply with a shaky voice.

"I'll start slowly," he promises.

I'm clinging desperately to the rope with my left hand and to Nyoman's arm with my right one. Gede gently pulls the swing backwards and then lets go. We're soaring over the edge and the green rice fields below.

What if one of the ropes breaks and we fall down? Would we die straight away or just suffer from multiple injuries? I can already see our lifeless bodies lying on the ground, covered in mud and rice. I want to scream, but I can't find enough air in my lungs to even breathe. I close my eyes and prepare to die. I imagine my friends, wearing sarongs and playing gamelan, as they walk in a Balinese funeral procession to my cremation pyre.

"Lucy, look, we're flying," Nyoman's voice is full of excitement.

I open one eye and am almost sick on unsuspecting Nyoman. We're even higher than I imagined. It isn't a rice field below, it's the Grand Canyon.

He puts his arm around my waist and whispers into my ear, "It's okay, Lucy, I'm here. You're safe with me."

There's something very reassuring about hugging his warm body. I tentatively open my eyes a little and take a deep breath. He's right. Miraculously, we're still alive, floating through the air with cool wind playing in our hair and a faint smell of mud rising from the paddies.

Gede is pushing our swing stronger and stronger until we can almost touch the sky. I shriek with delight. Now I can understand the emotions of the others around us. This feeling of flying, of being completely weightless is intoxicating.

When Gede finally stops the swing and we come back to the safe land again, my legs wobble, and I almost fall down.

"Watch out, Lucy." Nyoman wraps his arms around my waist to help me keep my balance.

"Thank you, Nyoman, it was amazing!" I fling my arms around his neck, look into his twinkling eyes, and do what I haven't done in a long time. I throw all my caution to the wind and lower my lips to his. At first, he seems surprised, but very quickly, he returns my kiss with great enthusiasm.

And so, we're making out on the cliff in the middle of the Balinese jungle. I don't care that his friend and other customers are watching. I don't care that I barely know him. Or that I have to leave Bali in less than two weeks. The only thing that matters is the kiss, long and intense, and the warm embrace of his lean body.

When our lips part, we can hear people around us clapping in approval. Someone even cheers.

"Wow, thank you, Lucy, this was amazing." Nyoman is positively glowing.

"Yes, it was," I say, even though I secretly wish that he was Antoine...

27

SPILLING THE BEANS

The next morning after my swing escapade, Sylvia, Mia, and I are having breakfast on the terrace of a small restaurant close to our villa. It's a very casual place serving typical English and European food, and —as far as I can judge from their accent—it's filled with Australian tourists.

"This doesn't look as good as the food at our wedding venue," Mia complains, trying to take a photo of her French toast with marmalade placed on a plain white plate.

"But it tastes delish." Sylvia cuts a piece of a plump fried sausage and pops it into her mouth.

"Oh, yes, how was your wedding venue yesterday?" I ask. "As good as you expected?"

"Yes, it was *magnifico*!" Mia puts down her phone and bites into the toast. "The whole restaurant is completely open-air, with a huge green lawn and a roofed dance floor in case of rain. It has a beautiful view to the sea."

"And they serve the best burgers I've had in my life," Sylvia adds. "And potato skins with cheddar cheese."

"Why are you eating burgers in Bali?" I ask. "I thought you wanted to explore the local cuisine?"

"I'm sick of the local cuisine," Sylvia spats, as she bites into a rasher of fried bacon. "Don't get me wrong, the food here is lovely, but why do I have to eat rice with vegetables all the time? I'm not a hamster, I need some proper food."

"Speaking of food, leave some space for dessert." Mia chews pensively on her toast. "Yesterday after the restaurant, Jack and I went to the cake tasting. We narrowed it down to three options, but you need to help us chose the final one. I've got the samples in here." She pats a thermal bag sitting on the table.

I'm glad that my friends are so busy with the wedding preparations that they haven't grilled me yet about my trip with Nyoman. When I came back yesterday, the villa was empty. And by the time they'd all come back, I was safely tucked in my bedroom. What's even better, Jack and Antoine are now on a hunt around Kuta, Legian, and Seminyak to find blue flowers for Mia's bouquet. Apparently, their chosen florist had only purple flowers, which isn't the same *puñetero* thing. Or so I'm told. If everything goes well, I might spend a whole day without seeing my ex.

Mia puts down her toast and interrupts my musings about seeing Antoine. I mean, about not seeing Antoine. "Luce, you still haven't told us what you were doing with Nyoman yesterday. What was his big surprise?"

"Hopefully, you did more interesting things than visiting temples and watching butterflies." Sylvia wriggles her eyebrows.

I muffle a sigh. These two are like bloodhounds that have found the scent of juicy gossip.

"We spent a lovely day together." I can tell them that much. "We went on a swing over rice paddies. And then we had dinner in Ubud. It was all very sweet."

"A swing? But you're scared of heights!" Mia widens her eyes in surprise.

"Yes, I was super scared at first, but Nyoman was holding me tight all the time. And we were flying! It was magical."

"Oh, so you pretended to be Aladdin and Jasmin on a Balinese flying carpet. And then what?" Sylvia wants to know.

I stare at the tropical fruit salad on my plate, debating how much I should tell them. Some things should stay private.

150

"Come on, Luce, spill the beans." Sylvia takes a sip of the luwak coffee and licks her lips with pleasure. "Speaking of beans, who would have thought that coffee that was extracted from poo could taste so good."

"The poo of some unfortunate, mistreated animal," Mia clarifies. "I'm still judging you for your poor life choices."

"Not everyone can be an environmental warrior like you," Sylvia retorts. "Some of us want to have a life without feeling guilty for stealing precious oxygen from the plants."

"You've got it completely wrong, Sylve. Plants produce oxygen, so we aren't stealing anything from them." Mia rolls her eyes. "And don't change the topic before Lucy tells us more about her date with Nyoman."

"It wasn't a date!"

"Really?" Sylvia seems disappointed.

Oh, what the hell, they are my friends, and I can tell them everything. And they'll be teasing me anyway, whether I tell them or not. That's the way our friendship works. "We got out from the swing and then we kissed."

"Ooh, finally some action. Atta girl!" Sylvia claps her hands. "And how was it?"

"It was nice, but I didn't feel the spark."

"At least you know your mojo is back." Sylvia pats my forearm. "We'll help you find a nice guy when we're back in London, you little minx."

"And what are you going to do with Antoine?" Mia asks.

"Nothing," I say, repeatedly stabbing a piece of mango with my fork.

"Don't pretend you're not interested."

The mango is now completely destroyed, so I start jabbing pineapple instead.

I stop massacring the fruit on my plate and look at my friends instead. "We had a serious chat and I feel that I'm finally over Antoine. For real. I'm free at last."

"Good for you, Luce!" Sylvia raises her cup of coffee. "Let's drink to that!"

"Well, enough about me. How are you both doing? Sylve, how's sexy Wayan?"

"He's gorgeous. And very good in the sack." Sylvia is almost cooing. "He's taking me to his hometown, Lovina, tomorrow. So don't make any plans with Nyoman, because he'll have to take care of Sasak Bar for the whole day. Or maybe even two days if we decide to stay overnight."

"Does it mean that you're serious about him?" I ask. "Do you think he has some potential?"

"I don't know, but I don't overanalyse things like you do. We're just having fun at the moment, enjoying each other as much as we can." Sylvia shovels baked beans with tomato sauce into her mouth. She accidentally bangs her fork against the plate, and a few beans are catapulted in my direction, landing on my leg. "Oops, sorry, Luce."

"It's okay." I flick the beans off my thigh and wipe the fingers on a napkin. I'm just glad that I'm wearing my black jeans, and not the new green skirt.

Sylvia and Wayan seem so perfect for each other. Wayan is helping her relax and forget about her stressful job in investment banking, while Sylvia brings so much energy and excitement that he can be anything but bored. But I understand that they come from two different worlds, and it might be hard for their relationship to survive the realities of the everyday life, especially long distance. Trust me, I know something about it. Still, one can dream.

———

Once we've finished eating our food, or least, in my case, stabbing it, Mia unzips the thermal bag and produces a white cake box with a name of a local bakery in Seminyak printed across it.

"Now you need to help me choose what to serve at the wedding." She unloads a piece of each cake on a clean plate provided by a friendly waiter. "Do you prefer chocolate sponge with Balinese coffee? Vanilla with mango? Or caramelized banana?"

Sylvia and I try each sample, clicking tongues and smacking lips.

"All the cakes are delicious, though they're a bit too sweet for me," I declare. "But I'm voting for vanilla and mango. It's the lightest and most refreshing of the three. And I like that they're using fresh local fruit."

"Definitely chocolate sponge with coffee." Sylvia is licking her spoon with relish. "Dark and sensuous. It'll be the highlight of your wedding."

"Thanks, *chicas*." Mia looks at us with dismay. "That's very helpful, because my favourite one is caramelized banana."

"And which one did Jack prefer?" I ask. "Or we can ask Anna to be the final judge."

"I'm not sure Anna can be a judge of something she hasn't tried. And Jack said that he wants me to be happy, so I can choose anything I like. And that the wedding isn't about the cake, but about our love."

"Aw, Jack's right." Sylvia's voice melts like buttercream. "But your love will be even better if you choose chocolate and coffee."

"And how are things between you two in general?" I ask. "You don't have any more wedding jitters, now that Jack is here?"

"He's great." Mia's face lights up when she's talking about her fiancé. "I can't believe that I almost cancelled the wedding."

"And have you changed your mind about inviting your father? Have you talked to him again?"

"Nope. I just told him to bugger off. Problem solved." Mia crosses arms over her chest. "But he still keeps calling and texting me, apologising for ignoring me over the years. It's like he suddenly had a personality transplant. It's very suspicious."

"What are you going to do about him?"

Mia shrugs. "I really don't know. It's stupid, because we're connected only by genetics, but I still care about him. It sucks."

"But he wants to come to your wedding, right?" Sylvia asks. "Maybe that's a sign that he's changed, that he'd like to patch things up with you?"

"I don't think so. I'm sure it's some trick devised by his new wife." Mia shakes her head. "And because of that, I can't properly focus on my wedding preparations."

"Another meditation session to help you relax?" I suggest.

"Maybe. But this time without loud meditation frogs. My head is still ringing from this horrible music at the Barong dance."

28

KILLER STILETTOS

"Today is the big day!" Two days after our cake tasting, Sylvia waltzes into the kitchen, where Mia and I are sipping our morning drinks—detox juice for Mia and builder's tea for me.

"You've lost track of time, Sylve. The wedding is in a week." Mia takes a big swig of her green juice and winces. "*Carajo*! I hate kale. Whoever asked brides to go on pre-wedding detox was a sadist."

"Kale is the invention of devil," Sylvia agrees, pressing buttons on the coffee machine. "Just like apples. They taste like wood."

"Why are you so chirpy, Sylve?" I ask, glancing at the clock on the wall. "It's barely 9:00 pm."

"My trip with Wayan was absolutely lovely." Sylvia adds three spoons of sugar into her freshly brewed latte. "Lovina is a real paradise —so peaceful and wild, complete opposite of Kuta. And after the dark, we had sexy time on the beach. Very romantic, though now I have sand in places in which sand has no business to be." She stirs her coffee and takes a big gulp. "Also, it's the big day!"

"The big day of what?" Mia asks and scrunches her face after drinking more juice.

"Of me throwing you a hen-do!" Sylvia puts down her coffee mug and starts dancing a Scottish jig on the white tiles. "You'll lurve it!"

Mia turns towards me with a suspicious look. "Luce, what is she

154

talking about? I explicitly told you that I don't want a hen-do. It's always so cheesy and rowdy."

I shrug and dip a biscuit in my tea. "Dunno. She just said it was going to be a big surprise and she'd organise everything herself."

"Does Jack know about this?" Mia pours her green concoction down the drain. "And what about Anna? We should have all my maids of honour at the party, but she isn't coming until the day after tomorrow."

"Actually, tonight Antoine is also throwing Jack a stag-do in another club close to ours. His groomsmen haven't arrived yet, but Wayan and Nyoman are joining them instead." Sylvia pops a minitart into her mouth and crunches it with visible pleasure. "And don't worry about Anna, she'll be with us in spirit."

"What's the dress code?" I ask, hoping against hope that she'll say casual.

"Glamorous. Elegant and sexy." This is Sylvia's default mode, and she always tries to impose it on her less fashion-savvy friends. Namely me. "But also take your swimsuit. There's a swimming pool in the club. And a lot of hot half-naked men."

"At least promise me there won't be any glowing dildos, strippers, or slutty costumes." Mia looks at Sylvia pleadingly.

"I can promise you just one thing, Mi. We're going to have the best time tonight."

———

One more step, and I'm going to fall down. I'm swaying on the uneven pavement, swearing at the stilettos that Sylvia has forced me to wear tonight. They're too small for me, pinching my feet. Sylvia and Mia are strutting in front of me as if they were born on a catwalk, but I can barely walk in high heels even under the best of circumstances. Who invented these shoes of torture? Probably the same person who forces Mia and other brides-to-be to drink kale juice. I hate this person.

The taxi driver has dropped us off in front of Potato Head, a fancy club in Seminyak, and now we have to walk through a never-ending alley to get inside. It's probably the longest and most painful walk of

my life. I almost weep with relief when we finally reach the club, a big round structure covered in old wooden shutters that look really chic, despite their mismatched shapes and colours.

I'm just about to sit on a small concrete wall and give some respite to my aching feet, when Mia's voice freezes me mid-air. "Don't sit on this! It's art."

I look past the concrete wall and notice a grassy mound covered in hundreds of old flip-flops attached to each other in a rainbow of colours.

"Look, there's more," Sylvia points towards a small tipi made of empty plastic bottles.

"That's the kind of rubbish Antoine and I cleaned from Kuta beach the other day," I say, peering at the artistically arranged litter. "But it looks much more impressive here than in our bin bags."

"Do you think it's a message to stop polluting the ocean?" Mia is already snapping pictures of the rainbow-hued flip-flops. "Or just a random artistic installation?"

Sylvia purses her lips. "Either that or a lot of people in this club have lost their flip-flops. Leaving the club drunk and shoeless like Balinese Cinderellas."

Mia snaps a few photos of the rubbish art and then gestures towards me and Sylvia to take a selfie with her. "*Chicas*, let's rock this party!"

We leave the art installations behind and walk through a dark corridor inside the rotunda to get into the club. As soon as we emerge on the other side, there's another surprise waiting for us. This time in a form of my favourite human.

29

VOLCANO DRINKS

"Oh my god, Anna! What are you doing here? You weren't supposed to come until the day after tomorrow." I forget about my horrible stilettos, as I run towards my best friends and squash her in a bear hug.

"Luce, sweetie. It's so good to see you," Anna replies, holding me tight. "It was Sylvia's idea."

"Why didn't you tell me?" I say, finally letting her go.

"She's sworn me to secrecy. And you know how scary she can be," Anna says.

"Scary? I'd rather say efficient." Sylvia smiles like a cat that has just learned how to use a tin opener.

"Anna, so lovely to see you." Now it's Mia's turn to embrace her. "I was afraid that Sylvia's surprise was a group of Balinese Chippendales performing a naked Barong dance. Or something equally horrific."

"That's your opinion of me?" Sylvia sends her a pained look. "You know I'm much more classy than that."

"Of course, I know, Sylve." Mia's trying to placate her. "But do you remember my twenty-fifth birthday that you organised in a strip-club in Soho? I'm still not over the trauma."

"Well, I was tempted to do something similar tonight," Sylvia admits. "But I knew you'd hate that. So tonight, we're going to stick to the old-fashioned drinking booze and dancing on the tables."

A smiling waiter, wearing a blue shirt with a beautiful bird-print, is guiding us through a maze of wooden tables, comfortable-looking sofas, and deckchairs. I'm clutching Anna's arm, to help me keep balance while walking on the uneven wooden boards. It's so great to have my best friend here in Bali. She'll know what to do with all my tangled emotions about Antoine and Nyoman.

I've read in my guidebook about Potato Head, one of the most famous clubs in Bali, and I expected something very posh and out-of-reach. But the atmosphere here is actually casual and friendly. People in swimsuits are lounging across this horseshoe building opening onto a big lawn and a famous infinity pool with a view of the sea.

"Look, there's even a pool bar." I point towards a mushroom-shaped counter serving drinks directly in the water, as one of the happy patrons is floating away with a cup of steaming tea.

"I wonder how often they take a loo break," Mia scrunches her nose.

"Why do you need a loo if you're already in water?" Anna asks sarcastically.

"Apparently, urea is good for your skin," Sylvia quips. "And I never say no to a free spa treatment, however unconventional."

We finally reach our table at the right end of the horseshoe, which gives us a perfect view of both the Seminyak Beach and the pool.

"So, what are we drinking tonight?" asks Sylvia, sprawling in a cushioned armchair next to Mia's.

"When I was waiting for you, I checked the drinks menu," Anna replies, making herself more comfortable on the sofa she's sharing with me. "It's quite impressive. We won't parch here."

"I love the names of their drinks," Mia's already leafing through the menu. "Barong Zombie, Koko-Loko, Volcano Agung."

Another waiter, wearing a shirt with the same bird print but this time in purple, takes our orders and disappears inside the bar.

"Speaking of the volcanoes, we have a great idea." Sylvia pushes up her oversized sunglasses to the top of her head. "Wayan told me that one of the biggest attractions in Bali is admiring the sunrise from the top of Mount Batur. We can't miss it."

158

"How romantic." Mia smiles wistfully. "But do we have enough time for a new expedition? The wedding is in just one week."

"It won't take long." It seems Sylvia has everything already planned out. "We can hire a special guide who will pick us up directly from the villa in the middle of the night and help us climb the volcano. Then, we watch the sunrise, go down, and drive back home. We will be back before lunchtime."

"Why can't Nyoman be our guide?" I ask, trying to remember what I've read about volcanos in Bali. "Also, isn't Mount Batur the active volcano that erupts all the time? Isn't it dangerous?"

"I think it's Mount Agung that keeps erupting. Batur is very safe." Sylvia's voice doesn't sound very convincing, and I feel an itchy patch of eczema forming on my forearm. I'm not even sure why I'm stressed —there's no way I'm getting close to any volcanoes, active or not. "And you need a specially trained guide, because it's hard to find a path to the top, especially at night."

"In that case, I'm out," I reply, scratching my arm. Hiking in the dark on an active volcano sounds like a suicide mission. Why would anyone want to do it?

I look at Anna, hoping that she will agree with my common sense, but she replies instead, "I haven't seen anything in Bali yet, and this seems like a good way to discover the island. I'm in."

"I love this idea. Let me text Jack to check if it works for him as well." Mia's already pulling the phone from her handbag.

"Jack and Antoine are already on board," Sylvia announces proudly. "I checked with them earlier. We can book the trip for the day after tomorrow."

"Luce, are you sure you don't want to go with us?" Anna turns towards me on the sofa. "It might be a fun adventure. Something to help you forget about your worries and get out of you head, living in the real world instead. Action is the best cure for anxiety."

"I'd rather stay in the villa and read a book in the garden. That's the best way to overcome my anxiety. Thank you very much." I turn my head and notice a waiter with a tray laden with glasses, goblets, and wooden cups. "Look, our drinks are here. Maybe I won't climb a volcano, but at least I can taste one here."

As I take a sip of my Volcano Agung drink, I close eyes in pleasure. The sweet and spicy liquid is making my tongue tingle. I can hear a buzz of conversations, laughter, and happy squeals coming from the pool. I'm surrounded by my friends, including my lovely Anna. Life is perfect right now.

"So, what's the goss?" Anna shifts her gaze from me to Mia and Sylvia on the other side of the table. "What did I miss? Tell me everything."

"Mia wanted to break up with Jack, because her father decided to invite himself to the wedding. But that's all sorted now," I say, raising my eyebrows. "And Sylvia's still going strong with the sexy surfing instructor. Even very strong, judging from the sounds coming from her bedroom."

"You're just jealous." Sylvia waves her hand dismissively. "You've got two hot guys chasing after you, and what do you do about them? Nothing. Wasted opportunity."

"Well, she did snog one of them on the swings," Mia adds, while I'm trying to hide my embarrassment by drinking more of the volcano drink.

"You didn't tell me anything about snogging, you sly thing." Anna turns her head towards me with avid interest.

"There's nothing to talk about." I'm avoiding her eyes. "Nyoman took me to a place where you can swing over rice paddies. It was beautiful and romantic, and I was scared witless. It was the adrenaline rush, nothing more."

"And what about Antoine?" Anna doesn't give up, so I check the menu, pretending I'm too busy choosing a new drink.

"You know what they did the other day, Anna?" Sylvia fills in the silence. "They went picking rubbish on the beach." She rolls her eyes. "Soooo sexy."

"At least we did something good for the planet," I reply with dignity.

The purple-shirt waiter comes back to ask if we need anything more. This time I choose Guava Good Day, described as fruity and fragrant.

"And what's going on with your dad, Mi?" Anna looks with concern at our bride-to-be. "Did you feel that cancelling the whole wedding would be a better option than facing your father?"

"When he invited himself to the party, I completely freaked out. But it's all under control now." Mia shrugs as she takes a sip of her Bali Pimms. "The fact that he gave me his DNA doesn't mean he has to ruin my big day."

"Maybe he genuinely wants to apologise for his mistakes and rebuild his relationship with you?" Anna is hopeful as always. I wonder if that's why she has become a therapist—to find hope in the most desperate situations.

"Maybe." Mia shrugs. Then, she's spared further questions, as her phone pings, and she picks it up from the table. "Jack's just texted me that their club sucks, and he's coming to join us. Better touch up your make-up, *chicas*, as he's bringing the boys with him."

30

THE BIG SPLASH

"You know that you're breaking the most sacred law of a hen-do." Sylvia's shooting daggers at Mia. "No guys allowed, unless they're Chippendales."

"It's not a hen-do." Mia turns her head towards the entrance in expectation. "And Wayan is also coming. You should be happy."

The afternoon heat is slowly dying out, and more and more people in Potato Head are getting pleasantly tipsy on the exotic cocktails. Our group is no exception. I look wistfully at the partygoers floating in the infinity pool, waiting for the best sunset view on Seminyak Beach. I'm dying to join them in the cool water, but I don't want to ruin my painstaking make-up. At least not now, when the boys are coming. Shallow, I know.

And here they are. Walking towards our table in this confident swagger that only young handsome men can pull off successfully without looking like complete muppets.

Jack, all tall and broad-shouldered, is leading the way, followed by sexy and mysterious Wayan. No wonder Sylvia's crazy about him. Nyoman, who's wearing a white shirt and a tidy ponytail, looks completely different from the bare-chested, loose-haired Nyoman from Sasak Bar, or even the snoggable Nyoman from the swings near Ubud. He does scrub well.

And finally, Antoine and his Clark Kent glasses, closing the rear. He isn't as tall as the other guys, but he makes up for it with his French charm and wicked smile. My heart skips a beat when I see him.

"*Hola, mi amor*," Mia stands up to greet her fiancé with a full mouth-on-mouth kiss. When their lips finally part, Jack looks at her with so much passion that I can almost smell pheromones cruising through the air.

"Hello, my little chorizo," Jack replies and kisses her again.

I've never been a big fan of that kind of "let's break up and then make up" relationship, but in their case, it seems to be working well. It's as if every breakup resets their passion levels and they fall in love with each other all over again. They don't even realise how lucky they are to have this kind of bond.

The waiters help us set up more chairs around the table, and we're finally settled after a flurry of more passionate kisses (Wayan and Sylvia), cheek kisses (Nyoman and I), introductions (Anna and our Balinese friends), and shaking hands (Antoine and I). Anna sends my ex just a cold nod. She doesn't easily forgive people who have hurt her friends, and she still remembers how shattered I was after our breakup.

After a short round of small talk and ordering new drinks, the discussion around the table breaks into smaller groups. Unsurprisingly, I'm yet again sandwiched between Nyoman, who's sitting on the sofa between me and Anna, and Antoine, who's got his own chair close to us.

What *is* surprising is that Nyoman is now engrossed in a heated debate with Anna about the local wedding rituals and then about the latest James Bond movie, which they loved and hated at the same time. Who knew that they had so much in common?

As the rest of my friends are all loved-up, chatting only to their partners and ignoring everyone else, Antoine and I end up sitting next to each other in awkward silence. I'm twirling a piece of sugar cane from my drink between my fingers and staring longingly towards the pool.

"Are you still making those funny collages for your friends?" Antoine moves his chair a bit closer and looks at me.

I nod silently.

"You know, I still have the card you gave me for my birthday in Paris." Antoine's voice sounds amused.

"Really?" I turn towards him with a sudden interest. "The one with a dolphin and an owl drinking champagne on the beach?"

"*Oui*, that's the one. *Le Dauphin et la Chouette* enjoying their life." He smiles, raising his glass. "And look, Lucy, our dream has come true. Here we are, drinking cocktails in Bali, having a perfect holiday."

That's all true, I want to tell him, but the circumstances are completely different now. If anything, it's the opposite of the honey-moon we planned back then. It's a bitter-moon.

"I've been watching a TV show recently and I think you might like it." Antoine isn't discouraged by my silence. He's always been able to make me talk, even when I was mad at him.

"Yes? Which one?"

"*Big Little Lies,*" he says and waits a beat for my reaction.

"I love that show!" I almost squeak with excitement. I watched both seasons a gazillion times and also read the book. But I'm surprised that he watched it. Psychological drama isn't his favourite genre. Or maybe it is now? "And why did you think I might like it?" I narrow my eyes with suspicion. Is there a catch here?

"I don't know." He shrugs and takes a sip of his wine. "Just the general ambiance, the music, the acting. And I know you love Nicole Kidman."

"And not because the story of Celeste and her abusive husband reminds you of my parents?"

"Ah yes, that as well." He looks down at his wine glass to avoid my eyes.

I sigh. My family situation played a big part in my mistrust of men and relationships in general. Just like Perry and Celeste from *Big Little Lies*, my parents had a very dysfunctional marriage, though without any physically violence, thankfully. One minute they were lovey-dovey, the next they were screaming at the top of their voices and throwing plates at each other. No wonder I was so clingy to Antoine. I thought I'd finally found my saviour, a man who would solve all my problems and help me overcome my childhood traumas. But we have to be our own saviours, as Anna is keen to remind me all the time. And your boyfriend can't be your therapist.

I shake off the memories of my miserable childhood and smile at Antoine. "So, tell me, Antoine, what have you been up to for the last four years?"

Antoine and I spend a very pleasant hour just catching up on each other's news, gossiping about our common acquaintances, and discussing books and films we both enjoy. It's nice reconnecting with my old flame, but my bladder is the size of a tennis ball, and I've downed five exotic drinks in the course of one afternoon. Time for a break.

Anna offers to go with me to the loo and I gladly agree. I can barely walk—alcohol and stilettos don't mix well.

"Why are you even wearing these shoes?" Anna asks, as we're weaving our way through the maze of tables and chairs. "You hate high heels, and you don't know how to walk in them."

"Sylvia made me." I wobble and almost sit on the lap of some random guy who happens to be in my way. "Oops, sorry."

Anna takes my arm in a steel grip and pulls me towards the bathroom.

"There are some steps down, watch out," she says without releasing my elbow. "You always let Sylvia and other people bully you into things. You need to grow more backbone, Luce. You have to protect yourself."

I have no answer to that. Maybe because I have to devote my whole attention to not slipping on the stairs and smashing my head on the black marble floor.

"Also, what's happening with you and Antoine?" Anna wants to know, after she's safely disposed me into one of the stalls. "Do you want me to stay here and help you with your dress?"

"Nope, I'm fine," I lie. As soon as Anna closes the wooden door, the floor starts swaying under my feet. "And nothing's going on with Antoine. Just friends. Just chatting."

I get out of the toilet stall to wash my hands while Anna is still in her cubicle. I don't want to hear any more of her questioning. She's like the bloody Spanish Inquisition, so I shout to her, "I'll meet you upstairs!" and sneak out of the toilet before she has time to protest.

When I emerge back in the club, I notice that it's almost dark outside, and the air has significantly cooled down since our arrival. I also feel a bit more sober, though the ground is still swaying under my feet. Maybe I should stop drinking now. I decide to take a longer route to our table and stroll along the infinity pool, the surface shimmering in the fading sunset. I imagine how lovely it might be to just jump into the golden water when I suddenly bump into someone.

I lift my head. "Antoine!"

He's so close that our bodies are almost touching. He's looking at me with his intensely green eyes, and my heart starts speeding. He smells so good, musky and manly.

"*Lucy, ma petite chouette*," he whispers. I can see that he's a bit tipsy as well.

He lifts his hand and gently caresses my shoulder. Goosebumps spring across my bare skin, and I can feel a warm pulse beating between my thighs. The air between us is charged with electricity.

"I was an idiot to ever let you go," he says, skimming his fingers up and down my arm, creating an electric shock with his every move. "I've been thinking about you all these years, unable to forget you."

I'm standing hypnotised by his words and his touch.

"Sometimes, I discover a nice bookshop in Paris, and I think, 'Lucy would love it,' only to realise that I'd lost you. Every day, I missed your laughter, your kindness, even your funny collages."

I'm so shocked that I can't utter a word. Is it happening for real or is it just a figment of my overactive imagination?

I look at his familiar face. He's my Anton, *mon dauphin*, my first real love. He's really here. I can just reach out and touch his broad jaw, his dark hair. I take a shallow breath and lick my lips.

My muddled brain doesn't protest, as my drunk body takes charge, and my fingers start caressing his hair. My hips move towards him in slow motion, my lips find their way towards his mouth. And before I know what's happening, we're locked in a long and passionate kiss. He tastes of red wine and something that's uniquely him. Something that feels like coming back home.

His strong hands are roaming my hips and lower back, sending little sparks through my skin, and also much, much deeper in my body. I don't want this moment to end, even though I have a vague feeling I shouldn't be doing this. If only I knew why?

I peel my mouth from his and take a step back. But before I have a chance to say anything, my ridiculously high heels get stuck on something on the floor, and I completely lose my balance. Antoine's arms are still holding my waist, so I take him with me, as we tumble down and land in the swimming pool with a big splash.

We spend a minute or so trying to disentangle in the cool water, but it isn't easy, as I'm still drunk and my clothes are clinging to my wet body. Maybe there's a reason why people don't swim in long dresses.

When we finally emerge to the surface, we burst into slightly hysterical laughter. My make-up isn't waterproof, so I probably look like a smudged panda. Antoine has lost his glasses in water, and his myopic eyes look so vulnerable and innocent now. I remember waking up with him back in Paris, without our contact lenses or glasses. We were both as blurry as Impressionist paintings. But it never stopped us from having impressive morning sex.

I remember all these beautiful moments with him, and against all logic, we start kissing again. Now he tastes of passion and chlorine. But after a while, my brain finally catches up with my body and tells me to stop. I shove Antoine away, gasping for air.

"Lucy." He pushes a strand of wet hair from my eyes. "I know that I fucked up, but we were so happy once. Do you think we could be together again?"

Oh my god, is he serious? I've fantasized about this moment so many times. I wished Antoine would realise his mistake and beg me to come back. But now, when it's finally happening, through the haze of alcohol and racing hormones, a thought is darting through my brain screaming, "Danger!" What am I doing? Kissing the man who broke my heart and dreams. I can't afford to have another major meltdown if he decides to leave me again. Breaking up with the Tindermen was painful enough. But being dumped by Antoine was a whole different level of suffering. Was it the same pain Voldemort felt splitting his soul to create Horcruxes? I can't make the same mistake twice.

What did Anna say in the bathroom? "You have to protect yourself." So, that's exactly what I'll do.

I trudge through the water, away from Antoine, and try to get out of the pool. I tumble back a few times, until someone gives me a helpful hand and I scramble out on the dry land. I was so caught up in our passion that I didn't notice a crowd gathering around the pool to watch our spectacle. Mia and Jack, Sylvia and Wayan, Anna and even our friendly waiter—they're all there, looking agog. It's a miracle the security hasn't kicked us out yet for unruly behaviour.

And then I realise that the helpful hand, which I'm still holding, belongs to Nyoman. Shit.

"Lucy, are you okay?" His voice is filled with concern. "I know you've drunk a bit too much tonight. Did he try to take advantage of you? Do you want me to beat him up?"

"No, it's fine, Nyoman. Thanks for the offer, but there's no need. I've got a handle on this."

I turn back to look at Antoine's handsome face bobbing on the surface. What I'm going to do will hurt both of us, so it's best to do it quickly. A clean wound heals faster. "It's over, Antoine! We have to forget the past and move on. For both of our sakes."

I notice one of these horrible stilettos floating on the surface. I take off the other shoe and chuck it into the water. And then I spin around and flee barefoot towards the exit.

31

THE PERFECT SOUVENIR
FROM BALI

What's wrong with me? Why am I so dramatic? Why did I kiss Antoine and then make a complete idiot of myself? Why can't I be a normal human being?

A merry-go-round of anxious thoughts is spinning inside my head. It's 11:00 am, and I'm still lying in bed in the crumpled dress from last night. But at least the shoes from hell are gone. Sylvia will kill me for throwing them into the pool and ruining them forever. Yet another reason to never leave my room.

After I fled from Potato Head yesterday, I hailed a taxi back to the villa and barricaded myself in my room. I pinged a quick text to my friends to let them know that I was safe at home and then turned my phone off. I spent all night replaying the events of the hen-do in my head and wriggling with shame and guilt. I cried so much that my contact lenses fell out.

I haven't left the room since (thank god for the ensuite bathroom), and my plan is to stay here forever. But now I've run out of mineral water, and I don't dare to drink from the tap like I do at home. The last thing I need right now is getting some exotic stomach bug and ending up in an Indonesian hospital.

What's wrong with me? Why did I ruin not only Sylvia's shoes, but also Mia and Jack's hen and stag dos? Why did I hurt Nyoman's feelings by publicly snogging another man so soon after our kiss on the swings? And why did I damage forever a chance of being friends with Antoine again? What's wrong with—

Before I have a chance to finish my thought, I'm startled by a gentle knock on my door.

"Luce, it's me, Anna. Can I come in?"

I glance at the wooden door, not sure what to do. What if Anna is a Trojan horse and everyone else will burst into my room and start yelling at me? Another wave of shame makes me sit up, as I grab at my dry throat and swallow the bile.

"We're alone in the house." Anna taps on the door again. "They've all gone on a trip to the Turtle Island. You're safe."

I get up and pad barefoot on the cold white tiles to turn the lock. I open the door a little and eye Anna suspiciously. She looks fresh in her safari-style linen dress, brown hair tied up in a ponytail, and her pretty face with no make-up. But she has dark shadows under her eyes, and she seems worried.

"I don't want to talk about last night," I inform her before letting her in.

"We don't have to talk about it," she promises, walking into the room and closing the door behind her. "But are you okay, Luce? Is there anything else you want to discuss?"

"Nope." I slump my shoulders, shuffle back to bed, and bury myself under the white sheet.

"Actually, I wanted to ask you a favour." Anna sits down next to me and strokes my hair.

It's a gesture I remember well from my childhood, but not from my own home. Every time my parents had a huge row or there was some problem with my brothers, I'd escape to Anna's house. There, her grandma Misia would prepare hot cocoa and chat about some trivial things to take my mind off my worries. Once I'd calmed down a bit, she would let me lie down on the old sofa in their living room, tuck me in with a fresh-smelling blanket, and sit down next to me, gently stroking my hair. I once read that during an anxiety attack, you should imagine that you're in your safe place. For me, it's Anna and Misia's living room, the smell of cocoa, and Misia's soothing hand on my head.

Anna stops patting my hair now and looks at me with her kind eyes. "Can you help me find a nice souvenir for Misia? It will cheer her up and take her mind off her health issues. Maybe a beer opener with some Balinese motif? Remember how we always brought her beer openers from our school trips, even though she never drinks alcohol?"

I smile at the memory. When Anna and I were in the sixth grade, we went on a school trip to Bath, and with our meagre pocket money, we bought a beer opener with a Jane Austen quote. On our return, we proudly handed it to Anna's grandma, only to discover that Misia was teetotal. Since then, it has become our silly tradition, and now poor Misia has a house filled with useless souvenirs she doesn't want to throw away for sentimental reasons.

"Can't you go with Mia or Sylvia?" I ask.

"I told you, they're all gone. Besides, they don't know Misia as well as you do."

I make a mistake of glancing up at Anna. Her face, which I know better than my own, is pinched with concern. I can see what she's doing. Her grandma doesn't need yet another beer opener. Anna just wants to draw me out of my bed of despair and connect me with the world outside of my troubled mind.

I remember how she and Misia helped me through the dark times after my breakup with Antoine. They patched me up as much as they could and sent me to a specialist to help me fix things that couldn't be healed with hot cocoa and kindness. I can't make Anna worry so much again. I'm a different person now. Stronger, wiser, more self-aware. That's why I rejected Antoine before he had a chance to break my heart again.

"Sure, I'll go with you. I'll just take a quick shower and change my clothes. Otherwise, people might think I've escaped from a zombie apocalypse."

Half an hour later, Anna and I enter a souvenir shop in the main Legian street not far away from our villa. We look around the tiny shop with no front wall or windows. The small room is filled with straw hats, round wicker handbags, and beach towels with I <3 Bali printed on the neon-pink fabric.

"Hello, do you have any beer openers?" Anna asks the shopkeeper, a middle-aged woman who's sitting on the front step of her shop, trying to cool herself with a big electric fan.

"Yes, over there." The woman stands up and brings us to a shelf filled with wooden—penises. They are all very colourful, decorated with flowers and "Greetings from Bali" signs, but this doesn't hide the fact that they're all more or less anatomically correct.

Anna takes one of them from the shelf and quickly puts it back. "Do you have anything, um, less penis-y?"

"We have different sizes." The shopkeeper opens a carton filled with wooden dildos—some as small as a thumb, some as huge as a forearm.

"Hmm, what do you think, Luce?"

"I know Misia is very open-minded, but maybe this is a bit too much, even for her?" I say, suspiciously eyeing the contents of the box.

We thank the shopkeeper for her time and go further down the street to find some less controversial gifts. But every shop we visit has the same range of wares: neon-pink towels, straw hats, wooden penises.

"It's a hopeless case." Anna rubs her forehead in frustration, as we leave yet another store in which we failed to find a beer opener that isn't a painted dick. "Do you think we might have more luck in Kuta or Seminyak? Maybe they have more choices over there?"

I squint my eyes at the sky, trying to remember the souvenir shops I've seen in Bali so far. "I don't think so. Kuta, Legian, and Seminyak are one touristy agglomeration. It's unlikely that we'll find much more sophisticated goods than here."

"So, let's go to Denpasar," Anna suggests, and before I have time to protest, she's already trying to hail a blue taxi. "I'm sure they'll have something more classy over there, it's the capital of Bali after all."

While we're waiting for the taxi, I start to wonder. "Why do people always create phallic objects, but never anything in the shape of the vulva?"

"Freud would say that some people have never grown up from the phallic stage of their psychosexual development, and they're fixated on their genitalia. But this doesn't explain why there are so many more depictions of male organs, and not female one," Anna replies, waving at the upcoming taxi. "Misia once told me that in Poland there's a huge monument of a vulva, complete with a huge stone clit."

"Really?" All I know about Poland comes from Misia's stories, but it never struck me as a very liberal country. "Where is that? And why did they decide to celebrate the female anatomy in this monumental way?"

"It's in a city called Rzeszów. And, well, it isn't really a vulva. It's just a monument of one Polish uprising or another, but it has a very unfortunate shape. Or fortunate. Depending on how you look at it."

We get into a blue taxi and we're now zigzagging through the stream of traffic taking us towards Denpasar. Anna and I make ourselves comfortable on the leather seats, and my anxious merry-go-round starts spinning again in my head. Hunting for non-phallic souvenirs was a good distraction technique, but now my stress is back. I have to do something, or I'll burst.

I glance at my friend, who's observing the world passing behind the car window. It must be so new and exotic to her, like it was to me just three short weeks ago.

After a while, Anna turns towards me with worry painted all over her face. "So, what happened yesterday, Luce? Why did you escape from the party and hide yourself in your bedroom?"

Now it's my turn to gaze out of the window. We're on the outskirts of Seminyak filled with shopping centres sprawled along the highway. It looks less like paradise and more like a horrible industrial area outside any big city. Why do we have to destroy the natural beauty with our Western ugliness?

"Sweetie, I'm so sorry about what happened," I say, trying to blink back the tears. "I don't even know where to start my apologies—to you, to Mia, to Nyoman."

"You say sorry too much," Anna cuts me off. "Stop apologizing for being alive."

"But I made a complete idiot of myself."

"At least you were entertaining."

"But I know you're angry because I kissed Antoine."

"Angry?" She raises her left eyebrow, and I realise she's annoyed, even though her tone is mild. "What are you even talking about?"

"I know you never liked Antoine, and I feel weak for falling under his spell once again."

"Oh, you, silly billy." Anna squeezes my arm. "It's not that I didn't like him. I just couldn't stand how you suffered after he'd left you. But I've never had anything against him personally."

I swipe away the tears and rummage in my bag looking for tissues. Is it possible that Anna doesn't hate my ex after all?

"Your breakdown was horrendous, but I don't think Antoine was the sole reason," she continues. "There were so many things going on in your life at once. You just started your first serious job, and your parents were going through an ugly divorce. I know you don't like talking about it, but I'm sure it must have been a very difficult time for you."

"But I wanted them to split. I was so relieved when it finally happened. Though, I think the divorce came too late for them. And too late for me too."

Anna nods. She's never been a big fan of my parents. Gosh, even my brothers and I haven't been fans of my parents.

"And Antoine was your first serious love interest. The first heartbreak always hurts the most."

I can see a flash of pain cross her face. I want to ask if this is how she felt about her first love, Sophia, but I notice tears glistening in her eyes and decide to change the subject.

"I always believed that love was supposed to bring you pleasure, not pain," I say instead. "So, if you don't feel completely happy, it isn't real."

"Oh, come on, Luce. We're fed all the Disney bullshit and rom-com ideals. Love isn't a Xanax. It's a process that can be hard, and dirty, and demanding. It doesn't fall from the sky, you have to work on it. And I'm not saying that anyone should stay in a toxic relationship, but you shouldn't run away because of the slightest inconvenience, either."

174

"So, what are you trying to say?" I ask. "That I should give Antoine another chance?"

"I don't know." She shrugs. "But I do know that letting anxiety rule your life is never a good idea. And sometimes the fear of pain is worse than the pain itself."

That sounds suspiciously like wisdom from Instagram, rather than a serious psychological advice. But who knows, maybe it's actually true.

32

THE BALI MUSEUM

Anna and I get out from the taxi in Puputan Square, a huge park in the centre of Denpasar. We're strolling through lush lawns and beds of pink flowers until we reach a huge sculpture surrounded by a calm pond filled with water lilies. The statue depicts three angry men wearing white sarongs and holding spears and long daggers in their green copper hands.

"What's that?" Anna jerks her head towards this unusual piece of art.

"No idea," I reply, looking around for some clues. "I didn't know we were going to Denpasar today, and I don't have my guidebook on me."

I switch on my phone to check the map, but we're just a blue dot in the sea of grey nothingness. I try to search for "famous sculpture in Denpasar," but my browser informs me that there's no internet connection. I'm scrolling through my phone with a rising sense of panic. I'm in an unfamiliar city, in a foreign country, with no connection to the rest of the world. Damn.

"I think they've turned off my roaming because I've exceeded the limit," I groan. "Can you check if your phone works?"

"I didn't even bother turning the roaming on. Too expensive," Anna replies without tearing her eyes from the sculpture. "Their furious faces are both scary and fascinating."

"Anna, how can we survive without the connection to the rest of the world? We won't be able to find the souvenir shop now. And how can we catch a taxi back home?" I start hyperventilating.

"Don't worry, we'll find a way, sweetie." My friend takes me by the shoulders and shakes me gently. "We'll just ask someone for help. Everyone here speaks English, we'll be fine. Think of this as an adventure. And if you're too stressed, remember to breathe."

I close my eyes and try the four by four breathing Mia taught me on the plane. I inhale to a slow count of four, hold the air for four, exhale to a count of four, and hold for four. After a few sequences, I open my eyes and start breathing normally again. Damn, this thing really works.

"Better?"

I nod and send Anna a small smile. She's right, it's an adventure. And I might even enjoy it.

Anna and I end up in the Bali Museum, which was recommended by a local woman selling lemonade in the park. She wasn't sure if there was a souvenir shop, but she assured us that it was definitely an interesting place to visit.

According to the info board at the entrance, *Negeri Propinsi Bali* (Bali Provincial Public State Museum) consists of four pavilions, each designed in a different regional style of Balinese architecture. The pavilions are surrounded by three courtyards connected by beautiful gates, one of which is currently occupied by a group of Chinese tourists taking photos and striking funny poses.

"As Mia would say, this place is very Instagrammable," Anna says, taking out her own phone and snapping a few pics.

There's no sign of a souvenir shop, but we still decide to buy tickets and visit the museum. We open the wooden door to one of the pavilions and walk into the wall of hot stuffy air that smells of mothballs. The first impressions aren't very inviting, but we soon find out that the glass cases are filled with real treasures.

The first thing I notice are silver daggers with wavy blades. According to the info board, they're called Krises, and they were the symbols of royal power. Some of the Balinese kings used their spears and daggers for Puputan, a suicidal attempt to defend themselves against the Dutch colonizers. I read the explanation on the board with a growing interest.

"Anna, I think this solves the mystery of the sculpture we saw in the Puputan Square. The Balinese nobles were trying to defend their island, but they stood no chance against the Dutch firearms. Puputan means 'until the last.' They didn't give up the fight, even though they knew they were going to an imminent death. It was like Braveheart but in the 20th-century Indonesia."

"What a horrible massacre." Anna shakes her head. "I think life is hard as it is without adding the war trauma to it."

"It was a long time ago, I'm sure it won't happen again." To lighten the mood, I pull her towards the fantastic masks and decorations, including the good lion Barong, evil witch Rangda, monkeys, and other characters from the music drama. "Look at these costumes from the Barong dance. We saw it last week and it was amazing. Maybe you can see it yourself if you find some time before the wedding? I'm sure Nyoman would be happy to take you."

"Sure, that might be fun. But what is this creature exactly? A horse from a Christmas panto?"

"It looks like it, right? That was also my first thought when I saw Barong," I babble with excitement. I love how Anna gets me. Actually, she's the only person in the whole wide world who communicates on the exact same wavelengths as me. Once, I also believed that Antoine was tuned into my feelings and needs, but clearly, it was just my wishful thinking.

From the monumental costumes and stage decorations, we move to tiny figurines made of rice leaves called *cili*. They were created to worship the rice goddess Dewi Sri.

"They remind me of the straw dolls we used to make to decorate a Christmas tree," Anna says, peering through the glass case. "Though, ours didn't have such ornamental headdresses."

"Yes, I remember how Misia taught us how to make angels and stars just from some dry straw and red ribbon. I think I still have them somewhere in my parents' attic."

In one of the glass cases, next to a clay sculpture of a woman holding her own breasts, Anna spots something that makes her giggle. "Luce, look at this." She motions me to come closer.

Behind the glass pane, in a little red niche, there's a huge clay penis adorned with floral decorations. The museum label calls it "A ritual artefact."

"Now I understand their obsession with phallic beer openers." I giggle as well. "They're just trying to keep their ancient tradition alive."

When we arrive back in Legian, it's already late afternoon. I'm in a much better mood than in the morning—I almost forgot about the whole incident in Potato Head last night. Instead of obsessing over my poor life choices or being glued to our phones, Anna and I spent the rest of the day exploring Denpasar, visiting the sights and chatting to locals. We even discovered a lovely vegetarian café serving soups and smoothies full of natural vitamins and delicious flavours. Mia would love it.

However, we failed to buy a non-phallic beer opener, and now we're standing in front of the very first souvenir shop in Legian we visited in the morning.

"What do you want to do, sweetie? Maybe we can buy Misia a nice fridge magnet with Barong dance or God Ganesha? Or this I <3 BALI towel? Apparently, older people don't see colours as vividly as the young, so maybe she wouldn't mind the horrid neon pink colour?"

"Hang on here, Luce. I've got an idea." Anna disappears inside the souvenir shop, while I'm looking idly at two homeless dogs sniffing the rubbish bin on the other side of the street. I take a mental note to donate to a dog shelter in Bali. I'm not sure what's the best way to help these poor dogs, but a donation can't hurt. Or so I hope.

A few minutes later, Anna emerges from the shop brandishing a life-size green dildo in her hand. "Do you think Misia would like it?"

I blink a few times, hoping the wooden penis will disappear. "But why? Just why?"

"The visit to the museum was eye-opening, We have to preserve the local traditions and share their unique culture with the rest of the world."

I look again at the dildo, then at Anna, and we both start laughing. Yes, I'm sure her grandma will be delighted.

33

THE LETTER

My good humour after the shopping escapade with Anna evaporates as soon as we get back to the villa and I realise I'll have to face Antoine. I squirm with embarrassment at the memory of our kiss in the swimming pool last night. And especially of what happened afterwards. The kiss itself was really enjoyable, too enjoyable for my own good.

When Anna and I enter the house, it seems to be empty. But then we notice Sylvia and Mia chilling out on the patio. They're both lying on the deckchairs next to the swimming pool, scrolling through their phones.

"*Hola, chicas.*" Mia lifts her head from the screen. "How was your day? And how are you feeling after last night, Luce? You gave us quite a fright!"

"There she is, the little eejit." Sylvia puts down her phone on a coffee table and sends me a disapproving look. But then she smiles. "Actually, I'm proud of you, Luce. You're not as wimpy as I thought."

"Thanks, Sylve. I guess." I slump into a deckchair next to Mia's, while Anna sits directly on the ground, with her long pale legs dangling in the pool.

"Sylvia promised me a memorable hen-do, and she didn't disappoint," Mia says. "Seeing you and Antoine falling into the swimming pool and then kissing like horny teenagers was the best entertainment I could ever ask for."

"Shush, he might hear you." I blush and glance towards the villa, fearing that Antoine will emerge from his room at any second.

"Don't worry, he isn't here." Mia puts a calming hand on mine. "He and Jack decided to be very manly and go rafting in the Ayung River. They'll sleep in the van and then climb the volcano with one of the trained guides. We'll meet them at the top at the sunrise."

In all the hen-do drama, I completely forgot about their volcano trip. Is it already tonight?

"Maybe you want to join us after all?" Sylvia asks. "Our guide will pick us up at 1:00 am, and now that Antoine and Jack aren't coming with us, we have a free seat in the car."

I shake my head, observing the ripples that Anna's legs are creating in the azure water. "No, I don't think it's a good idea. I'm really not fit enough. And I'd rather stay here alone than face Antoine."

"As you wish." Sylvia shrugs. "But I think you're missing out on life."

I take a deep breath and ask the question, dreading what I might hear. "And how was everyone after I left yesterday? Did Antoine say anything? And do you know if Nyoman is okay?"

"Antoine was a bit shell-shocked, and he wasn't sure how to interpret your behaviour. You played hot and cold on him," Sylvia replies. "And Nyoman seemed a bit sad, but not surprised. Maybe he already suspected that there was something between you and the French hottie."

"There's nothing between us," I say with a hint of melancholy. "Not anymore."

"By the way, he left you a letter." Mia picks up her phone and resumes her scrolling. "It's on the kitchen table."

I jump out of my deckchair and sprint to the kitchen. Before I leave the terrace, I can hear Sylvia's voice. "Anna, how did your shopping go? Did you find something nice for your grandma?"

"Oh yes, we've found a perfect gift. Let me show you, I'm sure you'll love it."

With trembling hands, I pick up the white envelope with 'Lucy Green' scribbled in Antoine's handwriting. I need to be alone, away from my kind, but noisy friends, so I head to the beach. The sand is still burning from the heat of the day, even though the sun is already descending into the sea. Feeling half-agony, half-hope, I sit down on the ground, as I tear the envelope open.

Ma chère Lucy,

First of all, I'm sorry about pushing you (metaphorically and literally) into an uncomfortable situation yesterday. I crossed the line, and I have nothing for my defence except my own frustration. You were so close to me, but still so unattainable.

When we parted ways four years ago, it was probably the hardest decision in my life. I had to choose between the duty towards my family and my love for you. I chose my family, foolishly thinking that you'd wait for me. I never fully explained the situation to you, as I didn't want to admit, even to myself, that my own family could be so closed-minded and snobbish.

I came back as soon as I could and was shocked to discover that you didn't even want to talk to me anymore. Now I realise that it was exactly what I deserved, but back then, I was arrogant enough to expect a completely different welcome.

Since then, I've done everything I could do to forget about you. But it never really worked. You were always my mètre de Sèvres, *my benchmark of what I wanted in a partner.*

When Jack and Mia told me about the wedding, I initially declined their invitation. I didn't want to wake up the painful memories. However, the more I thought about it, the more I saw it as an opportunity to reconnect. Maybe even become friends again. I missed our long disputes about the French literature and the superiority of French cuisine over British food.

Yesterday, I even believed for a moment that we could have a chance at a second beginning. But after you stormed out of the swimming pool, I lost my hope again. Did I misread the signs? Do you really want nothing to do with me? Are we really over?

I don't want to cause a scene during Jack and Mia's wedding. It's their day, and there's no space for my personal turbulence. To give you some space, I'm going on a rafting trip with Jack and then we're going to climb a volcano at night. Straight from the volcano trip, I'll get a taxi to the airport and take the earliest flight back to Paris. I think it will be best to leave you and the rest of the group in peace.

Enjoy the wedding, and if you ever change your mind, if there's even a small chance that we can be happy together again, you know how to contact me when you're back in Europe.

Ton Dauphin

I wipe away the tears that I didn't realise were falling on the letter, smudging Antoine's handwriting. I'm shaking, despite the heat on the beach. I tuck the letter back into the envelope, stand up, and wade barefoot into the sea. I need to distract myself from the drowning wave of emotions, so I focus my mind on the waves crashing on the shore instead.

Mother Nature has prepared an extraordinary show this evening. There are other spectators, sitting on the sand or standing in the shallow water like me, but I barely register their presence through the tears still running down my cheeks into the salty brine below.

The sky is blazing with an ever-changing kaleidoscope of navy blue, purple, and orange. The colours are fighting against each other and then peacefully blending together. As soon as the wind ushers in a new troop of clouds, they start their opulent dance all over again. If I ever tried to paint or even take a photo of this sunset, the result would seem cliché and kitschy. But in real life, it's really awe-inspiring. If it's so beautiful here, why am I still feeling so miserable?

Antoine has always been a good writer. He was sending me hand-written love letters by snail post whenever we were apart during our relationship, which I found charmingly old-fashioned. Once, I would do everything to receive a letter like this. But I don't know what to think about him anymore.

What exactly does he mean by the second beginning? Is it even possible to build a healthy relationship after a painful breakup like ours? Will I be ever able to trust him again? And if, theoretically, we get back together, does he want to move back to London? Or should I go to Paris again? Either way, it would be a huge change. Life-changing huge. And I hate changes, even if they are for the better.

I haven't noticed that for the past few minutes I've been furiously scratching my arms and hands. My stress eczema is really inflamed now, and some of the painful patches are even oozing water. Amazing, that's exactly what I need right now.

"STOP!" I shout at the top of my lungs, and a few people around me turn their heads to check why this crazy woman is screaming at the sea. "Stop, stop, stop!" I repeat, now under my breath. I have to halt the train of anxious thoughts before it gets out of control.

One of the useful techniques I've learnt from Anna is labelling my thoughts and feelings. This creates healthy space between me, Lucy Green, and the vortex of emotions that's been wrecking my body and mind.

I breathe in and out, trying to sort through everything I'm feeling right now. Fear. Nothing new here, I'm scared of almost everything. Next. Anger. I feel like this letter came four years too late. Why couldn't Antoine tell me all this when there was still a chance to salvage our relationship? Relief. He loved me, and I was an important part of his life. My biggest worry was that I was just a distraction for him and he'd forgotten all about me as soon as I disappeared from his sight. But it wasn't true. He cared for me—and he still does.

Next? Excitement. He wants to get back together. If I had any doubts after our kiss in the swimming pool, the letter dispelled them completely. Finally, hope. What if I allow myself to be happy this time? What if it could work? What if I could be with my *dauphin*?

The sun is exiting the stage in a purple glory. The warm water is lapping rhythmically against my ankles, with an odd rebellious wave jumping as high as my knees. And my panic attack is gone. I smile.

34

THE THREE WITCHES

I can't sleep again. Every time I doze off, fitful dreams about Antoine and Paris wake me up.

After my lonely evening on the beach, I sneaked back into the villa without bumping into any of my friends. It feels weird that there are no more noises coming from Antoine's room. I really got used to him moving around and playing music behind the thin wall. I even went to his room earlier to see if he was serious about leaving the villa and catching an early flight to Paris. I was hoping against hope that his clothes were still here, strewn around the mahogany furniture. But his room was completely empty, except for a faint smell of his cologne and sadness hanging in the air.

It's 1:00 am, and I can hear my friends getting ready for their hike to the volcano. I still don't understand why anyone would decide to wake up in the middle of the night to climb a fiery mountain. Soon, they'll be gone, and I'll stay completely alone in the dark villa. I feel suddenly very lonely, so I get up and go to ask them for advice. I need it more than ever.

Anna, Mia, and Sylvia are in the kitchen preparing food for their trip, chatting and laughing. When I enter the room, they all freeze mid-movement and stare at me for a moment, before Sylvia breaks the silence. "Ah, so she's alive after all. Our little Miss Hermit. We thought that you'd drowned yourself in the sea like Ophelia."

"Ophelia drowned in a river," I correct her automatically.

"How are you feeling, Luce? Any better?" Anna asks, as she spreads butter on a piece of bread.

"Never mind her feelings. I'm dying to know what was in the letter." Sylvia looks at me with an unabashed curiosity. "What did he say?"

"Are you sure Antoine isn't here?" I look around the kitchen, as if expecting him to jump out of the fridge.

"I told you that he and Jack went rafting," Mia explains patiently. "They're going to go straight from there to the volcano. They've decided to take a longer, more difficult route than us, so we'll meet them on the top."

"Ah, I see." I was stupidly hoping Antoine had come back and I could talk to him about the letter. I'm not sure what exactly I'd say, but I'm disappointed I won't be able to see him before his return to Europe. Should I try to catch him at the airport tomorrow morning? Or maybe I can just call him and try to convince him to stay until the wedding?

"What is it, honey?" Anna asks, putting aside the butter. "You know you can talk to us. Don't bottle it up."

"*Chicas*, I need your honest opinion." I sit down at the table next to Mia dicing fresh papaya. "Antoine says that he's really sorry about our breakup and wants to give us a second chance. Should I do it? I don't want to make another mistake."

My friends utter a collective gasp, looking at me with eyes as big as saucers. They remind me of the three witches from *Macbeth*.

"Of course you should do it, you bampot!" Sylvia takes a big spoonful of chocolate spread and puts it in her mouth. "He's sexy, he's funny, and he's clearly crazy about you. I thought you'd noticed it by now!"

"It's a big decision, Luce," Anna says gently. "But choose what will make you happy. Don't let anxiety cloud your judgement."

"Listen, I've known Antoine longer than you, and I know he's a

187

good guy," Mia adds, putting down her knife. "He was a fool to break up with you like this, but he's been repenting his decision ever since. I think you can be very happy together."

"You're both a bit weird, but in a good way," Sylvia adds. "I've never seen you as excited as you were after cleaning the beach with Tony. You were practically glowing."

"Weird? As if!" I scoff, stealing a piece of papaya from Mia's cutting board. It's sweet and juicy, unlike the plastic food we have in the UK. "And I was glowing because I spent too much time in the sun."

"Bollocks." Anna is putting slices of cheese on the sandwich. "You can try to fool us as much as you want, but you should stop lying to yourself."

I hope this isn't how she speaks to her clients.

"Try to imagine that you don't have any past with Antoine." Mia gives me another papaya chunk, and I eat it obediently. "That you met him for the first time here in Bali. Clean slate. Would you be still attracted to him? That's what I do after each breakup with Jack. I check if he's still the man I want to be with or if he's changed so much that I don't want to share my life with him anymore."

I chew pensively, pondering her question. I'm trying to separate Antoine from the past with the man he is right now. I remember how sexy he was when he appeared on Kuta Beach like a ghost from the past. How we shared a magic moment in the butterfly sanctuary. How we cleared the air while cleaning the beach. How he tried to help me understand Balinese temples and the Barong dance. And finally, how passionately he kissed me in the swimming pool in Potato Head.

There's no denying that I'm still attracted to him. Not in the innocent, almost naïve, way I loved him when we were living together in Paris. Now my feelings are much more grounded in reality. With more emotional baggage, but also more insights.

I nod slowly. "I like him a lot. But what if he dumps me again, and I have another breakdown? I don't think I'll survive it the second time."

Anna extends her arm across the table and puts her hand on mine. "Sweetie, even if it happens, you are not the same person you were four years ago. You're so much stronger and wiser. And now you have tools to manage your emotions. You can tap into them during any crisis."

"Life is like investment banking." Sylvia licks off the rest of the chocolate spread from the spoon and fixes me with a stern gaze. "You have to make a calculated risk. Do you want to give Tony another chance and risk a broken heart? Or do nothing and regret the missed opportunity for the rest of your life?"

"Sometimes making a bad decision is better than not making any decision at all," Mia adds sagely.

I look at my friends sitting around the table, as I'm trying to process all they've just said. Is it what they really think of me? That my life is ruled by fear and that I can't make calculated risks? Well, they are right —but that changes now. I don't want to be scared of my own shadow anymore. It's time to make bold decisions, whatever the consequences.

"Oh, you witches! You're just like Balinese *leyaks*, causing mayhem and putting your noses into other people's business," I say with a smile.

"It's because we love you, Luce." Anna pats my arm. "And we want you to be happy."

Suddenly, I realise what I need to do. I stand up quickly, toppling my chair. "*Chicas*, I hope you've got some spare sandwiches. I'm going with you to the volcano."

35

HATI-HATI

Climbing the Gunung Batur volcano seems easy-peasy. Much better than I expected.

With strong torchlights paving our way, Anna, Mia, Sylvia, and I are following our guide Ketut through a dark forest. The dirt road is quite broad and not too steep. The air smells of coniferous trees and wet ground. It must have rained here recently. Even though the drive from Legian to Gunung Batur took us two hours, and it's just 3:00 am, I don't feel tired. It's good to be outside of my own comfort zone and explore nature.

I've got this. I'm Lucy Green, and I'm going to climb a volcano.

"So, how was your trip to the Turtle Island?" I'm walking between Mia and Sylvia, while Anna is chatting with Ketut at the front. "I wanted to ask you yesterday but never got the chance."

"It was great!" Sylvia says. I've never seen Sylvia without high heels, but tonight she's wearing very sensible trainers. I think she had to borrow them from Mia. "We could pet turtles and parrots and even hold a snake. I looked like Cleopatra with a fat boa constrictor coiled around my shoulders. I'll show you a photo later. It was fabulous."

"Weren't you scared?" I ask.

"No, the boa was so fat it wouldn't be able to constrict anyone."

"Actually, I thought it was a horrible place. I didn't like it at all."

Mia's marching effortlessly with a big backpack filled with our food. I'm always amazed how fit and strong she is despite her petite frame.

"Why?" I ask.

"It's a sanctuary that helps animals that are ill or have lost their natural habitat, mainly because developers are cutting down the forests to build more hotels for tourists like us. But they keep animals in appalling conditions, especially compared to European standards, and I don't think that wild creatures are happy to be a part of a petting zoo."

"Oh, come on," Sylvia puffs out, though I'm not sure if it's from anger or exertion. "It was all very educational. Get down from your high horse."

We keep discussing animal welfare until the forest ends, and our path becomes steeper. This doesn't seem so easy anymore.

"*Hati-hati*," our guide tells us. "Slowly, slowly. It's very slippery after the rain. Keep close to me, and shout if you need my help."

I gingerly put my foot on a big boulder and lift my body, murmuring, "*hati-hati*," under my breath. It sounds like some Balinese mantra, calming me down and helping me get higher and higher on the rocky path.

Then, I step on something that's very wet and slippery, and I tumble down into the darkness.

"Help!" I scream, as I hurt my left knee on a sharp rock.

"Luce, is everything okay?" Mia says, as my friends and Ketut are coming to my rescue. "Are you hurt?"

"Don't worry, everything's fine," I lie.

Discarding my dignity, I climb on all fours, which is more difficult when you're holding a torch in your hand and have an open wound on your knee. But I'm not giving up, I'll go to the top.

Then, I slip again and bruise my right knee for a change. I'm Lucy Green, and I'm going to die on this bloody volcano.

The higher we go, the harder it gets.

Mia and Anna, who are the most athletic in our gang, are at the front, almost effortlessly climbing the steep slope and even chatting away with Ketut. But Sylvia and I are struggling, as we fight for life. Our bodies almost collapse, unused to all this physical effort.

"I think I've lost my stamina," Sylvia complains. "Or maybe I've never had it at all."

Why did I decide to come here? I thought it would be so romantic to chase after my true love like they do in all the rom-com films. Instead, I'm sweaty, dirty, and covered in dried blood. Romantic, my foot.

"Ketut, can we have a short break?" Sylvia asks, wheezing like someone dying from TB.

"Another one?" Anna says. I can't see her in the darkness, but I'm sure she's just rolled her eyes.

"Yes, sure, as long as you need." Thank god our guide is so easygoing.

"If we go any slower, we'll miss the sunrise," Mia complains.

But we all sit down on the ground, with our backs leaning against big boulders. I'm trying to see through the pitch-black darkness, but there's nothing visible outside the beam of our torchlights. I have no idea how long we've been on this godforsaken mountain. It might have been two hours or two years.

"Ketut, how far are we from the top?" I ask, hoping that his answer will motivate me to keep going.

But what he says has the opposite effect. "We aren't even halfway through."

"Not even halfway?" I blink back tears of disappointment. "In this case, I don't think I'll make it to the top. Can I go back and wait for you in the car?"

"It's too dangerous to go alone," he explains. "You can slip and break your leg, and there won't be anyone to help you. We need to stick together."

"Luce, if you don't feel well, we're coming back with you," Anna's supportive voice comes from the darkness.

"I think we should all go back," Sylvia agrees. "The whole trip was a very stupid idea. We're on holiday, not at a survival camp."

"It was your idea, Sylve," Mia points out.

"Yes, and now I regret it. Also, I'm hungry."

Mia opens her backpack and hands out the sandwiches and fruit they prepared back in the villa. We all stay close to each other, sharing the food and trying not to slide down from the slippery gravel slope.

As my strength and sugar levels rise, I start wondering if I should really quit right now. I've come so far, both physically and emotionally. I don't want to let my friends down. And more importantly, I don't want to let myself down.

Also, a hope that Antoine and I might be happy again is waiting for me at the top of the volcano. I'm young, I'm healthy, relatively fit, and we've got an experienced guide. I won't die here. I just need to take one careful step after another. *Hati-hati*, slowly, slowly.

I lick peanut butter from my fingers and announce, "I'm feeling much better now. Let's go to the top."

"Are you sure, Luce?" Anna's voice is filled with concern.

"Yep, I want to do it."

"We can pretend we're hobbits going to Mordor," Mia suggests. "I can be Frodo."

"And I'll be Pippin," Sylvia agrees, munching on a papaya. "I hope we'll have our second breakfast soon."

36

DANCING ON THE VOLCANO

We continue our quest to the top of Mount Doom, humming "The Misty Mountains Cold" song, taking a lot of short breaks, and helping each other with more difficult passages.

The grey pre-dawn light is gradually dispersing the darkness, and on the other side of the valley, we can see Gunung Agung. It's the highest and most holy mountain on the island and the abode of Balinese gods and family ancestors. It's also an active volcano that has killed many people, even in the recent years. An innocent-looking serial killer.

"Not far away now," our guide announces, and I almost weep with joy.

I probably look more like dishevelled Gollum than a respectable Hobbit, but at this point, my looks are the least of my worries.

What should I say when I see Antoine? How will he react? My heart is thumping, not only from the physical strain. I take a few deep breaths to avoid hyperventilation. Are we high enough to have the altitude sickness?

A few more minutes of the tortuous climb, and finally, the moment comes. We're on the top! As soon as we reach the summit, my legs buckle under me, and I sit on the ground, almost weeping with relief.

"Oh shit!" I can hear Sylvia's voice. "Look how high we are."

Cautiously, I peer over the edge and meet an impenetrable abyss. We're just a bit lower than Gunung Agung—the enormous mountain on the other side of the valley.

"Maybe it's a good thing we couldn't see anything in the dark?" I say in a shaky voice. "I don't think I would've made it otherwise."

"Look at the sea!" Anna's bouncing excitedly, pointing towards the expanse of water that's reflecting the golden light of the rising sun.

The view from the top of Gunung Batur is breathtaking. Literally. It's hard to breath with all the wind blowing in our faces.

"And what is this?" Mia's shading her eyes with her hand. "Do you think it's the Turtle Island?"

"No, this is Lombok," our guide explains. "The closest big Indonesian island east of Bali."

The sea, the green forest on the slope, the ginormous holy mountain in front of us—everything is painted with the warm brush of the sunrise light. My fear and fatigue disappear at the sight of this pure beauty. I'm so happy I made it despite the odds. And now I have to face the most difficult part of my quest. I have to talk to Antoine.

Jack and Antoine are standing a few yards away from a small wooden hut that provides shelter for tired tourists. They both look very manly, wearing mountain boots and feeding monkeys with pieces of banana.

What are the monkeys doing on the top of the mountain? Shouldn't they be in the Monkey Forest in Ubud or near one of the temples at the seaside? I step carefully around the cute little macaques and their less cute parents with vicious fangs.

I glance at Antoine's shapely bum and strong shoulders before he turns around, laughing at something that Jack's just said. Then, he notices me and freezes mid-laugh.

Jack follows his gaze and waves at me. "You've made it, Lucy!" He comes over to give me a brief hug. "And where's Mia? How's my little croissant?"

"She's over there with the girls and our guide." I point him towards the wooden hut.

"I'll go and check on them." And before I have a chance to reply, Jack's already gone, leaving me alone with Antoine and the hungry monkeys.

I'm trying to gauge Antoine's mood, but it's hard to read his face while he's still standing at a distance. Suddenly, I feel very self-conscious.

But as I take a tentative step back, Antoine shouts, "Lucy, wait!"

He throws the last piece of banana to a baby macaque, comes over, and stops a few inches in front of me. A frisson of excitement runs down my spine.

"I didn't know you were coming. But I'm happy to see you." He smiles, and I can see the sunrise reflected in his glasses.

I smile back at him, though I'm too nervous to say anything.

"Did you read my letter?" he asks.

I just nod, with my heart thumping in my ears. It's definitely altitude sickness.

"And what's your answer? Do you think we could be together again?"

"Yes," I croak with my dry throat. "My answer is yes."

"Are you sure?" He looks deep into my eyes. "I don't want to lose you again, Lucy."

"*Je suis sure.*" I put a hand on his arm. "Anton."

And before I know what's happening, he sweeps me up in his arms, and we're kissing on the top of the volcano. At first, shyly, trying to find each other again. Then, more and more passionately, until I lose myself completely in his familiar taste and smell, forgetting about the world around us.

When our lips finally part, I look around and realise that the monkeys are gazing at us with disdain. Their black beady eyes seem to be saying, "Get a room, humans! Or even better, give us more bananas!"

I never thought that one day I'd end up kissing Antoine on a volcano surrounded by judging monkeys, but I'm actually enjoying it.

"Lucy, *ma petite chouette.*" Antoine is looking at me with a mixture of happiness and awe. "I'm so happy you said yes. I can move to London for you if you want. Or we can try living in Paris again if you prefer. As long as we're together, I don't mind what we do or where we live."

"I'm sure we'll find a way." I smile and kiss him again, pushing all my apprehensive thoughts from the edge of the mountain. I know they'll find me soon enough, but I want to experience a few minutes of pure happiness with no anxiety in sight.

The way down from the volcano is much easier than the way up. I don't know why we had to scramble in the darkness like Hobbits climbing Mount Doom—on the other side, there is a much gentler slope with a wide stone path. Anyway, I'm gliding down on the cloud of pure endorphins, and I don't notice my fatigue and injured knees anymore. Anton and I are walking down holding hands, talking over each other, laughing like loonies, and singing patriotic French songs.

Yeah, that's our thing, don't ask.

We've also composed an impromptu song with a catchy chorus of "*Hati-hati,* slowly, slowly," repeated over and over again. The song is very bad, and we're singing it out of tune, but who cares? Well, actually, our friends do care, because they tell us to shut up.

Sylvia sends us an exasperated look. "The last time I heard such horrible music was during the Barong dance."

"What do you mean?"

"You're both singing so badly that you can join the gamelan orchestra. Even without any instruments."

The ride back home is a complete blur. I'm so exhausted that I fall asleep on Antoine's shoulder and wake up only when Ketut's van stops in front of our villa in Legian.

We walk into our side of the house, and there's an awkward pause in front of Anton's bedroom.

"What do you want to do, Lucy?" he asks. "Do you want to come in?"

I look down at my dirty clothes and shake my head. Also, the last two days were a roller coaster of emotions. I think I need a break.

I lift my head up and notice disappointment creeping into his eyes. I take a step towards my own bedroom, but then the new Lucy, the one that climbed the volcano, gets in charge. Oh, what the hell, we've already wasted four years, so what else am I waiting for?

"Give me ten minutes," I say. "I'll just clean up."

"Or we can take a hot shower together?" he suggests. "And then cuddle in bed."

Well, we might have done a bit more than just cuddling. Who knew that reconnecting with your old flame does wonders for your libido? Actually, we had the most mind-boggling sex in my life, even better than anything we did in Paris. It was amazing to rediscover Anton and his lean body. I close my eyes and murmur with pleasure, snuggling comfortably into his chest and falling asleep with a smile.

37

SASAK BAR

If the last four weeks in Bali have taught us anything, it's that when you need to relax, you should go to the beach. Or, more specifically, to Sasak Bar, where we can chill with some cold Bintang served by Wayan and Nyoman. So, this is what we're doing right now. We've already recovered after the volcano trip yesterday and we're full of fresh energy. While Jack and Antoine have volunteered to check on the final wedding preparations in the Boardwalk restaurant, our quartet of *chicas* is trudging on the hot sand along Kuta Beach.

When we approach Sasak Bar, I notice that something has changed. The place is teeming with tourists and poor Nyoman is rushed off his feet to meet their demands for cold beer and soda. He's so busy he doesn't even realise we're standing a few yards away. I give a small sigh of relief. I need to talk to him, apologise for my scandalous behaviour, but I shouldn't disturb him if he's working so hard. Right?

Instead, I look around the beach bar to take in all the changes since our last visit. I can't believe that it's the same place where I had my first (and last) surfing lesson almost a month ago. The horrible plastic chairs and beer crates are gone, replaced by red, orange, and yellow beanbags sitting on the sand. New wooden coffee tables are placed strategically in the shade of big parasols in matching colours, and Wayan's surfboards—placed vertically in the sand—create a natural backdrop for the bar. Instead of his old plastic icebox, Nyoman can now store the beer under a roofed wooden counter similar to the one we saw at the swing place.

I have to admit that the new bar looks much nicer and more comfortable than the original set-up, but it has also lost its laid-back authenticity and charm. It reminds me now of any hipster place around the globe. I tried to escape gentrification in London, but it caught up with me in Bali.

I turn around and notice Wayan coming out of the sea with a surf-board under his arm and water dripping from his black hair. He gives us a friendly wave, while Sylvia's already jogging towards him. As soon as she reaches him, she wraps her arms around his neck and engages him in a passionate kiss. We should probably demurely avert our eyes, but it's too late for this. The show is already on, and we can't peel our gaze off the embracing couple. So instead, we come closer, as Mia is snapping photos on her phone.

"Souvenirs," she explains. "Sylve will have beautiful memories when we're back in London."

"Don't talk about London yet. I feel like I've just arrived here," Anna complains.

I look away from our love birds and think of Anton, realising that going back to London doesn't feel so horrible anymore. Who knows how long I'll stay there anyway?

As if reading my thoughts, Anna asks, "Luce, how's it going with Antoine? Did you already make some plans for the future, or is the honeymoon haze still addling your brain?"

"We haven't decided yet where we're going to live, if that's what you're asking. He's willing to move to London for me, but maybe it's time for me to go back to France. After all, there isn't anything keeping me in England." I notice Anna's hurt look, and I quickly add, "Except for the two of you, of course. And Sylvia perhaps." I nod towards our Scottish friend still kissing Wayan's face off. "Also, living in Paris with my French lover sounds much cooler than being a senior PA in a boring law firm in London. All my colleagues will turn green with envy."

That makes Anna and Mia laugh, and I realise how lucky Antoine and I are to get another chance to be together. To fulfil our dreams that were squashed like an overripe mango four years ago. Well, maybe not all of our dreams, as I don't feel the same level of euphoria as the first time around. So, at the moment, any talks about engagement or wedding are off the table. And maybe that's where they'll stay forever. We'll see how it goes.

But living in Paris doesn't sound so bad. After all, I love the city, I love the language, and most importantly, I love a certain cute Frenchman. And maybe that's the push I needed to finally change my stressful job and uneventful life.

"Well, well, well, look what the sea brought up." Sylvia peels herself off from Wayan and smiles like a Cheshire cat.

"Hello, my goddess." Wayan sends her a killer smile. Mia clears her throat, and they finally notice us standing just a few feet away.

"Wayan, I didn't know you were planning a Sasak Bar makeover. It's amazing!" Mia gesticulates towards the colourful beanbags and parasols. "I love the new look."

"It was Sylvia's idea." Wayan puts his arm around our friend, who's beaming with pride. "She even helped me choose the colour palette."

"I didn't see the bar before, but I really like it," Anna admits, drinking in the hippie vibe, as she starts swinging in the rhythm to reggae music blasting from a portable speaker hanging from one of the palm trees. "And it seems to be attracting a lot of customers."

"Yeah, the redecoration wasn't cheap, but I think the investment will pay off." Wayan's voice is confident.

"Are you sure?" The question is out of my mouth before I can stop myself. I remember that Wayan and Nyoman invested all their savings into this bar, so what will happen if this new project doesn't work out? "Sorry, ignore me, this is none of my business," I add quickly, blushing.

"I prepared a solid business plan," Sylvia admits. "Don't send me that pained look, Mi. I know I promised to stay away from work for one month, but this had nothing to do with investment banking. It was actually fun, especially as it brought me closer to Wayan."

"And we're so busy now that we might have to hire more people to help us with the demand. It's the same cold beer, just in a more beautiful setting." Wayan shepherds us towards the bar. "Try it out for yourselves. The drinks are on us."

———

While my friends are making themselves comfortable on the beanbags, I pluck the courage to talk to Nyoman. He's behind the counter, pouring frothy beer into a glass. He looks so sweet and kind. I can't believe I let him see me snogging another guy just a few days after our kiss on the swings. I have no idea what to tell him, how to explain that I wasn't leading him on, that I cared about him, but not in the same way I care about Antoine.

The familiar metallic taste is back in my mouth, and I start scratching eczema on my forearm. For a second, I consider turning around and just going back to our villa. If I avoid him for three more days, I can just go back to London and forget about all the mess I inadvertently created. But now I know that running away doesn't pay off. It'll just haunt me as yet another unresolved issue, so it's better to face the music. Even if this music is played by the gamelan orchestra.

Nyoman looks up and notices me. Immediately, his usual smile is wiped off his face. Now that I think of this, I've never seen him without a grin before.

"Nyoman." I take a step towards him, but he turns away his head. "Can we talk for a second? Please."

He's motionless for a minute that feels like an eternity, but then he nods. I swallow hard, even though my mouth is bone dry. My mind is completely blank.

"Nyoman, I'm so sorry," I finally say. "You've been so kind to me, and I really like you. I didn't want to hurt you. I know that I behaved like a muppet, but I hope you can forgive me."

He's silent again, and I wonder if I'm making a fool of myself. Of course, he's furious with me, why wouldn't he be?

He turns his head towards me. "It's okay, Lucy, I always knew that our time together was short. You made me happy, but there must be always a balance between happiness and sadness, good and evil."

I sigh with relief and pat him awkwardly on the arm.

202

"No problem, no problem." He wipes away the tears, and his signature smile is back. "The balance in the universe has been restored."

I feel so relieved that I could hug him, but that may send the wrong message. So, I just ask, "Do you think we can be still friends?"

"Of course, we'll always be friends." He extends his hand in a firm handshake. "Also, what's a muppet?"

38

DADDY DRAMA

Later that day, I'm floating while the sun is drawing abstract patterns on my closed eyelids. My ears are submerged under the water, so I can't hear anything except the rhythm of my own breath. I know that my friends and Antoine are just a few yards away, chilling in the villa, but at the moment, I want to be alone, with two unicorns bobbing on the surface of the swimming pool as my only company. I feel safe in my private cocoon of the warm chlorine water.

Who knew that sex with your ex could be so relaxing? Even the discomfort I can feel down there from too much sexy time doesn't bother me too much. It was definitely worth it.

It's amazing how your life can change in less than forty-eight hours. I think back to the fear I felt before climbing the volcano. It paralysed me, not letting me open up to a possibility that maybe, just maybe, I could be happy with Anton again.

Don't get me wrong, I'm still scared and unsure how it'll all work out in the end. But I'm giving it my best shot. And even if we break up again further down the line, at least I'll know that I took the risk. I wasn't just passively floating through my life, even though floating is my favourite activity right now.

And so far, our new relationship seems very promising. Anton already knows that I'm weird and anxious, but he gets me. He challenges me and makes me step out from my bubble, but I never feel judged by him. And as much as I love talking to him, I love even more being in bed with him. For example, last night I was really excited when—

But before I manage to finish my thought, I can feel my drama radar tingling. And even though I can't hear or see anything under water, I can sense some commotion in the villa. I think my friends aren't chilling out anymore.

A shadow falls on my relaxed body, and I unwillingly open my eyes. It's Sylvia. She's saying something very quickly and animatedly, raking her hands through her auburn hair. It's funny to see her mouth moving, but no sound reaches my submerged ears. It's like watching a silent film.

She finally loses her patience and throws a flip-flop at me. She misses, but I decide to leave the pool before her Scottish temper erupts with full force. An angry Scott is worse than an active volcano.

"What is it, Sylve?" I ask, getting out of the pool and drying myself with my brand-new neon-pink I<3 Bali towel. A thoughtful gift from Anna.

"Mia's dad is here. They're having a big row in the kitchen. I can't even go there to make a sandwich, and I'm starving."

"Mia's dad?" I stop drying my hair and look at my friend with incredulity. "What is he doing here? And how did he even find us?"

"Apparently, he got the address from Jack's unsuspecting parents. He told them that he misplaced the wedding invitation, but he wanted to come and surprise Mia. They probably thought it was an early wedding gift or something."

"The wedding invitation that Mia never sent him?" I shake my head in disbelief, as we step from the sunny deck into the cool villa.

"Yep, that would be the one."

"Well, in this case, he surprised her alright."

Anna and Antoine are sitting in the living room on the leather sofas, scrolling nervously through their phones, pretending they can't hear the storm brewing in the kitchen, while Jack is pacing nervously around the room like a civet that's eaten too many coffee beans.

Antoine looks up from his phone and sends me a half-smile. "The drama meter is off the charts today."

Even though the kitchen door is shut, we can clearly hear two angry voices, getting louder and louder. Mia's shouting something in English and Spanish, but I can understand just a few swear words I picked when we were living together, like *mierda, cojones,* and *carajo.* And there's also a lower voice with a strong American accent that seems to be trying to placate her.

I instinctively cower, feeling as if I stepped back into my childhood and my parents' constant fights. I know that this is a completely different situation—I'm not a helpless child anymore, and this quarrel has nothing to do with me—but I still start to tremble.

Anna sends me a reassuring smile from the sofa. "Are you feeling fine, Luce?"

I nod my head unconvincingly, as a cold shiver runs through my spine.

Seeing what's happening with my body, Antoine gets up from the sofa and closes the distance between us in a few quick steps. "It's okay, Lucy," he murmurs into my ear, rubbing my shoulders. "You're safe, everything is fine." And then he uses a low blow and starts tickling me. I release a short burst of laughter, and a part of my stress evaporates. He always knew how to diffuse my tension.

"I'm so happy my parents aren't mental." Sylvia plops on the sofa next to Anna, as the shouts in the kitchen intensify. "I should send prayers of thanks to Saint Columba."

"This isn't right. I have to do something." Jack stops pacing for a moment and sends a pained look towards the kitchen. "Mia said I shouldn't interfere, but I have to go in there and give her my moral support. I can't leave my little cheesecake alone."

"What do you think they're talking about?" I ask, scratching my forearm. "We know so little about Mia's father, she never talks about him. Jack, do you think he could be violent?"

"No, I don't think so." Jack shakes his head. "He was neglectful, ignoring Mia and letting her down when she needed him most, but he was never violent. I'd rather worry about his safety—when Mia feels hurt, she turns her pain into anger. I just hope she won't decide to cancel our wedding again because of this daddy drama. You know her Spanish temperament."

As to prove Jack's point, the voices in the kitchen rise to a crescendo and then there's a crash of broken glass. And another. I can almost see our dinner plates smashing on the white tiles. Before the third plate has a chance to land on the floor, the kitchen door flings open, and Mia's father flees to safety.

Mia has never showed us any pictures of him, so I always imagined him as a typical wolf of Wall Street with shark teeth and a well-tailored suit. In reality, he's quite short and plump with a halo of curly silver hair. In his Hawaiian shirt and Bermuda shorts, he looks more like a friendly uncle than the villain of Mia's life. But maybe we're all villains in someone else's story?

Ignoring five pairs of eyes observing his hasty exit, he scatters to the main door and leaves our villa in a puff.

"What the hell was that?" Sylvia says, jumping up from the sofa, while Jack is already running to the kitchen to check on his fiancée. We should probably leave Mia and Jack alone to recover from this unexpected paternal visit, but curiosity takes the better of us, and we all flock to see the show.

Mia's standing in the middle of the crockery debris with one hand planted on the kitchen table and the other still clutching a plate. When she notices us, she puts the plate on the table and bursts into tears. Not dramatic at all.

Jack is at her side, enveloping her into a bear hug and making soothing noises. "There, there, my banoffee pie. Don't cry, my carrot cake."

"She looks more like Eton mess right now," Sylvia jokes, but she shuts up under Jack's angry scowl.

"So, what happened, Mi?" Anna asks gently. "Did your father attack you? Was he angry with you?"

"No, it was worse, much worse," Mia says between the sobs. "He apologised. Said he was sorry for abandoning me, for ignoring me all my life."

"So, it's a good sign, right?" I venture tentatively.

"It's a trap! I don't know how, but I'm sure it's a trap. A PR stunt to make him look better in front of wife number three. Apparently, she even came with him to Bali. *La puta!*"

We all look at Mia, not sure how to react to her outburst. Finally, Sylvia breaks the silence. "There's one thing your father didn't lie about. He really knows how to do surprises."

39

AFTER THE STORM

The storm in our villa has calmed down a bit, but I can feel it's still not over. After cleaning the broken plates in the kitchen, Jack took Mia to their bedroom upstairs, promising to prepare a bubble bath to help her relax, while we all heaved a big sigh of relief.

"Well, the show is over," Sylvia announces wistfully. "Now I'm really starving. All this shouting has given me an appetite." And she disappears in the kitchen, closing the door behind her.

"I'm just glad that I'm Mia's friend, not her therapist." Anna rakes her hands through her unruly brown hair. "I need a walk to shake off all these negative emotions. Also, a drink in Sasak Bar won't hurt."

Anton takes my hand and leads me to his bedroom, which has seen some steamy action over the last two days. But now we just lie down on the comfy bed and cuddle with my head pressed against his beating heart. I look outside the window at the palms gently swaying in the wind. I feel happy and safe in our cosy villa, as if nothing could hurt us here. Well, maybe except the hurricane called Mia.

"Wow, c'était impressionnant," Antoine says with a hint of admiration in his voice. "I didn't know Mia had such a fiery temper."

"You'd think she inherited it from her Spanish side," I say. "But actually, her mum is the coolest person I know, always chilled and down-to-earth."

"Unlike Mia's father, if we can judge by his performance today." Anton gives a short laugh.

"Mia rarely talks about him, but I always had the impression that he was a rather quiet, reserved person. I'm not sure what made him so upset today. Must be the bad influence of his new wife. Mia thinks she's another gold digger that just wants to use Rick's money and position to climb the social ladder. And now she's also determined to ruin Mia's big day just to pretend she's a part of the family and not trophy wife number three."

Anton drums his fingers on the mattress, thinking. "Rick is old enough to make up his own mind, not to be guided by his wife's whims. And I know Mia's holding a lot of grudges against him, but I don't understand why she still won't let him come to the wedding. Especially now that he's in Bali."

"And what would you do in her situation? If you were badly hurt by Monique and Jean-Pierre, would you still invite them to the most important event of your adult life?" I blurt out a split second before I realise that this question is much more loaded than I intended.

Antoine is silent for a while. "That's a tricky question. I don't want to put the blame on them, but it's true that their persuasions ruined our first chance at happiness. However, they're still my parents, and I know they care about me, even if sometimes their efforts are completely misguided."

"You see, that's the difference between you and Mia. Her father never tried to interfere in her life, but that might be even worse. Can you imagine being completely invisible to the very person who was supposed to love you unconditionally?"

I think of my own parents, always caught in their own world of quarrels and resentment. I sometimes felt that they needed me and my brothers only as spectators of their ongoing marital play. But I also have to admit that they were always there for us, at least physically. They turned up to our school events, took us on holiday in Dorset, gave us as much support as they could muster. That should count for something.

Anton brushes his fingertips across my bare arm, and his gentle touch gives me goose bumps. But before our cuddling has a chance to develop into something more, my stomach produces a very loud rumble. No wonder, it's already 4:00 pm, and I haven't eaten anything except for some yoghurt in the morning. With a sigh, I roll out from bed and land barefoot on the cold white tiles.

"I'm starving. Do you want something to eat?"

"*Non, merci,*" Anton replies. "I had lunch with Jack in a small *wareng* in Kuta, where we devoured a big crispy duck. I can take you there tomorrow if you want?"

"Sounds like a plan. But for now, I'll grab a quick snack. An avocado toast should do the trick. I just hope there's still something edible left after Sylvia's raid of the kitchen."

As I'm walking across the main hall of our villa, I hear a knock on the door. We aren't expecting any visitors, but maybe Rick decided to talk again with his daughter? Or maybe Anna is already back from Sasak Bar?

I open the heavy wooden door and notice a friendly-looking woman with a mass of black curly hair. She's wearing a flowery summer dress revealing her suntanned skin with the first hints of wrinkles. She smiles, showing dimples in her cheeks. "Hi, I'm Carla. I came here to see Mia."

"Hello, I'm Lucy." I wonder who she is, maybe one of Mia's count-less aunts? However, her accent is American, not Spanish. "Sure, can you wait here? I'll go and fetch her."

I climb the wooden stairs and stop in front of Mia and Jack's bedroom. I gently tap on their door, hoping that I'm not interrupting their bath, or anything even more intimate.

"Come in!" I can hear Jack's booming voice, as I press on the handle.

Mia and Jack are sitting amidst crumpled white sheets in their four-poster bed facing the huge windows overlooking the sea in the distance. Thank god, they aren't naked, but they're wearing matching silk dressing gowns and that might be even worse. Mia's petite body looks amazing in whatever she wears, but the skimpy blue gown with a floral pattern seems ridiculous on Jack, revealing his long pale legs and hairy chest.

"*Qué pasa,* Lucy?" Mia asks, turning her head towards me and swooping away her wet black hair.

"You have a visitor waiting downstairs. Someone called Carla."

"What? Carla? How dare she come here?" Mia jumps off the bed and stomps angrily across the room, rummaging in her wardrobe, probably looking for some more decent clothes.

"Who is she, my gelato?" Jack also gets up from the bed and tightens the belt of his dressing gown. I give a quick prayer to the Balinese gods that he has some underwear beneath the silk gown. Seeing the private parts of my best friend's fiancé might be the last straw of this already crazy day.

"She's my father's wife number three. The newest addition to his collection of stupid bimbos."

"I thought she was called Candy?" I venture to ask. I remember Mia mentioned her some time ago, and I found her name a bit bizarre. But who am I to judge? My middle name is actually Cassandra, as my mom was a big fan of the Greek mythology.

"I was being ironic. Don't take everything so literally, Luce," she replies quite harshly, throwing out a sports bra across the room until it lands on Jack's head. I don't like her tone and I decide to say something back, but then Mia looks at me, and her voice softens. "*Perdona*, it's been an emotional day. Can you tell Carla that I'll join her in five minutes? I want to make sure I don't start a relationship with my newest stepmother by mooning her with my naked bum."

"Mia will be here soon," I go downstairs and tell Carla, who's now sitting on the sofa and browsing though one of Mia's bridal magazines. "Would you like a glass of water while you're waiting?"

"No, thank you, Lucy," she replies with a smile. "I have no idea what Mia's wedding dress looks like, but from what Rick told me about her, she might like this one. What do you think?" She holds the magazine up and turns it around, so that I can see the photo she's referring to. A boho blue gown is exactly in Mia's style.

"Mhm." I nod, impressed by Carla's intuition. Or maybe just her skills at stalking Mia's social media, where she's posting a lot of photos of herself in flowy blue dresses.

Carla puts the magazine down on the coffee table and says wistfully, "I always envied the mother of the bride. I think's it's so wonderful to bond over the female rituals, choosing the dress, helping with the hair and make-up, calming the nerves with a glass of prosecco."

"Oh." I have no idea what to reply. I know next to nothing about this woman, and I feel a bit uncomfortable that she's sharing such personal thoughts with a perfect stranger.

"I have two teenage boys, you see," she continues in the same familial tone. "Mario and Luigi."

"Are you a fan of Mario Bros?" She looks more like an Italian mamma cooking homemade pasta for dinner than a hard-core gamer, but why can't she be both?

"Not at all." Carla laughs and makes herself more comfortable on the sofa. "I named them after my grandfathers. Back then, I didn't even know that this game existed."

"Is your family Italian?" It feels weird to be towering over her, so I sit down on the edge of the sofa opposite hers.

"Yes, my grandparents came from Napoli, the most beautiful city in the world," she says with an exaggerated Italian accent, gesticulating expansively with her hands, and I can't stop myself from laughing. There's something very open and charming about Carla, and for a moment, I forget that she's Mia's (potentially evil) stepmother.

"I grew up in the Italian neighborhood in NYC, where family is the most important thing in the world. Not just for Christmas and Thanksgiving, but also for the everyday life. That's why when I met Rick and discovered that he had an adult daughter, I couldn't believe his stupidity. How could you have a *bambina*, the most precious gift in life, and just discard it?" She shakes her head. "But then he told me his story, and I started to understand why."

40

CARLA

When Mia finally comes downstairs, fully clothed, she finds me and Carla chatting away as if we were old friends. Talking to Carla is surprisingly easy, she's asking thoughtful questions and listening attentively without any judgement. Before my usual reserve had a chance to kick in, I told her my own love story with Antoine, which she found very romantic.

"*Amor vincit omnia*, love conquers all," Carla says with a sigh. "I'm so glad you've found the courage to trust love again, Lucy. It's not easy, especially if you've been hurt before."

"Well, well, well, aren't you two looking cosy!" Mia says in her most sarcastic voice. If I didn't know her, I'd think she was being mean. But I can also see fear lurking in her eyes.

"Hello, Mia, I'm so happy I can finally meet you." Carla gets up from the sofa and extends her hand. "Rick told me so much about you."

Mia seems hesitant for a split second, but then she politely returns the handshake. "Funny, but he didn't say a lot about you," she replies unkindly.

"Maybe because you didn't give him a chance?" Carla raises her eyebrows.

"Did he send you here?"

"No, not at all. Actually, he wasn't very happy when I told him about my idea. Rick doesn't have the best communication skills, as you well know. So, if you don't mind, I'd like to try to explain what he wanted to tell you, before he got hit by flying saucers."

While they're talking—Carla with her arms folded on her chest and Mia with her hands planted on her hips—I retreat towards the kitchen. "I'll be here if you need me," I mumble, hoping they never will. Coming between these two would be like trying to pacify a corrida bull and an Italian mamma-wolf.

I shut the door behind me. The kitchen is cool and quiet, and it feels safe, even though just a few hours ago it was witness to the biggest row of this holiday. At this point, I'm so hungry that I feel almost sick. I might eat not one, but five avocado toasts, preferably with loads and loads of butter.

I take out bread, butter, and avocados from the fridge. We have to hide all the food here, otherwise it'll get devoured by the army of very tiny and very hungry ants that can march in through the openwork windows. Yes, that's right, there are glass panes in our bedrooms and the hall, but not in the bathrooms or the kitchen. So, we get constantly invaded by ants, mosquitos, and other creepy-crawlies. The only upside is that the holes in the windows are so big that cute green lizards can also troop in and eat most of our unwelcome visitors.

I put the bread into the toaster and sigh with disappointment. The Balinese eat mostly rice, so their bread is even worse than in the UK. White, soft, and mushy. Oh, how I miss the warm baguette from our local boulangerie in Paris. But who knows, maybe I'll have a chance to eat one sooner than I thought—

The toaster pings, and I cover my bread generously with butter. Another rarity in Bali, as they usually use coconut oil for cooking. And then the best part of my meal—fresh avocado that Jack and Mia bought directly from the local farmer during one of their trips to Seminyak. The avocado is so ripe and soft that I can spread it across the crunchy bread even without cutting. Just a squirt of lime juice, a pinch of salt and pepper on top, and my perfect snack is ready.

I bite into the toast with a crunch and murmur with pleasure. But as soon as I'm starting to regain my inner balance, I can hear some muffled voices in the garden. I peek out through one of the holes in the window and notice Mia pacing angrily between the barbecue area and the swimming pool, while Carla is standing still next to the deckchairs. They know that I'm in the kitchen and can hear everything, right? Eavesdropping is rude, so should I discreetly retreat to my room? To be honest, I'd rather not eat in the bedroom, as crumbs might encourage another ant invasion. Oh, what the hell, why do I even have to come up with an excuse? I really want to see the next act of this drama. So, I sit at the kitchen table and enjoy the show.

"Why are you both trying to be so nice all of the sudden?" That's Mia. "He already told me he didn't want to be my father. And that much is clear, given that he was never there for me."

"But did he tell you why? Did he tell you about his own family?" Carla's arms are still folded over her chest, but her voice is calm and firm. I imagine that's the kind of tone she uses to discipline her teenage sons.

Mia shakes her head and scowls at her stepmother. "No, I've never met my American grandparents. You see? He was too ashamed of me to even introduce me to his own family!"

"Or maybe he was ashamed of them?"

"*Que?*" Mia looks suspiciously at her stepmother.

"Do you know that your grandfather was an abusive alcoholic? Rick escaped from home in Kentucky to New York as soon as he turned eighteen. And he never looked back, pretending his crappy childhood never happened."

"So what? Is a crappy childhood an excuse for everything? Can you treat others like *mierda* just because you were mistreated yourself?"

"Listen, *bella*, I'm not trying to justify Rick and his behaviour. What he did to you was wrong, and there's no excuse for that. But maybe you can move on from the angry teenager phase and try to understand him as a fellow adult? For example, do you know how we met?"

"How would I know? I never talk to him!"

Carla sighs and sits down on one of the loungers, inviting Mia to sit next to her. To my surprise, Mia follows her instructions. This woman must be an Italian snake whisperer.

216

"It probably took him much longer than it should, but two years ago, Rick finally realised he needed help, and he joined the support group for Adult Children of Alcoholics. That's where we met and where his healing has begun."

"Oh, I didn't know that."

"There are a lot of things you still don't know about Rick. He's a good man. But he was always scared that he would be a horrible father himself. That he would hurt you."

"But he completely cut me off! It's even worse. It was as if I never existed for him. As if I was invisible!"

"That's not true. He was always watching from afar, and he regularly sent you and your mother money."

"But I didn't need his money! I needed my *pappi!*"

"Well, I think you needed both."

"What do you mean?"

"Mia, do you think your mom could afford living in central London and sending you to a private school all on her own? These things cost a lot of money."

"Why didn't I ever know about this? Are there any more family secrets to be revealed today? Do you want to tell me that I have a dozen of half-siblings waiting for me in New York?"

"No, nothing like this." Carla laughs. "Actually, Rick was really scared of having more babies, which was the main reason for his two divorces. He didn't want you to know about the money because he's stupidly proud. But he's always been really happy about what you've achieved, he just doesn't know how to properly express it."

Mia is sitting in stunned silence. I think Carla has found a mute button on my Spanish friend.

Carla gently touches Mia's hand. "I hope this wedding might be an opportunity for change. As you're embarking on a new life adventure with Jack, maybe you can find compassion and forgiveness for your father?"

I'm dying to know what Mia will do next. Even though she's as stubborn as a mule, I hope that she'll forgive Rick and give herself a chance to have the dad that she's always longed for. But before I have a chance to hear her answer, I'm startled by the sound of the kitchen door opening.

It's Antoine, looking sexy in his black boxers and tussled dark hair. "Where have you been, *ma chouette*? I started to worry that you decided to grow your own avocados for the toast. Come back to bed, we still have a lot of catching up to do."

41

CHOCOLATE MASSAGE

I'm covered in chocolate. Literally. Or at least some chocolate-scented paste. It smells so nice that I have to refrain from licking myself. I'm in a dark room with only candles flickering on the table and the relaxing flute music permeating the air, while a young Balinese woman in a well-pressed uniform is massaging my back.

"Is it nice, miss?" she asks, stroking my skin.

"Yes, it's heaven," I murmur. "That's the best massage I've ever had, Lina."

"I'm very happy to hear it." She presses her nimble hands against the small of my back, releasing tension from my muscles. This afternoon in the spa is Mia's pre-wedding treat for herself and her three maids of honour. She said that it would be a perfect way to unwind after the daddy drama yesterday. After her long conversation with Carla, Mia has calmed down and promised to reconsider her father's olive brunch. However, the jury is still out if Rick and Carla will be invited to the wedding the day after tomorrow.

Lina starts the massage from my back and shoulders, with all the twisted knots melting under her magic touch like a biscuit dipped in hot tea. I wonder why humans aren't as touchy-feely as other primates. I remember the macaques on the top of the volcano. They were constantly touching each other, cuddling, fighting, grooming. I'm starting to realise that even random Balinese monkeys have much more fun than most Westerners, especially if they're single. But do we have to be in an erotic relationship to stop being so touch-deprived? Shouldn't we get the warmth also from our family and friends?

Of course, it's all changed for me now, thanks to Anton. For the last two days, we've been doing almost nothing else then—well, monkey stuff. But what is going to happen when our Bali adventure is over? Can our freshly rediscovered relationship survive the distance dividing our countries? Can I just go back to my sterile life in London, where a handshake from a colleague or a hug from a friend are my only sources of human touch? At least in Paris, people air-kiss each other, surreptitiously sniffing each other's perfume and pheromones.

Lina is now moulding my buttocks and upper thighs, sending shivers up my spine. Her nimble fingers on my bum, the candlelight, the scent of chocolate—it's all deliciously sensuous. Just like the massage that Anton gave me after our descent from the volcano. What started as a way to relieve the pain in my sore muscles and aching feet, soon turned into foreplay, which lead to amazing make-up sex. It was definitely worth waiting four years for this moment of utter ecstasy. Also, it probably didn't hurt that I'd practiced in bed with all the Tindermen. At least now I am more confident between the sheets, and I don't feel like a blushing virgin anymore.

Lina flips me over like a pancake and starts to tap my face with her soft fingertips. She's so delicate that her touch reminds me of fluttering butterfly wings. I close my eyes and let my mind wander, but it keeps coming back to the only thorny plant in my garden of pleasure: what's going to happen next?

Antoine says that he can move back to London with me, but without his law job, without his network of friends, how can he be happy in a city that brought us so much heartache last time we tried to live there together? On the other hand, what do I have to lose if I move to Paris? I love my friends, but I hate everything else—my job, the long commute, the constant rush. But leaving my country is such a big commitment. What if I go to France, and we break up after two weeks? What if I stay jobless, friendless, and lonely once again? It's an important decision that will have a butterfly effect on the rest of my life.

While I'm debating the pros and cons of moving to Paris, Lina moves from tapping my face to rubbing my chest and breasts. It feels weird, even though I know that boobs aren't as much taboo in Bali as in Europe. Actually, before the Dutch colonizers arrived, Balinese women were walking completely topless, with just a sarong covering the lower parts of their bodies.

I feel ashamed for being so prudish, but I sigh with relief when the masseuse abandons my breasts and moves to my stomach and legs instead. She's kneading my body as if I was pizza dough, hopefully getting rid of the deep tissue tension and cellulite. When she gets to my feet, I giggle involuntarily.

"Is everything fine, miss?" she asks.

"It tickles," I admit through uncontrollable bursts of laughter.

Lina adjusts the pressure, and it doesn't tickle anymore. However, by touching some secret point on my sole, she sends a shot of pleasure up to my centre. Gosh, I just hope I won't start moaning. That would be so embarrassing.

Finally, she completes the chocolate massage by wrapping me in a blanket like a burrito and leaving me alone in the dark room. I'm now as high on endorphins as I was last night with Anton. Even the memory makes my body and mind dissolve in pleasure. A sweet cherry on top of our perfect reunion cake.

"So, how was it?" Mia asks, licking off hot chocolate from her spoon. "Did you enjoy your spa experience?"

Mia, Sylvia, Anna, and I are sitting on a shaded terrace in an open-door café in Kuta next to our spa, trying not to lose the after-massage glow.

"I loved it. Thank you for the treat, Mi." Anna sends her a warm smile. "I think I'll start recommending Balinese massage to my patients."

"This luwak coffee is amazing. I still can't believe it's been pre-digested by some poor critter." Sylvia purrs with pleasure. "But my Javanese massage was a bit painful at first—the guy was practically jumping on me. Now I feel like I have no bones. In a good way."

"So, you didn't go for the fish pedicure after all?" Anna is already sipping white wine, even though it's only early afternoon.

"Fish pedicure?" I scrunch my nose in disgust. "Does it imply putting dead fish on your feet?"

"No, you have to dunk your legs in a tank of water and little fish nibble at your dead skin," Sylvia explains.

"Sounds very unhygienic." I shake my head.

"I'll try it next time," Sylvia says. "I just hope the fish aren't piranhas."

"And how about you, Luce?" Mia turns towards me. "How was your chocolate treatment? And how is it going with Antoine?"

"And by this, we mean, is he still good in bed?" Sylvia clarifies, raising her eyebrows.

I blush as the flashbacks from the last night float through my brain.

"If it makes you uncomfortable, you don't have to tell us." Anna tries to be accommodating as always. "But we're dying to know."

Oh well, what the heck, they're my friends. They've been with me every step of the way. Without them, I wouldn't be in Bali, let alone reunited with Antoine.

"It's better than my chocolate massage and Sylvia's poo coffee put together," I admit and then fill them in on the details.

"Mi, how did the breakfast with your dad go?" Anna asks, once I stopped bragging about my newfound passion with Antoine. "Did you make any progress in your relationship?"

What? Mia met again with Rick, and I didn't even know about it? Living in my sex-fuelled bubble is great, but I think that I'm becoming a horrible friend in the process.

Mia nods reluctantly without peeling her gaze from a banyan tree growing in front of the café.

"And?"

"And I don't know." Mia sighs. "I was so sure he wanted to apologise only to impress his new wife. But after meeting Carla yesterday, I'm not so sure anymore. Maybe my father isn't such a ruthless *canalla* as I always thought of him. What if I misjudged him?"

"Did you tell him how you feel about this whole situation?" Anna, still unused to the tropical heat, swipes sweat from her forehead. We should buy her a straw hat before she burns to crispy bacon.

Mia heaves a sigh and dives even further into her armchair. "At first, it was very awkward. We were just sitting in silence like two strangers, which we are. But then we started chatting about Carla and found common ground. Even I have to admit that she's cool."

"Totally. I'm a big fan of your new stepmother," I say. I still can't believe how great Carla turned out to be. Warm, friendly, honest, the complete opposite of the bimbo bitch Mia envisioned. To be honest, after the incident with Antoine's mum, Monique, I don't trust my judgement anymore, especially when it comes to mother figures. But Carla has won over our whole gang. Even my shrewd Anna seems to like her, so I think she must be legit.

"Actually, my dad and Carla are inviting us all to dinner tonight at their hotel," Mia continues. "To get to know each other better before the other guests start arriving tomorrow."

"Does it mean that you're going to invite them to the wedding?" Sylvia asks. "After all, they travelled all the way from the US to see you. It must be really important to them."

"I'm not sure about my father, but I might invite Carla," Mia replies with a cheeky grin. It's the first time I've seen her talking about her dad and smiling at the same time. A little pre-wedding miracle.

42

DINNER WITH THE CELEBRITIES

We're back in Seminyak, the site of our shopping spree at the beginning of the holiday, and—more recently—Mia's infamous hen-do. But this time instead of hunting for a blue dress or falling into a swimming pool, we're going for dinner at one of the most famous Balinese hotels, The Oberoi.

Our whole gang, Mia and Jack, Sylvia and Anna, Anton and I, are strolling through the vast gardens dotted with frangipani flowers and palm trees. It doesn't look like a hotel at all, especially not the soulless one we had in Kuta. It reminds me of a traditional local village with wooden pavilions scattered across lush lawns rolling towards Seminyak Beach.

It's so peaceful and idyllic here that I could just lie down in one of the hammocks and fall asleep. If only I didn't feel so nervous about Mia's meeting with her father. Is she going to be civil and friendly? Or is she going to throw plates at him again? There's so much pain and anger that Mia has been hiding for years ready to explode, that I'm afraid it might be option number two.

Jack's squeezing her hand and muttering under his breath, "Relax, it's going to be fine, my chocolate pudding." But I'm not sure who he's trying to soothe more—Mia or himself. After all, he's meeting his future father-in-law and under unusual circumstances.

Anna's hovering around Mia, sending her supportive glances, while Sylvia's trying to distract us with a story of her date with Wayan last night. "And that's how we found out that you can't dance topless in Bali anymore. What a waste of a wonderful tradition," she concludes, but no one laughs at her joke.

The tension is becoming so palpable that I start scratching my arm again. Antoine notices it and gently stops me. "Whatever happens, I'm here with you, *ma chouette*," he says gently. "Do you think it's going to be a battle royal? How many points do you give them on the drama-meter?"

"Ten on the Beaufort scale," I reply. "You know Mia and her fiery temper. I'm afraid this dinner is going to end up very ugly indeed." To distract myself, I look around the posh resort, trying to imagine how it must feel (and how much it must cost) to live in this slice of Balinese paradise. "Is it really where Rick and Carla are staying?" I ask.

"*Si*," Mia replies. "Jack, we should come here next year. Maybe for our first wedding anniversary?"

"Whatever you wish, my chocolate fondant," Jack reassures her. "We can even try to get married here tomorrow. Do you think they take last-minute wedding bookings?"

"Ha, ha, that's very tempting, *mi amor*, but it's a bit too late for that. And Boardwalk is also a great choice. More boho and beach vibes, which is exactly what we wanted."

"I read in one of Lucy's guidebooks that Salvador Dali owned a villa here," Anna says, pointing at a stone hut with a black thatched roof. "Can you imagine sleeping in the same bed as the genius of surrealism?"

"They've probably changed the decor since Dali's visit," Anton observes. "But you're right, Oberoi is famous for its celebrity guests dancing and drinking during the full moon parties. Mick Jagger, Julia Roberts, even Princess Grace Kelly stayed here at some point."

"And now us," Sylvia announces with pride. "They should add Sylvia Mackenzie to their hall of fame."

"Of course, Sylve, they should have rolled out a red carpet and an orchestra to celebrate your arrival," Anna says sardonically. Sylvia's parents own a huge, draughty castle in Scotland and she sometimes forgets that living in a palace doesn't automatically make you a princess.

"I'm sure a red carpet wouldn't hurt," Sylvia replies with royal dignity, while we're all giggling at Anna's idea. "But they probably didn't even know we were coming. Maybe next time."

We turn onto a stone path winding through fragrant bushes to reach the hidden villa, where Carla and Rick are already waiting for us at the doorstep. Carla walks towards us with a big smile on her friendly face, while Rick is standing quietly behind her, shoulders slumped, head dropped. I feel sorry for this man, even though we've never exchanged as much as a word. Now that I know a bit more about his own challenges, I can understand why it was so hard for him to step up and be Mia's father. Don't get me wrong, I don't want to let him off the hook, just sympathize.

"I'm so glad you've accepted our invitation." Carla extends her arms towards Mia. "It's great to see you and your friends again."

There's a moment of tension, and I'm scared that Mia will say something rude. But instead, she smiles. "Thank you for the invitation, Carla." Then, she nods towards Rick. "And Dad."

Rick lifts his head and straightens his back, as if a big weight had been lifted from his shoulders. While they're so close to each other, I notice some family resemblance. Mia is lean and toned, while Rick is more on the plump side, but they're both quite short with a mane of curly black hair and stubbornly pointed chins.

"Mia, I'm so sorry. I fucked up as a father." Rick looks at her with big, sad eyes. "But I'd like to try again, if you only give me a chance."

"Is it all you have to say?" Mia lifts her chin defiantly. "You fucked up royally, failing to be my father over and over again. There's no way you can fix it."

"No, there's no way I can go back and make different life choices, no matter how much I wish there was." Rick shakes his head. "But if you let me, I can be a part of your present."

"And what about all the important events you already missed in my life?" Mia stomps her foot on the stone path. "All the birthdays, Christmas dinners, school performances, it was just me and my mum.

You didn't even bother to send me a letter or a card. You didn't think of me at all!"

Rick flinches, as if Mia had slapped him. "That's not entirely true. María Carmen was sending me the photos of you growing up. The two of you always looked so happy together, as if nothing was missing from your perfect little family." He clasps his hands on his belly. "Also, every photo was a reminder of my failure as a father. I kept all of them, but until recently, I wasn't able to look at your childhood memories without pain and self-pity."

"It's true." Carla puts a hand on her husband's shoulder. "Rick has albums filled with your photos, Mia. They're his biggest treasures."

I see tears brimming in Mia's dark eyes, building up until they over-flow. I want to come over and give her a hug, but Carla beats me to it. Bless this woman and her big Italian heart.

"But I've changed, I really have," Rick continues with a shaky voice. "Thanks to my support group, and especially Carla, I realised how selfish I was. I want to make it up to you, Mia. I hope it isn't too late to rebuild our relationship and create new memories? What do you say?"

I hold my breath, waiting for Mia's reaction. Is she going to throw blunt objects at Rick again, or is she in a more forgiving mood today? To my great relief, she takes a step towards her dad and envelops him in a hug. At first, I can see his whole body tense up, but then he relaxes and returns her embrace. I don't believe that a hug can magically erase almost thirty years of neglect, but it's a good start. There's hope for forgiveness and reconcili-ation for all of us, even for the prodigal millionaire fathers and their feisty Spanish daughters. I think of my own parents—far, far from perfect, but doing their best—and I swipe away a tear rolling down my cheek.

Once Rick and Mia stopped hugging, there's not a dry eye in the group. Even Sylvia is sniffing, and my usually level-headed Anna is surreptitiously wiping off the tears. I squeeze Antoine's hand, and he smiles at me with such tenderness and love that I might start crying all over again.

"Let me show you around our humble abode," Carla says jokingly to release the tension after the emotional scene on the porch, as we all follow her inside the stone pavilion. It feels even more luxurious than our villa in Legian, though both houses are decorated in the same traditional Balinese style. I'm treading on marble tiles, wondering how the same objects—a king-size canopied bed, bamboo furniture, purple cushions, wood carving artwork on the walls—can feel so much more opulent here than in our villa. Is it a matter of more expensive materials, better-quality craftsmanship, or maybe just my expectations to find pure luxury in the most famous resort on the island?

We cross the spacious bedroom and walk onto a patio with a private swimming pool and a huge table set for dinner. "That's a big table for two people," Jack assesses it with a professional eye of a restaurateur. "Do you share it with other guests?"

"No, we've got it set up just for tonight." Carla shakes her head. "The staff here are amazing. When we told them we were expecting company, they helped us organize everything. You can choose whatever you want from the restaurant menu, and they'll bring it directly to the villa."

We take our seats around the table with Carla and Rick on one end, Mia and Jack on the other, and me, Anton, Sylvia, and Anna serving as a buffer in the middle. While everyone's studying the menu, I look around, taking in the surroundings. The patio isn't very big, but it looks like a secret garden framed by frangipani and hibiscus trees. I imagine myself lying on one of the loungers, under yellow parasols with tassels, and just listening to the water trickling from a stone fountain into the swimming pool. I can't believe that in just three short days I'll be thousands of miles away from here, back in gloomy London.

"What are you having, *ma chouette*?" Anton's voice wakes me up from my reverie. "I think you might like *gado-gado*. It's an Indonesian salad with crunchy vegetables, boiled egg, and peanut sauce."

"Mmm, sounds tempting," I admit, feeling suddenly hungry.

"Carla didn't believe me when I told her that they have a real Italian chef." Rick puts his arm around his wife. "This was one of the reasons I chose this hotel."

"Their seafood linguini reminds me of my *nonna's* cooking." Carla licks her lips with pleasure. "I think I'll take it tonight."

"Again?" Rick rolls his eyes. "It will be the third time in a row."

"If I put on weight again, it'll be your fault, Rick. Next time book a hotel with a horrible chef. Or even better, no restaurant at all."

"Have you been here before?" I ask Carla.

"No, it's my first time in Bali. But it might become our favourite holiday destination. I think Mario and Luigi would really love it here. There are so many things to do for teenage boys. Rafting, hiking, snorkelling."

"That's a great idea," Rick agrees. "We just need to find someone to take care of Princess Peach when we're gone."

"Princess Peach?" Mia raises her eyebrows.

"It's our dog." Carla laughs. "Once I found out about Mario Bros, I decided to go all in. Do you want to see some photos?"

"Sure." Mia nods. "I love dogs."

Carla passes around her phone, so that everyone can see the pics of a funny Jack Russell playing with Carla and her teenage sons. They seem like a very close-knit family, hugging each other and laughing in most of the pictures. Even Rick seems happy and relaxed with them.

"Maybe you could come and visit us for Christmas?" Rick sends his daughter a pleading look across the table. "I could show you my favourite places in New York."

"Why not?" Mia replies. "But only if you take me to the Upper East Side. I love *Gossip Girl*. I'd like visit all the famous places from the show."

"That's actually where we're living." Rick raises his hands in surprise. "Very close to the MET."

"No way! I didn't know that my father was an Upper East Sider. Does it make me Blair Waldorf or Serena van der Woodsen?"

"I have no idea what you're talking about. But whatever makes you happy, dear." Rick looks at her with bemusement.

"You're definitely Blair," Carla declares, giving Mia a quizzical look. "Actually, I've never heard how you've met your Chuck. I mean, Jack. Lucy told me yesterday about her story with Antoine. So romantic! But what about you?"

"Our story is much less complicated than theirs." Mia smiles at the memory. "We were in a pub in Covent Garden, waiting to order beer for our friends and we just started chatting at the counter."

"The bartender was as slow as a sloth, so we had a lot of time to talk." Jack rubs his fiancée's arm affectionately. "Later, I tipped him extra for that, though he probably didn't even realise that it was for helping me woo my little pumpkin pie."

"That's a lovely meet-cute. Tell me more!"

And so, to our great surprise and relief, this turns out to be one of the nicest evenings we've had in Bali so far. The food is great, but the company is even better. Carla and Rick are genuinely curious about us. They ask loads of questions and share their own stories from New York. They make us all feel as if we were a part of their big family. Whatever my guidebook might say about the moonlight parties, I'm sure that the countless celebrities visiting Oberoi didn't have a better time than we're having tonight.

43

THE WEDDING

The wedding day is finally here. It's just 6:00 pm, but I feel more ready for bed than a party.

With all the guests coming to Bali almost at once, the last two days were very intense. Antoine volunteered to be the chauffer of our mini-van, cruising to and from the airport, fetching over forty friends and family members, regaling them with funny anecdotes about Bali. I tried to join him every time Mia could spare me from arranging flowers or running errands, but it wasn't very often. For all his work, Antoine got promoted to a groomsman. Also maybe because one of Jack's friends caught the flu and couldn't fly from London. But I prefer to think it was because he generously committed his time, soldiering through traffic jams and listening to Jack's grandfather complain about his gout. My taxi-driver hero.

And today, Mia, Sylvia, Anna, and I spent the whole morning preparing for the big event: showering, peeling, scrubbing, manicure, hairstyling, make-up, dressing up. Phew! I'm tired even thinking of all the things women have to do to pass for an elegant human being. Thank god, Mia and Jack decided to have a small, informal affair in a boho style. At least I can get away with no hat and no high heels. Yay!

The open-air restaurant looks charming in the falling dusk. The ceremony will take place in a white gazebo decorated with a muslin canopy and fairy lights, where Jack and his groomsmen are already waiting against the background of the sun setting over Kuta Beach. The spectacle of colour and light is even more magnificent than usual, with pink fluffy clouds gliding over the amber horizon.

Anna, Sylvia, and I are standing at the beginning of the gravel path leading to the gazebo. We're wearing our blue dresses that we bought in Melody's boutique in Seminyak. My dress is soft and surprisingly comfortable, and it also makes me feel like a character from a Jane Austen novel. I almost feel ready to elope with an eligible bachelor myself. I smile at the thought, as I imagine Antoine in riding breaches and a Regency-era velvet jacket. Dashing!

Behind us, Mia is rhythmically stamping her feet, as if she was starting a flamenco dance, and we all turn towards her. She looks fabulous in the boho ivory dress, long dark hair cascading in natural curls down her back, and a wreath of real flowers on her head. She's clutching a bouquet of blue delphinium and white roses in her hands. As planned, she's going to walk down the aisle on her own, like the strong and independent woman she is. But both her parents are somewhere in the crowd, standing on the lawn along the gravel path.

"Ready?" Anna asks with a reassuring smile.

"Ready." Mia nods her head. She gives a signal to the band placed on a platform closer to the gazebo and they start playing a jazzy version of Mendelssohn's "Wedding March." I'm not a big fan of this particular musical cliché, but it sounds much more fun performed on the piano, guitar, trumpet, and bass, rather than the usual church organ or classical orchestra.

"Such a pity you didn't hire a real Balinese band after all," I say with a wink. "I'm sure Nyoman is disappointed."

"*Dios mío*, I don't want to hear the bloody gamelan ever again. My ears are still ringing from the last time we heard it during the Barong dance."

As we walk down the aisle, or rather down the gravel path, with Mia gliding behind us, I see the happy faces following our small procession. Jack's gouty grandfather and other relatives are tipping their hats and waving royally. Mia's Spanish aunts are clapping with glee, surrounded by a bevy of excited children. As classy as always, our friends Victoria and David, at whose party Antoine and I met for the first time, are holding their cute baby Rose in their arms. I wave at Rose, and she giggles. What a cutie. Our uni friend, Simon, and his husband Robert are waving at us with their impeccably white handkerchiefs. I love these guys.

Our new friends from Bali, Wayan and Nyoman, are also here. They're beaming with their snow-white teeth that match their crispy shirts. I'm so happy that Nyoman isn't holding any grudges against me and that we can still be friends. And who knows, maybe if things work out between Sylvia and Wayan, we'll be all coming back to Bali more often than I thought.

Mia's mum, María Carmen, with her long silver hair and floaty patchwork dress, reminds me of a good witch. It was her who taught Mia how to practice yoga and how to be a free spirit. I wonder how she feels, seeing her daughter get married to an English aristocrat, while she herself has always been fighting against patriarchy and class divisions. But she just smiles at us and sends Mia a quick blessing with her hand.

Jack's parents ignored the memo about the casual dress code, and their clothes are completely over the top. His mum, Camilla, is wearing a mint formal dress with a matching summer coat, fascinator, and even white gloves, while his dad, Philip, is sporting a tuxedo and a top hat. They probably think they've been invited to a royal wedding at Downton Abbey, not a boho party on the beach. They both look completely out of place, not to mention that they must be boiling in this tropical heat.

Holding their hands like a pair of giddy teenagers, Rick and Carla are cheering and waving at us with huge smiles on their faces. After their reconciliation yesterday, Mia decided that the wedding without her dad wouldn't be complete after all. "This time my mom won't be sending you any photos, so you'll have to take plenty yourself," she told Rick, making him cry again. I'm so happy Mia has finally found peace in her rocky relationship with her father. And, as a bonus, we've also invited Carla to be an honorary member of our group of *chicas*. This means an open invitation to all our shopping sprees and gossip with wine whenever she comes to London.

And then, finally, Jack, and his groomsmen, including Antoine. They're all wearing cornflower gingham shirts, navy-blue chinos, and yellow suspenders. Very dapper, very boho, very sexy. Especially a certain Frenchman, who's sending me a wicked smile from behind his glasses.

The wedding ceremony is simple and short. The representative from the British Consulate in Denpasar turns out to be a Black woman in a red linen suit. She's conducting the ceremony with warmth and humour, which I know is exactly what my friends wanted for their big day.

"It's so sweet it's giving me diabetes," Sylvia complains, furtively wiping tears. "It also ruins my mascara."

Mia and Jack seem to be in their own world, looking at each other, oblivious to the crowd of friends and family surrounding them on this beautiful balmy evening. It's amazing how much their on-and-off relationship has survived. The ups and downs of their student days, the challenges they faced when he was working low-paid restaurant jobs to become a chef despite his family's objections, while Mia was setting up her own yoga studio, and even a year apart when Jack was studying in Cordon Bleu in Paris. I don't believe in soulmates or halves of the apple, but maybe this is real love. Being friends, supporting each other in all their projects. Not clinging too hard to the other person, giving them space to be themselves, even if sometimes it means parting ways.

I glance across the aisle towards Antoine. His face is so familiar and new at the same time. I still can't believe how lucky we are to have another chance. I think this time it's going to be even more amazing.

I can hear a lot of sniffing behind me, so I turn my head and see that almost everyone is crying, even Jack's posh parents have glistening eyes, and Mia's father is sobbing on Carla's supporting arm.

"I, Mia Valeria Romero, take you, James Charles Musgrove, to be my husband, to have and to hold from this day forward, for better, for worse, for richer, for poorer, in sickness and in health, to love and to cherish, till death do us part."

I turn back just in time to see Jack take Mia in his strong arms, sweeping her into the air and exclaiming, "I love you, my Spanish paella!" before engaging her in a long and steamy kiss.

And this is when I start to cry as well.

4 4

CHEEK TO CHEEK

The wedding party is now in full swing. The band is playing jazz versions of all the modern pop hits. Who knew that Justin Bieber could have some decent songs if you played them on bass and sax?

Now the guests are boogie-woogie-ing on the wooden dance floor decorated with frangipani garlands and fairy lights glowing in the darkness. Both young and old are on the floor, with little children spinning close to the stage. Jack's parents are cruising in a dignified attempt at a waltz, completely out of time with the music. Mia's mum is swinging in a circle with her sisters and cousins, her robes and silver hair swaying in the wind. Victoria and David are slow dancing, their arms wrapped around each other, with baby Rose snuggled between them. Even Rick is jiving with Carla, his potbelly jumping with every step.

Mia, Anna, Sylvia, and I are standing barefoot on the lawn, cooling our sore feet in the dewy grass, our shoes long ago discarded under the table. Even though I'm surrounded by my friends, I start feeling tired and restless. As an introvert, I enjoy spending time with others, but then I need to be alone to recharge my batteries. And weddings are especially trying for me, there's just too much noise, too many emotions.

"This is the best party I've ever been to." Sylvia throws her arms towards the starry sky and starts dancing her signature Scottish jig. "Delicious food, great music, sexy men." She gestures towards Wayan, who's drinking beer at the bar and chatting with Jack and Nyoman. "And the chocolate sponge cake with coffee ganache was a great choice. I've already had three pieces."

"It's amazing here, Mi," Anna confirms. "Now I wish I had come to Bali even earlier. I didn't realise how much this beautiful island has to offer. Much more than bike rides through rice paddies and toothless healers we saw in *Eat, Pray, Love*. Maybe there's even a handsome guy or gal waiting for me somewhere in the crowd."

"I can't imagine a more romantic place for a wedding." I take in the sound of the waves murmuring in the distance, the jazz band playing another mellow cover, the lights twinkling with magic. "Perfect, just perfect."

"Aw, thank you, *chicas*. And thank you for your thoughtful presents. Luce, the collage of a chorizo sausage wearing a veil and getting married to the Swedish Chef from *The Muppets* made me and Jack crack up." Mia looks lovely in her boho dress, slightly tussled hair, and face glowing with happiness. "But the wedding wouldn't be complete without my *chicas*. Heck, I'm not even sure if it would be taking place if it hadn't been for your support." She wipes away a tear from her cheek and extends her arms to envelop us in a big hug. It's so good to feel the warmth of my friends, the smell of our perfumes mixed with a sweet whiff of frangipani around us.

Now we're all blinking back tears and sniffling. Damn, those invisible ninjas cutting onions.

For a moment, I feel overwhelmed by the uncertainty of my future with Antoine. But then I realise I'm not really scared. Is it possible that this time I'm feeling excitement, and not his evil twin sister—anxiety? I'm sure she'll be back again, but now that I think of it, I haven't had an anxiety attack since the day I climbed down the volcano. Five whole days. A personal record.

The jazz band changes the tune, and we break our group hug. I hear the first few notes and immediately recognize the tune—"Cheek to Cheek" by Ella Fitzgerald and Louis Armstrong. Our song.

"I think this one is for you, Lucy," Anna says with a smile. "I've seen Antoine talk to the band a few minutes ago. Go to him."

I scan the crowd for Anton and notice him standing on the other side of the lawn, sipping a glass of red wine. He must have sensed that I'm looking at him, because he turns his head towards me, puts down his glass on the table, and extends his hand towards me as an invitation.

This song brings back so many bittersweet memories. It was playing when we met each other at the fateful party at Victoria and David's house. But it was also supposed to be the first dance at our wedding. The wedding that never happened. This doesn't matter now, because we are together again, and we can create many more lovely memories.

I walk barefoot on the dewy grass. When I reach Anton, I take his hand—strong and firm. Dependable.

"I'm so happy you're here, Lucy." He gently rubs my hand with his thumb. "And that you agreed to give me another chance."

"I just hope we'll be happy together. That we won't make the same mistakes." I shiver at the sheer thought.

"I solemnly promise you, *ma chouette*. We won't make the same mistakes." His eyes are twinkling with humour, already diffusing my apprehension. "Though, I'm sure we'll make a lot of new ones."

I smile back at him and feel like I've just come back to a safe haven. He's right. I can't be sure what happens with us next. But if I bail out now, I'll regret it forever.

He leads me towards the dance floor and puts his hands on my waist. I link my hands behind his neck, as we're dancing cheek to cheek under the Balinese sky.

EPILOGUE - ONE YEAR LATER

I open the squeaky door and get enveloped in the familiar smells of beer, cider, and French fries. As always, Approach Tavern, our favourite pub in London, is full of patrons drinking, eating, and playing board games.

I'm walking through the laughing crowd until I notice my friends sitting around a big wooden table at the back. Anna's chatting animatedly with Sylvia, who's playing flirtatiously with her gorgeous ginger hair. Jack's glancing protectively over Mia's shoulder at a small bundle she's holding in her arms. Mia's face has this angelic look that you can see in the paintings of Virgin Mary with baby Jesus.

Anna notices me as I come over, and all my friends scramble to give me a hug.

"Lucy! Luce! Great to see you, dear! So happy you're back!"

As soon as we settle back at the table, Mia proudly presents their latest addition to their family. "Lucy, meet Fudge."

I look at the shining black eyes, wet nose, and velvety black ears. "Oh my god, he's so adorable! Can I pet him? Or is he scared of strangers?"

"He was extremely shy at the beginning, but now he's a bit more confident." Mia carefully hands me the little puppy. "He's a rescue from the Battersea Shelter. He had a rough start to his life, but he's blooming now."

"I still can't understand how anyone could have abandoned this little sweetie." Anna's caressing his soft black head, while Fudge is trying to lick my fingers with his pink tongue.

"What is he exactly?" I ask, sitting at the top of the table between Mia and Anna, cuddling the warm pupper in my arms.

"A cockapoo," Jack says with fatherly pride in his voice. "A cross between a Cocker Spaniel and a poodle."

"And I'm officially his godmother." Sylvia's beaming. "I'm going to take care of him whenever Mia and Jack are travelling. Can you imagine how many guys I could pick up with a cute doggo like this?"

"And what would Wayan say?" I raise my eyebrows.

"I said I could pick up. Doesn't mean I would."

"And how's Wayan anyway? Are you going back to Bali any time soon?"

"Actually, he's coming to the UK this time. We're going to spend Easter together with my family in Scotland."

"Oh, that's a big step. I'm so happy for you, Sylve." I squeeze her hand and steal one of her French fries. "And how about you guys?" I turn towards Mia and Jack. "How's married life treating you? Are you still breaking up and making up?"

"Not anymore. The divorce fees are too expensive." Mia winks at me.

"I would never break up with my little chorizo," Jack says, wrapping his arm around Mia's shoulders. "Especially now that we have little Fudge. But she sometimes threatens to dump my sorry ass if I get too wrapped up in work."

Mia shakes her head, but then smiles. "Maybe I sometimes overreact. We now agreed that instead of splitting up, we just have bubble time. Each of us stays in their own bubble, giving each other space to process our emotions, and then usually things come back to normal."

"And what about you, Luce?" Anna asks. "How's Paris been treating you since we last talked? How are Antoine's horrible parents?"

"Paris is lovely, and his parents are still horrible. But I don't care anymore."

"And what's this ring on your finger?" Sylvia leans over to inspect my hand. "I didn't know you like bling now."

"Anton and I got engaged again!" I announce with a blush, waking up Fudge, who's just fallen asleep in my arms. "He proposed on the same bridge as the last time. But this time he gave me his grandmother's ring." I show them the old-fashioned silver band with a huge emerald.

"Congratulations, Luce! So happy for you!"

I hand over Fudge to Jack and then get squashed in a triple hug from my friends.

"It's really brilliant news, Luce." Anna sends me a smile across the table. "And I can see that even your eczema has disappeared."

"Well, it still comes back in the times of stress, but it's much better."

"And when's the wedding?" Mia asks.

"That's the trick, there will be no wedding."

"What? No wedding? What do you mean, you pair of eejits?" Sylvia's strong burr is back. I missed her Scottish temper.

"You know that I've never been a big fan of flashy ceremonies." I glance at Mia and Jack. "Though of course, your reception in Bali was amazing. So instead of a big hutzpah, we'll just get PACS, a civic union. It gives us almost the same rights as a marriage, but there's so much less hassle. And the ceremony will be so small that we don't even have to invite our families, which is a blessing. It'll be just us and you all if you can make it to Paris."

"That's amazing. Congratulations! We have to hear the full story," Mia demands.

"How long are you staying in London?" Anna asks once I've filled them in on the details of my second engagement.

"Just for the weekend. I have to go back to work on Monday. Who knew that I'd be enjoying working in an American bookshop in Paris? Maybe my degree in literature wasn't so useless after all."

"And where's Tony?"

"He was just meeting some old friends from his London days. He should be here shortly."

As if summoned by my words, he walks through the creaky door and smiles at me across the pub. My Anton. Mon dauphin. Mon amour.

Sylvia pours prosecco, and we all raise our glasses. "To friendship, sexy men, and Bali!"

THE END

BEFORE YOU GO

If you enjoyed *The Bali Adventure* and you want to read more about Lucy and her friends, join my email list. I hate spam, so I promise to send you notifications only when the next book in the series is ready.

You can also stay in touch by following me on Instagram and Facebook —all the links are available on my website: www.katedashwood.com.

As an independent author, I really appreciate my readers' feedback. If you enjoyed the book, please leave your review on Amazon, Goodreads, Barnes and Nobles, or any other platform of your choice. You can also email me directly on kate.m.dashwood@gmail.com

Thank you for joining me on this amazing adventure!

ACKNOWLEDGMENTS

The events and characters in this book are completely fictional, but they might have been just a tiny bit inspired by my friends and our trip to Bali. Sadly, we didn't meet sexy Antoine, Wayan, and Nyoman, but we still had loads of fun on the beach, the swings, and even in the temples that Sylvia despised so much. And yes, climbing Gunung Batur volcano was super hard, and no, you really can't pee on local spirits in the rice paddies.

This book would never have come into existence if it hadn't been for my amazing friends with whom I shared a house in London—Edyta, Milena, and Anna. The time we spent together was one of the happiest periods in my life. I loved our parties, barbecues, and trips. But I valued even more our daily life, drinking mimosas in the garden on lazy Sunday mornings, talking in the kitchen long into the night, and watching *Downton Abbey* and *Oh My Venus* in our living room.

Special thanks to Edyta, who not only was my best friend and housemate, but also helped me come up with the plot of the book and flesh out my characters and story. This book wouldn't be the same without you, Edi! And many thanks to Aisha for being my writing buddy and for helping me overcome my writer's block.

Kass and Alex, from Birds of Feather critique group in Paris, your weekly feedback on my chapters was extremely helpful and it kept me motivated to write, revise, and push myself to become a better writer. And I'm so happy that we've become friends in the process!

Many thanks to my beta readers, who gave me their invaluable feedback: Agatka, Aisha, Alex, Ania, Anna, BB, Daria, Edyta, Emcia, Gosia, Grzesiek, Justyna, Kamcia, Kasia, Kass, Liz, Maja, Milena,

Orianne, Pawel, Sara, Syrine, and Zoe. Thank you for being my Guinea pigs!

Big kudos to my editor, Rachel Garber, and to Whitney from Whitney's Book Works, who proofread the manuscript. This book is so much better thanks to your amazing feedback and expertise. Huge thanks to my hawk-eyed friends, Liz and Zoe, for spotting typos and grammar issues that were missed in the editing process. As always, all mistakes are mine.

To my therapist, Ewa, and my doctor, Cecilia, who helped me manage my anxiety. They improved the quality of my life by continuous therapy and suggesting antidepressants when things got really hard. I hope that everyone who suffers from anxiety, depression, or any other mental health challenge can also receive professional help and start their journey towards a full recovery.

And last but not least, my family. My late grandmother, Irena, who taught me how to write and read. My parents, who filled our house with books and encouraged me to read from a very young age. My sister, Justyna Williams, who's also a talented painter. The Bronte sisters have nothing on us, Sis! BB, your book about spies, war, and dragons was such a pleasure to read. Please keep writing! My fourteen-year-old niece, Mila, who is one of the most creative people I know. She writes, dances, sings, draws, and sews. Our writing power hour in the house in the forest pushed me to finish the first draft of the book. Thank you, sweetie!

And my own mini-family, Flavien and our dog Cirilla. Thank you for being with me and supporting me every day. With you, life is even better than with a floating unicorn!

KEEP READING

THE FRENCH ADVENTURE IS COMING SOON

Stay tuned for the second book about the *Chicas*—Lucy, Anna, Sylvia, and Mia.

After the loss of her beloved grandmother, Anna doesn't know what to do with her life. She's no longer able to do her job as a therapist—now she needs professional help herself.

Thanks to her friends, Lucy and Antoine, Anna ends up house- and dog-sitting in a quaint village in the South of France. Will the sunshine, French food, and friendly locals help Anna overcome her grief?

THE FRENCH ADVENTURE

I step out from the air-conditioned Eurostar train and bump into a wall of heat. The air is heavy with the smells of hot metal, rotting garbage, and piss.

So, this is the wonderful Paris everyone's in love with, I think, trying to breathe through my mouth. I weave my way through the crowd of passengers who are rushing to leave Gare du Nord station and lose themselves in the bowels of the city.

Once I've left the platform, I stop and look around, disoriented, not sure where to go and what to do in this foreign country. I blink a few times, trying to gather my thoughts. My brain, usually sharp as a razor, is lagging like an old PC from the 1990s. Why? Ah, yes, the brain is full of chemicals, neurotransmitters, whatever— And mine aren't working properly right now. Probably because of a horse dose of Xanax I took just before boarding my train back in London.

I scan a small group of people waiting at the end of the platform with a hopeful look on their faces. One of them seems familiar. Tall, blonde, slim, slightly frazzled. It must be Lucy, my best friend in the whole wide world.

"Anna, Anna, I'm so happy you made it!" Lucy runs towards me and squeezes me in a bear hug.

I automatically return her embrace, though I feel nothing. Emotionally, I mean. Physically, I feel Lucy's warm body and a faint scent of her vanilla-based perfume. I let her go and notice that she's wearing the same sleeveless black dress she bought for Misia's funeral. I wonder if this is her subtle way to tell me that she's still in mourning? Or is it just a coincidence? After all, Lucy's wardrobe is full of black clothes.

"I'm also happy to see you, Luce," I reply on autopilot. I'm so numb from my medication that I don't even know what happiness means anymore.

"Let's go, I parked in a forbidden place, and I don't want to get a ticket." She takes my hand and leads me through the crowded station. "I hate driving in Paris, so I usually take the metro or bus to go to the city centre," she keeps chatting. "Have you heard of this girl who tried to find a car park in Paris, but took a wrong turn, and ended up on the highway to Calais? Well, that was me. True story. But today I thought it might be nice to drive you home in an air-conditioned vehicle, especially if you had a lot of luggage."

"Thanks, sweetie. Though, you know I travel light." To prove my point, I pull forward a cabin suitcase that I've been dragging behind me all this time. It's packed with only the essentials—underwear, toothbrush, a few T-shirts, linen trousers, and a summer dress elegant enough to wear for the non-wedding ceremony.

"Do you remember how Sylvia took six pairs of stilettos to Bali?" Lucy laughs at the memory. "She had the heaviest suitcase on the whole plane."

Ah yes, Mia and Jack's wedding in Bali. It was just over a year ago, but it feels like an eternity. My life is now split in two—before and after my grandma's death. Bali was definitely before, full of sunshine, happiness, hope. We were all so carefree, so innocent. Though, the shadow of Misia's illness had already started creeping into my life.

When we leave the train station, the sun slaps us with its full force, made even hotter by the hot concrete building walls and countless taxis producing hot fumes. I feel like a fly exposed under harsh laboratory lights. If the Inferno exists, it probably feels like a heatwave in Paris.

Printed in Great Britain
by Amazon

24944420R00148